The Realms Series

Book Three

Enchanted Forest

Emory R. Frie

Dear Hayley,
Face the Monsters
with a Smile ♡
with love,
Emory R. Frie

1

For Kendra, who fights dragons and wears the tiara;

A true Princess.

The Forest is dark, dearie, The Forest is dark;
The moment you think that you're lost in the woods, then you are.

Do not lose your way, dearie, Do not lose your way;
The monsters are lurking not far from the path should you stray.

Things aren't what they seem, dearie, Things aren't what they seem;
Kind grins are bared teeth; Please don't answer the calls from the trees.

Do not pay them heed, dearie, Do not pay them heed;
Hear footsteps behind you, beware but don't fret, they're just checking.

The air is alive, dearie, The air is alive;
To help and to hinder, but it's how some learned to survive.

These woods are too old, dearie, These woods are too old;
Watch for crimson wraiths, keep your strength and wits close should you go.

Deep in the Forest.

-The Woodsman

Chapter One

The Bounty Hunter

Ebony gates loomed over him in the haunting darkness. Such magic was made to keep out the monsters of the Forest, the creatures so inhuman no mortal could control them. But the grey wolf never broke stride. He morphed into a man with eyes of the moon and hair as black as the foreboding fortress he approached. With tense demeanor, he passed straight through the gates, iron bars turning to smoke at his presence. They solidified behind him once again as if they'd never vaporized at all.

Approaching the dark castle, he fingered the cuff clamped around his wrist. It was shaped like a dragon wrapped tightly about his forearm. He'd worn it for five years. What was originally supposed to be a simple job had turned into half a decade of servitude. The dragon cuff was a shackle, a constant reminder of what really controlled him.

It didn't matter now, though. Enough was enough. The cuff, his client—or *master*, really— even the actual reason he'd taken this job in the first place; none of it changed the fact that this time he failed.

Even so, this couldn't go over well.

Doors opened at his presence, allowing him entry. Gargoyles along the walls glowed orange in the mouth and eyes as he walked by in determinate strides. The grotesque creatures carved into horrific scenes on the walls stared at him hollowly. He ignored them all.

Great doors blocked his path and he came to a halt. Confidence wavering, he tugged on the cuff once again. If everything went right, he wouldn't have to wear it anymore. But if it didn't...

The doors opened so suddenly they might as well have blasted open. He flinched at the startling sound.

"Hello, bounty hunter."

There was no backing out now.

Fang stepped forward, head high in approaching. In a way that used to feel so foreign to him—and even now made his stomach clench at its present ease—he *knelt* before his client. He fought past a tight throat to greet her, "Carabosse."

The smile she had was fit for the devil. Forebodingly and dangerously beautiful, Carabosse lounged in the intricately gothic throne. Hair black as living night swept back from her brow. Reflective eyes bored right through him. Shadows highlighted jutting cheekbones and a sharp chin. The inky feathers bleeding through her gown and her talon nails completed a demonic façade.

Does the devil himself cower before her? Fang wondered. It wouldn't surprise him.

"I've been expecting you," Carabosse crooned, a voice that crawled eerily over his skin. "What brings you to my humble home?"

"It has been nearly two years," Fang began, keeping his eyes at her feet, articulating every word. "In all that time, I've not found the girl."

He could feel her cold eyes boring into his bared neck. "Yes?"

"For nearly seven years, I've been more than faithful to our agreement," he added to soften what he was about to propose.

"Do you have a point, wolf?"

"Please," he couldn't keep the anxious plead from his voice, "I've done everything I can do! I've gone above and beyond what you initially asked of me. All I want, all I beg for, is my payment."

There was only silence.

This implored Fang to look up, taking in the sorceress' reaction. Both she and the raven stared at him with the same beady evaluation. The bird seemed ready to pick his eyes out. *Diablo*, many called it. Its true name had long been forgotten, if it ever had one.

Fang tried to keep his composure. But at the lack of response, he felt his steel ebb away to the worry he felt in the pit of his chest.

Absentmindedly, Carabosse reached over to a bowl of green apples sitting beside her and plucked one from its pile. She inspected it with calm demeanor. The slap of the fruit against her palms as she tossed it between her hands echoed in the chamber.

"I have an old friend who was a queen," Carabosse spoke almost to herself, tracing its skin with her fingernails. "She's long dead now. But I've long marveled her. She was renowned for her beauty, but she had a nasty temper and boiling jealousy. She also had a talent for potions, a mastery beyond my own; but what good is a potion if you must rely on its consumption?" She laughed bemusedly, the sound echoing. "The most impressive of her creations was so wonderfully brilliant, so deceivingly innocent, so perfectly evil that no one else has yet been able to replicate it. I believe you're familiar with it: The Poison Apple."

His blood ran cold as the hairs on the back of his neck rose. Suddenly, the apple in Carabosse's hands didn't seem like a mere prop anymore. Every slap it made against her skin caused his throat to tighten.

"I've yet to see the effects of one myself, despite my possession, but one hears stories," Carabosse continued. "Juices drip in and the poison shoots instantaneously through every vein, artery, and nerve in the body. Weakness comes first. Then pain, more pain than I can even attempt to describe. I've heard a scream gets lodged in the throat just as you swallow. But then comes nothing. Numb chill overtakes the body as you collapse. You can't move, or speak, or breathe, or feel anything. Your body becomes your prison. And while life continues on, you can do nothing about it."

Reflective eyes suddenly fixated on him. Fang held her piercing gaze, but the effort made his hands tremble and shoulders tense. Sweat lined his brow.

It's a fate worse than death.

Carabosse leaned forward like a cat stalking its prey. "Imagine what would happen to your precious wife if you were to meet such a fate. She would soon turn to gold because you could not stop it."

She crushed the apple in her hand, juice dripping from her knuckles. Fang watched the pieces fly in every direction. Some hit his chin, but he didn't bother to wipe it off. He felt incapable of doing anything.

But her message was clear even before she stated it.

"You shall get your reward when you have finished your job."

Chapter Two

Second Skin

Just as the words left her mouth, a blood sucking pain erupted through Red Daim. She shrieked despite herself. The ground met her quickly. Spots dazzled her vision like the sparks of a bonfire, and her ears rang with agonizing howls.

The vision pressurized inside her skull until she saw it all clearly behind her eyelids.

Her body contorted.

She couldn't stop it.

Running. Heart racing quicker than a gunshot. Breath heavier than a meteor plummeting to earth. Trees zipped by. Never look back. Never look back.

She wasn't fast enough.

All she had was one mirror clutched tightly in her fist, the only thing she'd had time to grab. Her cloak had been abandoned. Not that it would help her now. The warning had already come and was barreling upon her.

She wasn't fast enough.

A gnarled root caught her foot. She fumbled, hastened to return speed. But the delay was too long. She heard him behind her, catching up right on her heels.

She wasn't fast enough.

The wolf threw her to the ground in one final leap. Claws raked over her skin. She screamed and crashed with him onto the forest floor. She caught one glimpse of the full moon looming in the sky before the savage clamped onto her shoulder. Teeth sank into her flesh. Her pupils dilated.

She wasn't fast enough.

Having overpowered her, Fang shifted his form. The man scared her more than the wolf. She tried to fight him off, desperate despite her lingering stupor. Muscles quavered. It was pointless. He was too strong. Still she fought, trying to use the only weapon she had in her possession.

She wasn't fast enough.

Fang wrestled the mirror from her grasp before she could land a hit. Exhaustion weakened her. He raised that blasted mirror overhead, to stun her, to knock her out, to kill her, it didn't matter. She couldn't stop him.

She wasn't fast enough.

His arm plunged down. Air pressurized around her. The sound of glass shattering was all that remained.

Bottle green eyes flew open and caught the sight of blood and glass. Her muscles cramped from holding her knotted position. As her senses cleared and expanded, Red realized what she was leaning against, or rather *who* she was leaning against.

She jerked up out of Jack Caldwell's arms, trying to calm down her shaking. Her friends surrounded her in concern. But snarls filled her mind, and her skin itched beyond the possibility of potential satisfaction, and her muscles tightened with a strength she tried desperately to keep at bay.

Blood dripped down Wendy Darling's finger onto the glass that littered the ground.

It was the same glass from the same mirror that had taken Red into the dense wood of France, the mirror that had taken her away from Fang and the Enchanted Forest.

She squeezed her eyes shut, pressing her forehead to her knees. It felt like her head was going to explode.

"Are you alright?" Alice Liddell questioned—*the bloody girl never ran out of questions!* "What happened?"

Red took in a deep breath, trying to calm down, trying to push past the discomfort. Someone touched her shoulder. She let him keep his hand rested there, appreciating its warmth. But all she wanted to do was run away and give in to these horrible sensations that threatened to destroy her from the inside out.

Kai Ødegård looked at her as if he knew precisely what she wanted to do.

Forcing her voice to level, Red barely spoke above a whisper, "It's back. The Wolf's returned."

Chapter Three

The Golden Maiden

Taking the steps two at a time, Fang hastened to the tower room. He stopped just outside the entrance. His heart skipped a beat when he saw her standing there by the window.

She was still as beautiful as ever, but in his eyes, she always was. Long blonde hair cascaded down her back in soft curls, strands of gold growing bolder and more apparent as the sun's rays bounced off them. Milky skin and soft features, she had every appearance of a goddess. A gown of sheer white fell loosely over her shoulders and ended at her ankles in a waterfall of fabric. The effect gave her figure a glowing aura in the sun's light.

His heart swelled. *I don't deserve her*, he thought for the thousandth time. Yet he was the one to hold her heart, just as she held his all.

He drunk in her peaceful presence a moment more before he stepped in. "Zoë."

Zoë turned, her expression brightening upon seeing him. He felt a pang at seeing her difficulty in widening her smile on the right side of her face. He wondered if it hurt. But Zoë would never admit to it.

"Fabien," she breathed his given name with more familiarity than he had in hearing it.

It pleased him when she spoke his name. It was as if that name spoken by her alone was one of the few things that kept the man in him alive. It kept the beast tame. But Zoë was the only one who loved him for both man and beast as one. He loved her all the more for it.

Zoë ran into his embrace, left arm wrapped tightly around him. The right hung useless by her side. But Fang made up for her half hug in bringing his strong arms around her. Always, he remained soft and tender as if at any moment she would shatter if he handled her too hard.

It had been much too long since he'd been with his wife.

When she pulled away, he examined her in more detail. His throat tightened at the sight of her right arm. It was almost solid gold now, immobile. Tendrils of gold were starting to crawl up the right side of her neck as it continued to spread. It was like a disease spreading gradually throughout her system, killing her slowly as it made its way toward her heart. It was already inking down her side and leg.

When his gaze fell to her left arm where her skin was still pink, the blood drained from his face. He took Zoë's left hand, trembling, rubbing his thumb down her knuckles. The tips of her fingers were dusted with gold. It hadn't been there before. A knot formed in his throat. He pressed her gold infested fingers to his lips, kissing each one.

"How fast?" Fang found his voice strained and cracked with the effort of pushing the words out.

"Fabien…"

"How fast?"

She swallowed in hesitance before confessing, "Too fast. I'll be unable to move in under two weeks by my calculations."

Fang cursed under his breath and turned away, pacing. He raked his fingers through his dark hair in frustration.

The golden rose caught his eye. It perched upright on its own pedestal, covered in clear glass for protection. Hatred filled his gut. There were petals at its base, having fallen off in its ever-wilting process.

Why must his wife's fate rest on the wellbeing of an accursed flower? Why must a merciless death fall on the one who least deserved it? Why should she be punished for the selfish choice of a father she never chose to have? But magic was a force of balance, and this cruel world thrived off of magic.

"Fabien," Zoë took a step toward him, her foot giving a heavy chink, "you must stop worrying!"

"How am I supposed to stop worrying when you are slowly *dying* right before my eyes?" Fang questioned helplessly.

Zoë shook her head. "We can't do anything about that."

"No," he refused. "No, I *can* do something about it. I *am* doing something about it, or at least trying to."

She sighed. "Not Carabosse again. She's the reason I'm turning into gold!"

"No, she's not. Your father did this to you. He was given a choice to give up his curse. It was his life or yours and he chose to sacrifice you!"

"And who was the one who cursed him with the golden touch in the first place?"

Fang grabbed her hand in his. "I'm *not* going to lose you."

Zoë sighed again, looking down at him with a calm he couldn't imagine ever obtaining in this situation. "I would rather spend my last days with you than have you sell your soul to chase after a false hope."

"Carabosse will give us what she promised," Fang assured, trying to convince himself as much as her. "She will break your curse. I only need to find the girl."

"Fabien..." Zoë tried, but he was already starting towards the door.

He turned back quickly, pressing his lips firmly to hers. She brushed his hair out of his face with her gold tipped fingers as Fang pulled gently away.

"Stay," she whispered, kissing him softly. "This time, stay with me. Just for tonight."

Everything in him wanted to stay.

He pulled away, barely a breath from her lips.

"I won't let anything happen to you," he whispered. "I promise."

Then Fang turned and left.

*****

Red stared into the crackling flames. Sparks flew into the air. Smoke curled in strange shapes. She was aware of *everything* for the first time since Wonderland. Her senses inflamed while her body continued to get accustomed to the Wolf again.

Her friends' steady breathing; rustling leaves as the night wind blew through the trees; skittering of a late-night critter in the forest. No footsteps. Not yet.

Strong scents of nature, heavy pine, wholesome oak, the stench of a squirrel hiding in the branches overhead. No monsters. Not yet.

But she sensed magic with every nerve in her body. It made her skin tingle, the hairs on the back of her neck bristle. The sensation made her eyes sharp and heavy at once, her body relaxed yet tense. Magic was so indecisive, able to inflict anything so long as the right person used it. And anyone could use it.

This place filled her with such fear, more so now than ever before.

She wished she had her cloak.

Someone rose, walking towards her in slow strides. She wasn't surprised when Kai stood beside her. His breathing hadn't been deep and rhythmic like the others'.

"I'll keep watch," Kai stated. "You get some sleep."

Red laughed to herself. "That's exactly what Jack said two hours ago. I denied his offer, too."

"I'm not Jack."

As if I don't know that, she thought.

He continued, "I don't take refusal so lightly. No matter how stubborn Jack is..."

"Which he can be pretty stubborn," Red muttered.

"... I'm nearly unmovable," Kai finished.

"I'm a Wolf with teeth and claws, not to mention inhuman strength. I think I can be more than persuasive."

"Maybe," he shrugged. "I wouldn't count on it. I've wrestled a few wolves back in Anders. Worse in the Snow Queen's realm."

"I need to keep watch over you all," Red argued. "You have no idea what it's like here."

"Danger around every corner? You can't be too prepared? You're constantly on your guard?"

Red nodded grimly. They had no idea what the Enchanted Forest was like. There were incredibly good things here… But with every good thing there seemed to be a bad one.

"Sounds familiar," Kai muttered, taking a seat beside her, not close.

Icy blue eyes fell on the flames, but she knew how deceiving it was. He was focused, attuned to everything around him that he was capable of. Kai could survive in the Forest, that Red was sure of. But could she do it this time?

At least I'm not alone this time.

But even that thought wasn't completely reassuring.

Kai's low voice slipped through the silence, "How are you holding up?"

She shrugged. "I'm fine."

He glanced at her out of the corner of his eye as if to let her know that he sensed her lie. Red didn't correct herself, though. She could think of better lies later.

But Kai didn't press. "I didn't know that your wolf abilities were suppressed back in Neverland."

"It was nice while it lasted."

"And now?"

She sighed, hanging her head to hide her eyes. "Now I get used to it. The Wolf isn't going anywhere. Nothing's going to change; I need to accept it."

"That's not true." His counter struck her so much that she raised her gaze to him again. "Everything is going to change. We just need to see how those changes are going to play out, for better or worse."

Red looked around at the sleeping forms of friends. "I'm going to make sure they're for the better, if I have any say about it."

Her eyes locked on the figure cloaked in shadow standing at the edge of the campsite. Her blood chilled.

"Do not move," she warned under her breath just as Kai also became aware of the figure. They couldn't afford him doing anything stupid... Like trying to save Wendy, who lay curled up at the wraith's feet.

His eyes were hard, but thankfully he remained staring at the flames.

The wraith grinned under the shadows shrouding its face, or rather where its face ought to be. Red had never seen a wraith grin. But now, she *heard* it: the moist pull of muscle and flesh over wet gums and rows of razor teeth. As far as she could tell, this was how it could taste the air... and the magic.

It lurked there a moment more, drifting from Wendy to Jack and back. It never stepped too close to the fire's heat. Then the wraith disappeared into the dark of the Forest, as silent as when it arrived.

"It's gone?" Kai muttered.

Red nodded slowly, twisting her hands. "A wraith. One of the Forest's known monsters," she answered his unasked question. "It was just... checking."

A song inked its way into her mind. She shook her head, trying to be rid of the unwanted thing for now. Later, she knew she'd have to reminisce. Not tonight.

"Will it come back?"

"Perhaps," she responded. "That's why I have to keep a look out always. The Forest is full of monsters."

* * *

Kai grunted, looking around at the dark shadows. Did he think that he could see them coming if he looked hard enough?

Red huffed. *Once you see them; if you see them, it would be too late.*

"Seems like the perfect place for this Master to be hiding," he said.

A shiver ran down her spine. Too many faces and names came to mind as possibilities. But Kai was right; if this cruel power were anywhere, it would be here. And if it was here, did they even stand a chance?

"What or who will we need to watch out for?" he questioned much too casually for the circumstances.

Her throat tightened. The past was on the brink of coming back to at last expose itself. How soon would she have to break down her defenses? Relive the horrors?

She swallowed hard. "Monsters in the Forest, wraiths and shapeshifters, but they're something like animals. It's the others who you can't predict their appearance that we have to look out for. Wolves like Fang and the savage Lupa; the whole Pack holds allegiance with one or the other. There's a sorceress, Carabosse. I've never seen her and I'd like to keep it that way."

"Another witch?"

"Not just another witch," Red corrected. "She practically rules this Forest with her impending powers."

He dipped his chin in a nod of understanding. "Anyone else?"

"There's a man they call Bluebeard." She took a quick glance at Alice and Wendy before lowering her eyes. "He does... *terrible* things to girls."

Kai's fists clenched. "Have you faced him?" Was that a growl in the back of his voice?

She did her best to force the images from her mind. "Once. I was in his fortress; I saw him. But I never let him touch me."

"Good."

She wondered what it would be like now, though. What if she faced Bluebeard in person again, now that she was a Wolf? One strike and she could end him forever. Or she could make him suffer for every life he'd destroyed. One glance at Kai told her he'd gladly jump to help her do it.

Maybe we don't have to avoid that monster after all.

"Any others?" he asked.

Red shrugged. "There are always others. Witches, trolls, cannibals."

"Cannibals?"

She jumped at the sound of Jack's voice. She hadn't even realized he'd gotten up, much less been listening.

He looked disgusted, which complimented his mussed-up hair. "Can we at least avoid the cannibals? I prefer not to vomit when screaming for my life."

Red smiled, holding back a laugh. Why was he so good at that?

"Regardless, you'll need your sleep just as much as the rest of us," Kai put to her, "if not more so. No one is any good if they're half asleep and jumping at shadows."

"We'll do that regardless," she retorted halfheartedly.

He gave her a look that made her want to shrink back like a scolded pup.

Jack pulled himself up onto his knees, crawling closer to them. He sat promptly as if he still didn't look half asleep.

* * *

"Kai and I will both keep watch. We'll wake you up when it's your turn."

Red huffed, but both boys appeared quite satisfied with themselves. If she didn't do as they insisted, they were just going to stay up anyway.

"Fine. You win," she groaned, shoving Jack's head when he gave that stupid grin as she stood. She lay between Wendy and the Forest, facing away from the fire.

"Night, Rubes," she heard Jack whisper.

She hardly closed her eyes.

Chapter Four

How to Survive

At first light, when their journey was to continue, Red snapped awake when the monster burst into camp and shattered the fire pit with an explosion of sparks. Kai already stood erect with cutlass raised. Jack quickly rolled out of the way before the wide mouthed creature lunged at him. Wendy was nowhere in sight, and Alice was reaching for the firewood with unusual ease.

Shaking out of her shock, Red took a quick analysis of the monster before instinct took over. Wiry hair, lean body, large paws and a flat face. But it had a tail like a snake with a deadly spike at the end, and a sharp toothed grin that stretched up to those fiery eyes.

Why did all monsters smile?

She leapt forward and latched onto its flank. Bitter fluid filtered through her teeth and seared her gums, forcing her to recoil back. The wound smoked like a campfire. With a shrill, the monster whipped around, proving its large size did nothing to hinder its agility.

Red scrambled out of the way as its maw lunged toward her. Growling, they stood frozen with eyes locked. Everyone moved at once, the monster pitching forward, Red skirting away to find an opening for the throat, and Kai bringing his blade right onto the monster's iron plated spine. The monster yelped loudly. In one bite, it tore the sword from Kai's hands and consumed the entirety of the weapon before he had time to react. Red's heart skipped a beat as the monster advanced on a retreating Kai without any hindrance at having eaten a sword.

Iron spine, smoking wound, and swallows blades, she thought with horror and calculation.

With Kai defenseless, and Jack now thinking twice about his own sword, Red shot forward to draw the monster's attention. It whipped around instantly and knocked her aside with its tail. She twisted to bounce back up, but the monster leapt right on top of her, pinning her to the ground. Its weight knocked the breath right out of her. Those fiery eyes looked right down at her, ears perked up.

This is child's play to it, she discerned with a snarl.

Then fire exploded right against its head. The monster screamed, turning away. Red saw another blow coming and squeezed her eyes shut before the sparks showered full force once more. Bone crushing weight leaped off her, leaving her gasping.

With one hand, she clutched her ribs and the other propped herself up. She hadn't even realized she'd changed form.

Alice stood facing the now angry monster, a fiery log in each hand. She was smiling at it much the same way it was doing to her. Her sling seemed to have disappeared. Without hesitation, she sprang forward, not taking heed of the claws and teeth waiting for her while she bashed her fiery weapons against the monster's head. Red shouted at her when that tail plunged toward her, but instead of jumping back, Alice jumped closer.

"Are you insane?!" Red exclaimed. "You're going to get yourself killed!"

Alice laughed at that.

She plunged one of her logs directly into the monster's left eye socket. The monster screamed and threw Alice away with one swipe of its paw. She landed not too far away, but her other weapon was lost.

Before anyone else did anything stupid, Red took a deep breath and let the Wolf take control.

She rushed forward, colliding with the monster at maximum speed. The Wolf dodged a sweep of its arm before springing up to latch onto its neck just to the side of the spine. The monster tried to shake her off, but she just locked her jaw and snarled as the bitter juices filled her mouth. With a shriek, it vainly tried to bite her and dash her aside with its tail. When that deadly spike came too close, the Wolf released to snake under the monster's belly and snatch the other side of its neck. Smoke billowed.

The monster sent them rolling. The Wolf ripped a single iron plate from its spine. And a shot split the air, stopping it all.

With a new smoking wound right in its ribcage, the monster scampered off into the Forest. The Wolf stood stock still, heart racing and breath heaving as Red controlled herself. She turned to find Wendy standing at the edge of the clearing, solemn, a smoking pistol in hand.

Wendy lowered the weapon and looked around at the others. "Good morning." She indicated her arm that cradled some eggs to her torso. "Anyone up for breakfast? Or do we have another unwanted guest we need to take care of first?"

Shifting form, Red spat out the unpleasant monster blood before thanking Wendy for her help. She just shrugged, stowing the pistol away again.

While Jack worked at frying the eggs—after they were deemed safe—Wendy examined Alice's bullet wound. The bandage had to be readjusted after the skirmish with the monster.

"You reopened the wound some, despite the stitches," Wendy muttered. "Not that it had time to close…"

Alice winced. "If that's all that beast did—"

"But that's not all it could've done," Red interjected with more accusation than she intended. "What kind of insanity drove you to keep getting closer like that?"

Her expression waned, blue eyes falling to the ground. "I don't know."

Red almost regretted what she'd said, but she didn't apologize for it. Alice didn't say anything more about it, though.

By the time Wendy had finished patching up Alice, Jack finally got the cooking thing figured out. Wringing her hands, Red tried to plan how they were going to survive the rest of the day.

*****

Carabosse stroked her bird, long fingers trailing down its back. Power coursed through her veins in waves, a sensation she found pleasure in. Reflective eyes snapped up suddenly as a foreign tingle touched her spine. A small smile formed dangerously on her lips.

"It's been a while since you last visited me," she stated without turning around. "Have you come to visit or is this another business proposal?"

"What is it you expect?"

"I expect that you have come to inform of your findings," Carabosse proposed as she at last faced her visitor. "But that's not your style; is it, Lupa?"

Lupa grinned, revealing teeth filed to a point. "You know me all too well."

"Not as much as I would like," Carabosse admitted, "but enough."

Gold eyes glimmered under her arched eyebrow at that. Chocolate caramel hair fell in a thick, curly mess over her deteriorating blouse. Layers of skirts brushed the floor over her bare feet. The dim light reflected off her brown skin, making her glow.

"I do have much to share," Lupa said, her accent making every word distinct, "but only if the right questions are asked and, of course, if you answer mine in turn."

"You are a strange wolf. One I like, to be sure, but strange none the less." She strolled to her throne and took a seat. "Fine, I shall play your games. You always answer truthfully."

"Questions are made to be answered," Lupa said simply. "I have found that most times the truth can bite worse than a lie."

"How many do I get this time?"

Three long fingers tapped Lupa's nose, pearly nails sharpened to claws.

Carabosse sat back against the bones that constructed her throne. "I should have guessed. My first question, then: how many imperfects are left in this realm that you know of?"

"None. I have only found two of late, both found final solace between my teeth."

She masked her relief with a satisfied smirk. "And has the wizard kept out of trouble?"

"Isbjørn has not been seen since you banished him."

"Then he's being smart," she commented. Hardly a breath came before she ritualistically asked her final question, "And has the girl returned to the Enchanted Forest?" She chuckled, enjoying the feel of bone against her skin. The raven perched on her shoulder, bowing down next to her face to stare at the wolf.

Lupa grinned again, her white teeth gleaming. "Yes."

A jolt shot down her spine, snapping to attention in keen interest. The room darkened. Diablo flew from her shoulder with a caw.

"When?" Carabosse inquired. "Where?"

"I apologize, oh great sorceress," Lupa crooned, turning away toward the door, "but you're out of questions."

*****

No plan had been verbalized, but one thing was clear: they had to keep moving. After Red relayed the information about the monsters and villains to watch out for—as well as the visit from the wraith last night—to those who hadn't heard the first time, it was clear the safest thing was to not stay in one place for too long. Being visited by two monsters in one sitting has a certain effect on a person.

Red led the group, on high alert but remembering the warnings of venturing through the Forest. If only she had a path to follow. Or her cloak. Either one would make everything so much easier.

"Wendy," Red's ears pricked at the sound of Kai's deep voice behind her, "I need to talk to you about something back in Neverland."

"Sure." Wendy leaped over a protruding root. "I've been meaning to ask about what happened with you back there anyway. Where'd you get the limp?"

"Mermaid attack."

Red caught the look on Wendy's face, some mixture of shock and sympathy and no shortage of being impressed. She wasn't surprised though. Of course Kai got away from a mermaid attack with nothing but a limp to show for it.

"How much do you know about the ghosts on Skull Rock?" Kai continued.

"Not too much. They kept to themselves, and most try to stay clear of Skull Rock if they can help it. Although, I won't deny having been part of a few treasure hunts that led to that place."

"But you don't know about their curse?"

Wendy's face darkened. "I know they came from the first battle between Lost Boys and pirates. But I don't know about any curse. Just the visions, or hauntings, that can happen when you encounter them."

He gave a nod and grunt in acknowledgement. Red could practically hear the gears in his head turning.

"Does this have anything to do with when you were at Skull Rock?" Jack spoke up.

Wendy gawked, "*That's* where you were?"

Kai didn't say anything at first, collecting his thoughts by the look of it.

Red shivered at the thought of being with ghosts for so long. She lived with enough ghosts; she didn't need to meet someone else's.

"I met some of them," Kai finally spoke up. "They told me how to find you, and about the spy."

Wendy didn't say anything at the mention of Jane. But Red could hear the race of her heartbeat in instant anger. Hearts had a habit of exposing even the most suppressed of emotions.

"They told me about their curse, how they're stuck between life and death, the pain and memories they feel," Kai continued. "And they asked if I would help release them."

"Why you?" Alice questioned quickly.

He shrugged. "Because I might know people back in the Snow Queen's realm who can."

"What are you going to do?" Wendy asked curiously, voice quiet in thought.

Again, Kai didn't respond right away. Red wondered what else happened with the ghosts to make him care so much. Was he even telling them the whole story? Or was he only telling them what was necessary?

"I told them I would try to help them," Kai confessed at last. "I'll keep my word. I just thought you should know and see what you thought."

This time it was Wendy who took a long moment to answer. "In general, I think anyone should be careful when listening to those ghosts. But I trust your judgement, and if you want to help free them then I think you are doing the right thing." She paused again. "And if I can, I'll help you do it."

Kai didn't say anything after that, but there wasn't any need to. He gave a small smile, which she easily returned.

Red wished she could trust anyone so easily.

It was almost noon before they stopped to rest and eat the food they'd brought back from Neverland. Red couldn't sit still, even as she knew she needed a break just as much as the others. After passing around the bread and cheese, Wendy made sure that Alice's bandages were still secure. Jack sat near them and stretched.

The air tightened.

Red noticed instantly.

"Don't move!" she barked immediately. "Jack, don't you dare move a muscle!"

He froze on the spot, eyes wide at her tone. But her gaze was fixed on the small boulder hovering in the air just behind his skyward-reaching elbow.

"What?" Jack asked, looking at her with a mixture of concern and panic. "What is it?"

"I said don't move!" she scolded in a hiss. "One wrong move and that rock might crush someone's head."

Now everyone sat frozen, all except Jack able to see the flying boulder. His eyes rolled around trying to find it. He accidentally moved his arm. With a jerk, the rock sailed straight over Kai's head as he ducked for cover and stopped abruptly in front of Wendy's nose. She squealed unintentionally.

"I told you not to move!" Red exclaimed sharply.

"Sorry!" Jack apologized, now seeing the rock in its entirety.

Wendy didn't move a muscle, close enough to kiss the thing.

Red took a deep breath, trying to figure out the best way to control the situation. One false move and Jack could do more than just crush Wendy. The boulder could explode, or fly everywhere at once, or melt on the spot. And if Jack had enough strength to work the magic, it could even transfigure into something else entirely. Since he'd never worked magic before... This could get messy.

Figuring things out, Red began slowly and firmly, "Listen very carefully. I need you to..."

A sharp caw cut her words off abruptly.

Blood drained from her face. She dared not look up in the trees where the sound came from. Brow knit in confusion, Alice opened her mouth to ask something. Red gave her a look that promptly made her clamp it shut.

Moistening her lips, Red changed tactic. "Jack, do *exactly* as I say. Roll your right shoulder back slightly."

Jack did as instructed. The boulder glided away from Wendy and stopped in the center of the group. Wendy breathed again as if she'd been holding it.

"Good. Now lower both arms slowly—*slowly*—and make sure your right fist touches your opposite hip."

As he did so, the boulder sank down into the ground, the earth forced to accompany it. Even so, the air was still tight in their ears. They weren't done yet.

"This is the most important part, alright?" Red risked a quick glance up at the trees. "Throw your fist behind you in a sweep with all the force you can muster."

"What?"

"*Throw* your fist behind you," Red enunciated every word as calmly as she could, "as hard as you can."

In one fell swoop, Jack swept his arm back as quickly as he could. The boulder flew up at lightning speed and crashed into the tree. There was a bird's scream, the crack of wood, and then the whole branch came crashing down. But the boulder was still stuck in the tree trunk high above.

The group jumped to their feet, except Jack who dutifully remained frozen on the spot. Red pitched toward the wreckage, letting the Wolf take over. Sniffing around, she found the raven's remains. By the array of feathers and its crushed body, she knew the boulder had done the trick.

"You can move now, Jack," Red disclosed after she changed form again.

He gladly obeyed, leaping to his feet with the others.

"What was that about?" Kai questioned.

"We need to get moving again," she stated, gathering their things before leading them away from the scene. "There could be more coming soon."

"More what; ravens?" Jack asked, taking one last look at the suspended boulder in the tree.

"Diablo's ravens are Carabosse's spies," Red explained without breaking stride. She handed Wendy back her satchel. "It must've sensed the use of unstable magic. More can't be too far behind."

"Unstable magic?" Alice echoed.

Jack protested, "I don't even know how to use magic!"

Red huffed at that. "Anyone can use magic here, but not everyone knows how to control it. Many animals can sense its use, like ravens and... wolves." She shook her head to suppress a shiver at the realization. She'd never been able to sense magic's use before. She hadn't even noticed the change this time until now.

"Where are you taking us?" Alice spoke up suddenly, the first time that question was asked.

Red didn't look back at them to hide her face. "There's a kingdom called Grimrose. We should be able to find safe haven there."

Chapter Five

Grimrose

Thankfully, they were closer than she'd thought. Early the next morning, after wading straight through the prickling underbrush, Red found the road. The air wasn't buzzing as terribly here, and the day seemed brighter.

Now to stay on the path...

But she never had to warn the others about the consequences of wandering because soon they reached their destination.

The fragrance hit first. Sweet and tickling, the roses overpowered the scent of the trees. They crawled up the city's stone walls with blossoms in every shade. The gate was open, thankfully. Though Red didn't know many times when it was otherwise.

Tiny fairylike creatures flew along the edge of the wall, humming to an unknown tune. Some buzzed up to them curiously. Small blue faces crinkled into funny expressions as they tried to tug on their hair. Red swatted them away, weaving her hair into a tight French braid quickly.

"Sprites," she explained to the others. "They're cute, but pesky. Keep an eye out; they'll steal your hair for their nests... and they like shiny things, too."

Sprites were already snagging at Jack's brown waves despite their short length. Another one snatched the thin chain around Kai's neck. It pulled up to fly off with its prize. Kai waved it away agitatedly. He popped his collar up over the chain to keep the annoying insects from taking it again. Alice did the same.

Before they passed under the entrance, Red glanced up at the wall. She felt eyes on them though she couldn't see the sentries.

As soon as they stepped into the village, she knew something was wrong. The cottages seemed cozy enough with the flourishing gardens and inviting aura. Statues stood in front of a few homes, ivy crawling up the stone and sprite nests tucked into the crevices. It was too quiet.

"Where is everyone?" Wendy voiced.

That was the problem. There was not a soul to be seen or voice to be heard.

Red didn't bother to answer the question. She'd only ever visited Grimrose a few times, and most times drifting through as invisibly as possible. Festivals would excuse the town's barrenness. But she heard no music, though she supposed they were still on the outskirts. Even so, something felt wrong.

Trekking onward, the townhouses grew closer together to borderline the streets. This place should've been bustling with activity. But again, there was not a living soul in sight. Buzzing sprites were the only things disturbing the eerie silence, congregating in corners and nooks. Statues became more frequent and strange.

The possibility of a festival ebbed away. Dread slowly took its place.

Red was drawn to a large building, a market that was overflowing with unique statues that increased the pit in her gut. The others followed.

"Where are the people?" Alice questioned, weaving around the statues.

Red bit back a huff. "Look around," she said, voice lowered. She gestured to the stone figures crowding the open market. "They're here. They're everywhere."

Indeed, the more she looked at the statue's faces, the more she was sure of herself. Somehow, by some curse or unimaginable beast, the people of Grimrose has been turned to stone.

Rotting fruit sat stinking in the baskets. Flies and sprites zipped about the horrendous stench and moldy bread. Fabrics once on display for sale now sat frayed and moth eaten.

How long have things been like this?

The sound of stone against stone thudded behind her, causing her to jump around with every nerve on edge. Jack caught the first statue quickly, the one he'd knocked over. Wendy stopped the second from causing a chain reaction while Kai swiped Alice from being crushed. The noise echoed.

"Careful!" Red scolded through her teeth. She wasn't sure why she continued to whisper.

"Sorry." Jack winced as he righted the statue once more. It had been caught frozen in stone mid-sneeze.

Alice thanked Kai quietly, stepping away.

"How could this happen to an entire kingdom?" Wendy voiced, she too fixing her statue. It was a woman with a basket over her arm. There was a kid by her side.

... an entire kingdom...

A hollow pit formed in Red's stomach.

Turning on her heel, she sped out of the market place. Her heart pounded like a drum pronouncing doom. Stone cold villagers came in greater quantity and thicker crowds. A prayer came under her breath in hopeless desperation.

There was a ditch between the village and the walls, a small stream running at the bottom where there might have once been a moat. But she didn't need to worry about the ditch since the gate was open and drawbridge lowered. It was like a mouth ready to swallow her whole. Red glided past the guards that were thrown to the side and left frozen on the ground.

Across the courtyard, through the doorway that stretched high overhead, Red entered the castle where a congregation awaited. She felt as frozen as the statues before her. She didn't even move when her friends joined behind her.

A hand was placed on her arm. She didn't ask for it, but she didn't reject it either.

Before her stood a score of knights, a crowd of soldiers, and a king and queen staring right at her with shock and anger permanently etched in their faces. Behind them were fleeing lords and ladies. Servants bordered the entirety of the group amongst the columns. All were stone.

Red hated being where she stood, right at the source of their glares. Anxious, she stepped closer to the king. Out of their glares. Away from the accusing king's reach. But a lump still formed in her throat.

"Did you know them?" Jack's voice sounded in concern.

Red didn't know exactly how to answer that. "Not directly. But they were my—*our* only hope." She hid her fumble as best as she could. Then she pointed the royal couple out one by one. "This is King Thrushbeard and Queen Euna. I've only seen them twice before."

"How did this happen?" Alice repeated Wendy's earlier question. She stood at the source of the curse now, looking around at the faces now glaring at her.

Red swallowed a foul taste in her mouth. "Grimrose has long been known to be under scrutiny of Carabosse for not bowing to her will. She's cursed them before; I wouldn't be surprised if she cursed them again."

"What now?" Wendy asked.

"We should scour the castle, look for anything we can use," Kai suggested. "Weapons, clothes, even food if we can find it."

Red noticed Jack's reaction before anything else. He turned suspiciously around in a circle, eyes sharp, muscles tightened. That's when Red saw something skitter out of sight behind the columns. The hairs on the back of her neck stood on end.

"Uh, guys," Jack warned, "I don't think the statues are the only ones here. And I'm not talking about the little blue people."

Eyes narrowed, senses spiked. Red sniffed the air and was awarded with the stench of mud, gravel, and sweat. Her skin crawled.

"Goblins."

*****

Nose pressed to the floor, the grey wolf searched for a whiff of a scent to track. Anything would do at this point. But Fang's confidence was so low that even the Forest and its strange ways of path finding could do nothing to help. Years of hunting this girl, and this is where it's gotten him. He'd had her in his claws once, and…

Something caught his nose in the dirt. His heart skipped a beat. There was no way that it could be possible. Sniffing again, Fang made certain his senses were not fooling him.

Morphing into his human form, his hand pressed to the ground. The earth sent a shock of new energy through his arm. Silver eyes sparked with hope. He couldn't help the smile that flicked at the corner of his mouth.

Finally.

Fang sighed, relief swelling in his chest.

Switching back into the grey wolf, Fang let out a loud howl. The call to his pack pierced through the Forest. With instant quickened pace, he rushed toward Grimrose and the girl.

Chapter Six

Fleeing the Castle

Creatures emerged from the shadows, scraggly and grotesque with colorless cracked skin. Pointed noses, beady eyes, and nasty teeth convulsed on their faces. They slinked out from behind pillars, hunched over on knuckles and skinny legs.

Red and the others backed away slowly as the goblins advanced. Every step produced more creatures climbing around statues. Black eyes were filled with hunger.

"Go," Red hissed. "Run, *now!*"

She spun around a moment after her friends and together they bolted from the castle. Goblins chased after them, much faster than they appeared. They blew through the castle grounds and over the drawbridge. At the gut wrenching sound of claws against wood, Red dared to glance back to discover the crowds of gathering goblins squeezing through the entrance. If only they'd had time to pull the drawbridge up.

But it turned out not to matter anyway. Goblins protruded from the town as soon as they entered, ugly sneers pulled on their faces.

They ran.

Red took a breath and let the Wolf take over. Speed increased. Power jolted through the muscles in her limbs. She ran ahead of the others, digging her claws and sinking her teeth into the goblins closest to them. Their flesh was like elastic, but once torn they bled freely. Blood like ink filled her mouth.

They were fairly easy to kill, but came in overwhelming numbers. An ugly face sneered at her, batting at her. Nails ripped her muzzle, pain stinging. She snapped its neck.

Pausing to check on her friends, she found them running for their lives. Jack had his sword drawn, as did Wendy. But the next moment a horde of goblins leaped *onto* Alice's cutlass, forcing it out of her hands. At least she had the sense to keep running. Kai was weaponless, thanks to the blade-eating monster from yesterday.

Talons raked through Red's ribs while she was distracted. She yipped, flinching away from another strike. With a leap, she took out three more goblins thanks to their brittle bones. But she saw the look in their beady eyes. They'd drawn the Wolf's blood. By the time she realized what they would do, she was too late.

Four of them jumped at once, only two managing to land on her back. Snarling, Red tried to wrestle them off. Razor teeth latched onto her ribs right on the scratches. Whipping her body around, she threw them off. Flesh tore instantaneously. The goblins were gone, but they both had her fur and skin in their bloodied mouths.

She ignored the pain, but was too aware that her wounds were oozing now. It was too tempting. Passing the market and eight more slaughtered goblins later, they began jumping again. The Wolf dove into a roll, forcing them off. As soon as she popped up, they were on her again.

A savage instinct took hold. She didn't even fully process her senses. Blood and elastic skin between her jaws.

Snapping bones under her weight. Still, they came in multitudes.

Goblins threw themselves at her so they were all she could see. Her feet were yanked out from under her, landing her on the ground with blood and stars. The creatures piled up and weighed her down. She couldn't get her feet under her.

When she shifted form, she tried to wrestle them off, but it only pushed them back briefly before they attacked again, still aiming for the bleeding ribs. Stars specked her vision. Her ability to gather energy for a fight ebbed away. The pain in her ribs numbed all other sensation. But she was still conscious, however altered it was.

Someone screamed her name before Red disappeared under the flood of goblins.

They were eating her alive.

And she wouldn't black out.

Wendy turned back first when she noticed Red's absence. She caught one glimpse of her friend in human form vanishing under a horde of those creatures.

"Red!" she cried, but her exclamation turned into a scream when a goblin collided into her and dragged her down.

It was just as big as she was, and it landed right on top of her. Wendy panicked, wrestling first to grab her short sword that landed beside her before having to give up and keep the goblin's teeth from getting at her throat. Hands pushed against its cracked face, the tactic working to an extent. The goblin dug its claws into her arms and raked them over her skin frantically. She didn't budge despite the burning stings. A grey tongue waggled at her from between her fingers.

Heart pounding, Wendy risked it. In one movement, she dropped an arm and snatched her sword. The goblin broke from her resistance. It lunged. She skewered it just as it went for the throat. Suddenly, the goblin was gone, kicked in the face and thrown from her in one fell swoop.

She lay there, adrenaline pumping. Kai extended his arm to hoist her up. Before Wendy could protest, he wrapped an arm around her and sped off. Her legs couldn't keep up with his pace. At this point, he was practically carrying her!

"What are you doing?" Wendy exclaimed when she could catch her breath. "The others are back there! Red—"

"Jack and Alice are taking care of that," Kai spoke to the rhythm of his breathing.

"We have to help!"

"We have to get out of here!"

Kai fumbled, a goblin snatching at his ankles and leaving scarlet lines. Picking up the pace to as near a run as he could manage, he had to hold Wendy tighter. She couldn't match his step at all.

"And that means leaving the others behind?" she questioned, about to wrestle out of Kai's grip to go back. They were quickly nearing the wall bordering Grimrose.

"It means everyone is getting out," he responded, passing through the open gate, "even if it takes one of us at a time."

"I will not be the first—Hey!"

Taking her around the waist, Kai nearly threw Wendy into a tree just by the path and outside the Forest. She clung to the branch, too stunned to formulate a coherent response.

"Climb higher," he ordered, kicking a goblin away full force.

Still shocked, she scrambled up the tree until she was a good deal higher than Kai could reach. When she looked back down, Wendy found him throwing goblins off. They landed sprawled out on the ground.

"Stay there!" Kai shouted, icy eyes shooting a warning. "Wendy, *stay* in that tree!"

With that, he took off back into Grimrose, disappearing behind the wall. A swarm of goblins followed at his heels.

Snapping out of her shock, she felt a surge of hot frustration. She was not about to stand to the side—or sit in a tree—when her friends needed her help! With a huff, she made to climb down.

A growl like gravel rolling over stone sounded below her. Stomach knotting, Wendy looked down from her perch. More of those nasty creatures were slinking to her tree. Teeth gnashing, they glared at her hungrily.

She reached for her sword only to realize it had been left in the carcass of the goblin that'd attacked her. Her pistol was still strapped to her pants, but she didn't want to risk wasting her bullets. Pulling her legs up, she realized she was trapped. Then one of them dug his claws into the tree bark. Her heart pounded.

The goblins were climbing the tree, and the only way to go was up.

Just as Jack reached the violent swell of vicious rock monkeys, Alice appeared in a dangerous whirlwind of terrified monsters and her pitchfork. He didn't bother to question where she got the thing. It seemed to be an effective enough weapon.

Together, they charged into the horde. Jack hacked away at the creatures with his blade, blood spraying like black rain. He even dared to rip the beasts off the pile with his bare hands. Killing them wasn't his priority. Alice was doing a fine job of that; a constant reminder not to anger a girl with a pitchfork.

This deep in the crowd revealed that the evil monkey creatures didn't necessarily care which blood they went after so long as it was edible. Jack grimaced as goblins attacked each other in the confusion. But maybe that meant there weren't so many attacking the Wolf at the bottom of the pile.

Goblins flew in all directions, screaming. Then he saw a bloodied hand—scarlet, not black. It was outstretched and limp. He grabbed it, dropping his sword to pull her out with both hands. Muscles burned. Finally, Jack managed to pull Red out of the stinking pile. The goblins were too distracted with eating their own kind, or avoiding a pitchfork-wielding maniac, to notice him drag her body away.

She was limp and sticky with blood, both black and scarlet. One glance was enough to notice pale ribs exposed behind her side. While Alice fended off attackers, Jack ripped off his jacket and tied it tight around Red's middle to protect her open wound. Green eyes fluttered.

"Blasted bloody—" Jack cursed under his breath. "You're awake."

At least she was alive.

He hoisted her up onto his shoulders so her wound wasn't rubbing against his neck. Then he ran as fast as he could under Red's weight. She was heavier than she looked.

Alice took position as bodyguard, keeping the goblins away so all Jack had to focus on was running. Then after she shouted at him, he focused on running the right way.

A cry split the air. Jack whipped around just as Alice skewered the goblin and flung it aside. Her calf was bleeding from fresh bite marks.

"Keep running," she barked at him, walking now with a limp.

Turning to do just that, his heart plummeted. Kai was heading their way... with a wave of goblins in his wake. There were more between them.

"As if running wasn't hard enough," Jack exclaimed as he barreled through the evil rock monkeys.

Alice rushed after him, trying to clear a path. When Kai finally caught up, she nearly stabbed him had he not stopped the pitchfork with his strange weapon. For a moment, they stood frozen. Then Jack trotted past them, and that seemed to snap them out of their daze.

"Was that a frying pan I saw?" he called over his shoulder when the two threw themselves into fending off the goblins again.

"Iron skillet, I think," Kai corrected just as he bashed aside a creature so hard it flew back, skull crushed. "It's all I could manage at short notice."

Jack didn't have the energy to question how one happened upon an iron skillet when running through the village.

Feet pounded under him. Shoulders ached. He wasn't running, not really. He couldn't under his current circumstances. Sweat ran down his face and arms, heat and exhaustion pulsing through him. He clung to Red's body so she wouldn't fall off. Sticky blood trailed down his back. He ignored the fact that it wasn't all Red's blood.

His stitches snapped.

Burning legs carried him on.

They barreled through the village, Alice and Kai losing agility with running and fighting. Jack's lungs were on fire. It seemed like the exit was a spot in the distance. Suddenly, Kai appeared beside him.

"You're losing energy," Kai pointed out, bashing a leaping goblin in midair with his skillet. "I can carry her the rest of the way."

Jack shook his head, panting, "I can't stop. If I keep going, I can make it. I can't fight off the monkeys."

"We're running out of time. We need to get out of here now!"

"You think I don't know that?!"

"Boys!" Alice snapped so sharply that the goblins closest to her flinched away. "I hate to break it to you, but *shut up*! The sooner we leave this place, the better. But let's get out in one piece!"

Seeing her point, Jack met Kai's gaze and they came to a wordless agreement. Slipping Red off his shoulders, Jack pulled her arm over his neck and held fast to her waist. Kai did the same, sharing the weight and increasing their speed. Of course, Kai still had the frying pan to whack aside any goblins that got too close. Meanwhile, Alice held her pitchfork before her to break through the awaiting goblins. The path cleared in her wake.

Then Red woke up.

Really, she just came to full consciousness, but Jack felt the change when her fist closed over his. Her legs moved next, somehow managing to keep a pace that almost matched theirs.

Jack's skin crawled and a shiver ran down his spine. He'd felt this sensation before. It sent his adrenaline pumping. He almost expected a boulder to be floating beside them. But it wasn't like before. This time, the magic hurt.

"When I say so..." The tortured voice swept past his ear. It took a split second to realize it was Red. "... turn around and stop."

Jack's mind raced. What was she thinking? But he didn't have the energy to argue, and he already knew what he was going to do anyway.

Even though Kai clearly hadn't heard, Jack nodded in comprehension to let Red know that he understood.

It took a few more foot falls before a hot wave washed over his skin. His ears rang. His fingers numbed. Somehow, he knew even before she shouted for it.

"*Now!*"

Jack whipped her around so fast that she was yanked from Kai's grasp. Red raised her arms and shoved them away from her. An invisible force slammed into him. Next thing he knew, he was on the ground a few meters away from her. A cloud of dust filled the air. Jack looked around, but the only one standing was Red.

A second later, the dust cleared. Goblin bodies littered the landscape, all dead and broken, thrown aside like ragdolls. Jack struggled to catch his breath. Another glance at Red and he shot over to catch her.

"We need to move," she muttered before her knees gave way.

He nodded, tossing her arm over his shoulders again. Her head slumped. This time, she was unconscious.

Alice helped Kai up, both having been thrown aside by the invisible force as well. The skin-crawling heat was gone. No longer running, the four of them passed through the gateway.

Kai led them to the tree he'd left Wendy in, as he explained. But when they found the tree, Jack's stomach tightened. Goblin carcasses were all over in gruesome angles. Some dangled from the branches. Others were sprawled on the ground.

Wendy was nowhere to be seen.

Kai's face had gone ashen. "Wendy!"

"Up here!"

Jack craned his neck to find her barely a smudge in the treetops. After a slow and cautious descent, Wendy was on the ground once again. Though glad they were safe and together, there was not a smile among them. They decided to brave the Forest, staying on the path of course. But they wanted to put some distance between them and Grimrose before tending to their wounds.

Good riddance, Jack thought with a last glance back at the kingdom's walls.

Chapter Seven

Wolf Pack

"Are you going to call her?" Quinn asked, pushing her short caramel-accented hair out of her eyes. "Because I'd like a warning before that witch decides to pop up out of nowhere."

"I'd say she's more of a sorceress than a witch," Lev countered. "Witches are more of the sort told at bedtime to scare cubs into behaving properly."

"Witch, sorceress, fairy, all the same!" Quinn waved it off. "Point is, when are we telling Carabosse?"

"Don't say her name!" Lev's arrowhead eyes darted around as if expecting the sorceress to emerge from the shadows.

Quinn rolled amber-shot eyes to the star speckled sky.

Fang smirked, ripping off a strip of meat with his teeth. "I'm sure she already knows. She has eyes and ears everywhere."

Lev looked around with new vigor at that.

Rolling up his sleeve, Fang relented, "But just in case…"

With the dragon cuff exposed, he closed his eyes and balled his fist. He released his breath through the nose. Muscles in his arms tightened. His eyes snapped open just as the dragon's eyes glowed and a single puff of smoke twisted from its nostrils. Quinn stepped back; Lev tensed in his seat. When the dragon eyes faded to empty darkness, Fang relaxed and lowered his arm.

"There," he acknowledged. "Now she knows."

Lev shivered. "Give us a warning next time, before your eyes start glowing like you're possessed."

Fang dropped his gaze to his meal. He hadn't realized that the dragon cuff's eyes weren't the only ones glowing.

"If Carabosse is so capable," Quinn muttered, "why doesn't *she* just find this girl?"

"I don't know, nor do I care." Fang shrugged. "So long as I get my payment, I'll find the devil himself if she requested."

"That's too easy!" Lev retorted. "Just give her a mirror."

"How is Zoë?" questioned the last member of their group, ignoring the younger man's quip. His grey hair was pulled back in a knot and crow's feet etched the corners of his eyes. A pale scar slit the olive skin across his right eye.

"*Thaddeus*," Lev raised his eyebrows mockingly, "you dare to ask the forbidden question?"

"I can ask whatever question I wish to ask," Thaddeus responded calmly. "I also know when to speak and when not to, which is something you could learn from."

Quinn burst out laughing, nose crinkling in a wide smile. She laughed even harder when Lev's brown complexion reddened to a blush. Fang suppressed the urge to smile at his friends.

Lev ran a hand through his wild hair shot through with white strands that had nothing to do with age. Blush diminishing, he looked up at Quinn deviously. An arctic wolf before the blink of an eye, he sprang from his seat and sailed straight for her. Lev collided with Quinn, sending them rolling. She changed form instantly.

* * *

53

Arctic and red wolf sprawled around the campfire, snarling and yipping. Fang and Thaddeus did nothing. After all, neither of the younger wolves did any damage despite their strikes with teeth and claws.

Eventually, Lev ended up on top, teeth bared. Then Quinn kicked him in the stomach and sent him rolling too close to the fire. A yowl split the air as the arctic wolf's tail went up in smoke.

Quinn morphed back, dirt smudged over her tan skin from the tumble. She laughed hysterically as Lev jumped around to snuff the heat. Fang couldn't help but grin at the sight. Switching form, Lev's trousers smoked at his rear. He cursed as he beat out the burning fabric. That earned a chuckle from Thaddeus.

Lev snatched Quinn around the waist and pulled her down in his lap. His arms wouldn't permit her to escape. Whispering things in her ear made Quinn either snicker or elbow him in the ribs. But her amber-shot eyes glittered all the same. He took the liberty of playing with her messy hair.

Ignoring the couple's flirtatious giggles, Thaddeus turned back to Fang. "You still have yet to answer my question."

Silver eyes fell to the bare bone in his hands. "She'll be alright. I promised her that, and I don't intend on breaking it."

Thaddeus scratched his goatee and moustache. "And now? How long do you think it will take before that curse runs its course?"

The words came like burrs in his throat, "About two weeks. The rose is wilting so fast. Once it fades away..." He stopped, the rest of his sentence caught in his throat.

Thaddeus nodded as if he understood. "You are certain that Carabosse will do as she promised, even if she is able to undo it?"

"She can, and she will." Fang threw it at the dirt like a vow. "She started it with cursing Zoë's father. Now she'll finish it."

"I just wish it had not taken you so long to ask for help," Thaddeus huffed. "The Pack will follow you wherever you lead. After everything you have done...Even those two over there will run to the ends of the earth after you, though they might get a little distracted along the way."

Fang laughed half-heartedly.

Ahead of them, Quinn and Lev had fallen asleep slumped over each other. They were sure to fall over soon.

Thaddeus patted Fang on the knee. "Get some sleep, son. You are going to need it if we want to make it to Grimrose by tomorrow."

"And hopefully," Fang sighed, "to Red."

Chapter Eight
Blood and Dust

Red screamed.

Whoever was peeling off the shirt from her ribs—Wendy, she thought—didn't let her cries stop them. Blood was everywhere. It stained Wendy's arms up to her elbows. It soaked Jack's back. Crimson drops speckled the road in small pools. And from what Red could tell, it was all hers.

The wind hit her open wound and set her nerves shrieking. Tears leaked from her eyes. Clenching her jaw, she tried her best to control herself. But even though she knew that her friends were helping, everything in her wanted to fight them off.

Someone was holding her hand. She squeezed it so hard she was afraid she'd break his fingers. In fact, she was certain of it. That's why she forced herself to let him go.

"Red, are you listening?" It was Wendy.

Neck stiff, she dipped her chin slightly.

"How do I help you?"

"I can't move my legs."

"Kai is holding them down," Wendy explained steadily. "You keep fighting us off; we have to keep you relatively still."

Fabric rubbed against sensitive skin around her wounds, the stinging causing every muscle to contract. But still, the fabric was held firm, shoved against her wound to stop the bleeding.

"Red," it was Wendy again, "how do we help you? Is there anything in this forest that can help heal you?"

She could barely get the word out, "Sprites…"

"What? Alice, hold this."

Next thing she knew, Wendy was right there kneeling in front of her. She waited expectantly.

Red tried again, fighting through clenched teeth, "Sprites have dust…"

"Like pixie dust?"

"It can… help with the bleeding…"

Wendy nodded and then she was gone. She heard them arguing, but couldn't make out the words. Someone ran past her. Then Jack was there again, holding her hand this time.

"It'll be alright, Rubes," he insisted as if trying to convince himself. "It'll be over soon."

But neither of the others said anything to affirm or deny this. Red didn't blame them. She could feel her energy ebbing away. If it wasn't for the Wolf fighting inside of her, she wouldn't even be conscious. And if help didn't come soon, her state of consciousness was the least of her worries.

Wendy burst out of the Forest a thousand sprites swarming around her like insects. Grimrose's walls were infested with the creatures and roses. They pulled at her curls before darting away fast as lightning. Too many licked at her bloodied arms. Even so, they darted out of her grasp. No amount of snatching, sneaking, clasping, or pouncing helped at all. The pesky sprites were too speedy. They had no intentions of being caught.

The more she tried and failed, the more anxious she became. But if she couldn't catch a sprite, if she couldn't get its dust...

She *had* to catch one.

Chilling laughter sounded behind her, making her stumble. Sprites scattered. Wendy whipped around.

"Look at you flapping around like a bird!"

She froze.

A woman stood there, tall and muscular with frizzy caramel chocolate hair and striking gold eyes that looked at Wendy like fascinating prey. Somehow, she knew that if she tried to run away this woman would catch her. Wendy itched to grab her pistol.

When the woman spoke again, her voice came in a purr, "What are you called, bird?"

She cringed despite herself. Only two people had ever called her *Bird* before, and the thought of either of them made her blood boil. Wendy had never considered herself a loathing person. That is, until Hook came into her life. And then Jane.

"Wendy," she answered at last. Best not to anger a woman with pointy teeth.

"Ah, a Wendy Bird," the woman crooned, "quite a rare creature."

"Please don't call me that."

"Do not worry. I never cared for birds."

Wendy didn't respond to that. Her heart pounded heavily in her chest, but she wasn't frightened. Too many emotions scrambled inside for her to be frightened of this woman. Her confusion made the stranger smile.

"Who are you?"

The woman ignored her question. "You will not catch one that way." She indicated the sprites that returned to flit around Wendy and get a lick at the blood on her arms. "They can sense your emotions, and unless you match theirs, they will continue to tease you."

"But don't they care?!" Wendy questioned, frustrated.

She gave a laugh that held a sickening amusement. "Of course not! Sprites are not fairies. They have no soul."

Wendy swatted at some sprites trying to lick the blood off her arms. Again, she could not hit them, only scatter them. The stranger's gold eyes glittered at the sight of the crimson blood coating Wendy's arms. She felt the urge to run.

The woman examined her as if Wendy were a puppet who's strings she desired to control. "So young. You are not much older than Little Red was when we first crossed paths. Such responsibility and destiny lie on young shoulders. It must be suffocating."

Cold fingers crawled down her vertebrae at those words. What did this woman know? And somehow, she knew Red, which made Wendy distrust the woman even more. *Little Red* was a title that Red had always loathed. Perhaps there was good reason.

The woman shrugged. "But then again, it cannot be helped."

"I am not as young as I look," Wendy muttered. She really was tired of the assumptions that just because she looked like a child meant she was one.

The woman cocked her head. "No, I suppose not."

They stood that way for a moment, examining each other. Wendy was trying to figure out a way to escape with a sprite and her life, when the woman pulled a small vile from her bodice and tossed it to her. Catching it, Wendy stared at the vile. Cyan substance filled it, a color matching the sprite's moist skin.

"What is it?"

"Sprite dust," the woman answered simply. "Enough to last for enough time."

Suspicion crawled in her skin, pulling her brow together. "Why give it to me?"

"I have an investment on Little Red; I cannot have her dead." The woman smirked, revealing those sharp teeth. "That would be catastrophic. I need her very much alive, but she would not take help from me directly. Besides, it is not time for us to meet again."

Wendy swallowed down a sinister thought that came when she heard those words. She clutched the vial.

The woman turned away to slink back into the Forest where the trees seemed to part way for her to enter. "Just tell Little Red that Lupa sends her regards."

Everything was a haze now. There was pain and noise and hands covering hers and someone holding her legs and fabric shoved against her ribs. Red felt like her head was filling with cotton. It all gave her a headache.

She just wanted the pain to go away.

Then a new commotion took place. The pressure applied to her wound lifted and peeled away. Her spasm reflexes reacted against her accord. Her tongue felt dry in her mouth.

Something cold and sticky was smothered over her ribs. She gasped. The sensation itched over her wounds,

* * *

seeped into her muscles, and shot down her veins. And Red breathed, slowly, heavily.

Her senses returned to her in stride, vision clearing, the pounding in her ears diminishing. Soon she could move without being awarded with a shot of pain. Jack and Alice helped her sit up while Kai pressed a canteen to her lips. Red let the water slide down her parched throat.

Though still weak, Red could at least sit up on her own and take in her bearings. Her friends gathered around her.

"It worked!" Wendy exclaimed with both excitement and relief.

Kai frowned, capping off the canteen. "But how long will it last?"

Red glanced down and struggled to get a look at her wounds. Through her torn shirt, she saw a blue-green film spread over her ribs like an instant scab. It didn't look as bad as it felt a moment ago. But then again, she was only seeing the aftermath. Wendy's arms were stained up to her elbows with blood, as were Alice's hands. And pools of it speckled the road.

"It won't hold over a day," Red informed, voice strained.

"We have more sprite dust," Wendy told her, holding up a strange vial.

Red stared at it a moment, processing. "Where did you find that?"

Wendy lowered her eyes guiltily. "I couldn't catch a sprite, and then this woman found me. She gave me the vial. I think she called herself Lupa."

* * *

Instantly, her blood ran cold. But she didn't say anything about it, despite her instantaneous urgency to run. Swallowing the bitter taste in her mouth, Red explained, "The sprite dust is only a temporary reprieve. We need to find more permanent methods."

At that, Kai started ripping the ruined jacket into bandages and began wrapping them around Red's middle. She didn't protest.

"Where are we supposed to find help?" Jack questioned. "Grimrose is full of statues and evil rock monkeys, and I don't like the sound of this Lupa person, no matter what she gave us."

Red groaned, rubbing her eyes. "I really don't know."

There was a moment of silence, the intensity of recent events settling down with the reality of the present situation. Red's mind struggled to regain a sense of direction. What were they supposed to do now?

"Jack," Alice's voice was quiet and laced with pain, "you're bleeding."

Jack huffed. "Most of it's not mine. Besides, you're bleeding too!"

"No—I mean, yes, I'm just now realizing that." She sat on the road with her knee up, revealing a bite on her calf. But Alice was more annoyed with the fresh stain blossoming from her bandages to prove her wound had reopened. "But you are actually *bleeding*."

Wiping the blood tickling her face with the back of her wrist, Red strained her neck to see Jack's back better. Her blood indeed stained all down his shirt. But the dark mass flowering through, that was fresh. A sickening feeling crawled in her gut.

"You broke your blasted stitches!" Red groaned, reaching out to prove her words true. Jack flinched back before she could touch his shirt.

"I'm fine!" he protested, pulling a smile as if to ward off suspicion.

She was still too exhausted to tell if he was lying or not; but from experience she knew that anytime someone claimed that they're fine, it was usually a lie.

"Stitches?" Kai muttered in confusion.

"He had an incident with a cougar back in Neverland," Wendy explained, fidgeting with the vial of sprite dust. Kai grunted in acknowledgement.

"Honestly, I didn't even notice they'd snapped until Alice pointed it out," Jack insisted.

Red frowned at him. "Fine. But you'll need some of that sprite dust, at least until we find a way to stitch you up again. And that goes for the rest of you as well! Only the serious stuff, though. We have to make it last."

"I'd hardly call a few scratches serious," Jack muttered.

"I don't care what *you* call serious," Wendy spoke up, obviously taking it upon herself to distribute the sprite dust. "I'll decide that."

It didn't take long for her to decide what to use the sprite dust for, to which the others had various input. In addition to Red's exposed ribs, Jack's shredded back and Alice's bullet wound were deemed the most serious of injuries. A bit of the dust was spared for the bite on Alice's calf and the deep scratches down Red's nose. If the stuff worked on bone, Kai would've been given some for his ankle. Unfortunately, it didn't.

The aquamarine dust fell like sand, turning to a kind of thin paste upon contact with skin and blood. It served as a painkiller and instant scab all at once. And they only had one small bottle of it.

The shadows lengthened and darkened with the setting sun. Night was approaching quickly. Kai gathered wood from just off the road for a fire after they decided to camp there until tomorrow. Red knew she needed to figure out what their next move was. But her eyelids grew too heavy. With assurances that someone would be on continuous lookout despite their being on the road, and a last warning not to listen to whatever whispers came from the trees, Red lay back down and fell asleep faster than she had in a long while.

Dreams eluded her, which was a blessing.

Chapter Nine

The First Question

"I want a new deal."

Carabosse's words echoed through the chamber as soon as Lupa stepped foot in the room. Her timing was impeccable as always. No one could manipulate the Forest like Lupa. Except for Carabosse. She could bypass the Forest without a second thought.

Lupa smirked. "That is not how our relationship works."

"I wish to know the location of your *Little Red Riding Hood.*"

"That is information I would only give for a deal." She twiddled with the multiple necklaces around her neck. "Which, as I have explained, is not a proposition for you to make."

"I want a new deal!" Daggers in her tone came with every annunciated word.

"You always want to control everything." Lupa drew her finger over the surface of a fearsome statue, inspecting the dust she picked up. "But not this. I make the calls."

Carabosse's face darkened, a dangerous fire in her eyes.

Tongue clicking, Lupa absentmindedly stroked the visible charms attached to her clothing. "Do not waste your breath on threats, sorceress. You cannot force anything on me. And I hold nothing of personal value to manipulate me with."

She kept her lips pressed firmly together. Unfortunately, thanks to those cursed charms, she wasn't going to get anything out of this wolf unless it was in her best interests. And Lupa knew that. She reeked with the knowledge of her power.

"I have come to collect an answer." Lupa turned gold eyes amusedly on Carabosse. "And I will know if you answer truthfully or not."

"I do not need to be reminded of your talent in lie detection," she growled.

"I would like to know your technique. How is it that you are able to control the will of man with limited need for physical involvement?"

An odd question. But Carabosse didn't need long to come up with an answer. She flashed her white teeth in a malicious sneer. "Love. It can bring the strongest of men to their knees. When one is able to control and manipulate its abilities, one has the power to control the will of any and all of man."

Lupa raised a thick eyebrow. "Thank you. I shall consider that for future reference."

Just like that, she turned to leave. Carabosse took a few strides after her, determined to somehow get the information she needed. She stopped a few paces away when her hands began to burn.

"Is that all?" Carabosse inquired, not revealing a trace of discomfort.

Lupa turned back, a smirk playing at her lips. "Do not worry, I will be back. I still have two more answers to collect."

A shadow darkened a slit in the wall before Diablo flew into the room. His hoarse voice cawed frantically. Swooping down, he landed on Carabosse's shoulder and pressed his beak to her ear. Diablo clicked his beak in a message only she understood. Reflective eyes brightened.

"It seems my bounty hunter finally found a trail to our Little Red," Carabosse boasted. "Looks like I don't need your help after all."

"I know of Fang's pursuits," Lupa called back as she walked away. "But you are still far from not needing my assistance."

*****

Excusing himself from Wendy's fretting and insisting she get some sleep, Jack took next watch. He passed Kai, who he knew was only on the brink of waking, and Alice who looked like she was trapped in a bad dream. Jack sighed. He used to have nightmares, too.

Red lay curled next to the fire, so still and quiet. She was a terrible fake-sleeper.

"How are you feeling?" Jack asked casually, sitting promptly next to her.

She didn't move, but a groan sounded in her throat. "Like I'm going to pop at any moment like a bloody balloon."

"Sounds messy."

She huffed something that was almost a laugh. He took that as a good sigh of her improved health.

"At least they went for your side," he muttered, eying the various scratches over her skin, "and not your throat."

Her eyes cracked open so she could peer up at him. "What was it you called them? Evil rock monkeys?"

When Jack nodded, she smiled.

"Anyway, as soon as they drew blood, that's the spot they went for." Red grimaced. "I guess you could say I'm lucky."

He looked away to hide his face. "If you were lucky, you'd have been unconscious."

The silence sat uncomfortably between them for a moment. But it faded away.

Jack watched the shadows play around her face like dancers. Her neck was stiff from a pain she would never admit. He felt the urge to brush the tendrils of black hair away from her neck, but refrained.

"Well, Rubes," Jack started, aimlessly drawing in the dirt, "where are you taking us next?"

Red sighed. "That's what I've been trying to figure out."

"Do you have any friends here that could help us?"

She took a lot longer to answer than he expected. "Any friends I had were back in Grimrose or are impossible to find."

"Impossible to find?" Jack raised an eyebrow. "Well, I know we have one girl here who would probably argue with you about that…"

"I don't care what Alice would say." Red paused as if realizing how sharp her words had come and regretted it. "What I mean is, I wouldn't know where to start looking for them. They don't exactly stay in one place for long."

"Alright, so maybe not," he relented. "You mentioned before that there are lots of kingdoms here, right? So, where is the closest kingdom besides Grimrose?"

"I'm not particularly friendly with any other kingdom."

"All we need are supplies and a good healer. Then we can either figure things out from there or take the watch out of here." Jack pondered over her expression. She was closed off again, thinking inside herself. Why was she such a mystery? Would she ever let him know what lay behind the walls she'd built around herself?

"Chliobain," Red said at last. "It's the closest kingdom. They call the queen a giant killer."

Jack's spine prickled, fists closing involuntarily. "There are giants here?"

Now Red gave him the analyzing look. "No, not since long before I was here. If there even was any giant. It could just be legend, or stretching the truth. After all, we're not strangers to twisted stories."

"I guess not." He sighed, allowing himself to relax again. "Then we go to… wherever you just said."

"Chliobain."

"I'm telling you now, I won't ever be able to say that right. I'll just call it Whuppie or something."

"Because that sounds so similar."

"It doesn't! That's the point."

Red laughed, a real one despite its quietness. He liked it when she laughed. She didn't seem so guarded then. Unfortunately, it ended too soon.

Jack studied her distracted face. "When are you going to let us in, Rubes?" he spoke softly. "You were here for three years. Something happened here besides what you've told us."

She didn't affirm it, but she didn't deny it either. He took that as a good enough sign.

"Will you ever tell us?"

The expectant silence stretched on so long he almost gave up hope for an answer. But then she muttered, "Before we reach Chliobain."

He took it as a promise.

Chapter Ten
Run for Cover

"Is it faster?"

"The road will lead us around Grimrose and directly to Chliobain."

"Is it faster?"

"You don't realize what's in those trees! Taking on one monster does not mean anything."

"Is it faster?"

Red sighed, annoyed at arguing about this with him. But talking to Kai was like talking to a wall. He wasn't going anywhere until he got some answers.

Gritting her teeth, she relented, "It's safer."

He grunted as if he got exactly what he was looking for. She bit back a retort that it didn't matter anyway. If they could avoid going back into the Forest, she would hike ten times the distance with her legs tied together if she had to.

The morning was dying and Grimrose was far behind them when she heard her name, and all aggravations fled.

"*Rubina.*"

Her head snapped up at the voice. Her heart raged, but it wasn't in fear. Red looked around, knowing all too well whose voice she heard. When it came again bearing her name, it came like a purr in her ear, a seduction calling her forward. But she couldn't see him.

"Red," Alice questioned, laying a hand on her arm and snapping her out of her stupor. "Are you alright?"

Red flinched at her touch. It took a few seconds for her heart to beat regularly and for her to realize what happened.

"I'm fine, just hearing things," she confessed, glancing around at the trees again. "No matter what you hear, do not go into the Forest. If you hear something, or someone, in there... don't listen to them."

Alice smirked at that. "Don't worry. I can still tell the difference."

Red didn't bother trying to interpret what she meant by that.

Even though the voice stopped calling for her, the echoes still lingered inside. Her demons were crawling back to the surface.

It has begun.

Something gave and Red let out an involuntary moan. Pain flooded through her nerves. Touching her ribs, her fingers came away bloody.

"We should stop..." she announced with a grimace.

Wendy caught on instantly, vial in hand and readying the sprite dust. Helping Red sit, she unwrapped her bandages as carefully as she could. Red got a glance at her wounds before Wendy spread the sprite dust over it. She suppressed the urge to vomit.

Red had been stabbed, shot, broken, bitten, and wounded in a hundred different ways. But she had never had the flesh torn from her body so bad that it exposed bone. If it wasn't for the sprite dust... she wasn't sure she would be alive.

The pain subsided to a numbing sensation as the sprite dust sealed her wound. When Wendy started to wrap her up again, Red waved her off.

"The other's will be coming undone, too," she explained, finishing the job herself.

On cue, blood began to seep through Jack's shirt. Wendy hastened to tend to his wounds.

Red sighed, tying the bandage off. Raising her head and wiping her brow, she wondered why Wendy was taking so long with Jack's back. She was probably taking out the broken stitches before applying the sprite dust.

Alice didn't accept the stuff, seeing as her wound hadn't bled through the bandages yet. Of course, Wendy didn't let that stop her from pealing back the bandages and lathering on the blue-green paste. She was somewhat intimidating when she played nurse.

Kai sat patiently on the other side of the road, that iron skillet in hand like a weapon. He was looking in the Forest, eyes trained on the trees. Red wondered who he heard calling for him.

"Don't listen too hard," she warned.

His icy eyes flicked to her. The emotion behind them was too complex to discern.

Red didn't offer comfort, only fact. "No matter how convincing, or how much you hope, they're not real."

*****

Bursting from the underbrush, Lev came screaming into the group, face pale and eyes wide. Giggling at the sight, Quinn stood to meet him. Thaddeus scowled disapprovingly at his state of hysteria.

Fang raised an eyebrow. "What's got you screaming like a pig this time?"

"They're coming after me!" Lev exclaimed, hardly sliding to a stop, "A whole swarm of them!"

"What'd you do now?" Quinn laughed. "Did you disturb another flock of lucky piggies? Or did a shapeshifter get you with your pants—"

"I was out looking for food," Lev panted, cutting her off, "and I found a bunch of fruits and such just lying there in a neat pile. And I thought it'd be nice to avoid getting scurvy."

"I see where this is going," Thaddeus mumbled. "When will you learn that nothing comes on a silver platter in this Forest?"

"And now they're coming, and they're beyond angry!"

Fang grasped his arm to get him to calm down. "What's coming?"

The ground vibrated under foot, barely detectable. Lev blanched. When the battle cry erupted, it finally dawned on him.

"Gnomes," he growled, melting into the grey wolf.

"You messed with the gnomes' lunch!" Quinn scolded, shoving the culprit.

"I didn't know it was a horde!" Lev cried defensively.

When Fang yapped at them, they snapped out of it. Then, before he saw them shift form, he bounded away into the Forest. The silver furred Himalayan wolf was right at his heels. A flood of gnomes charged after them, far too speedy for their size.

Feet pounding, Fang tried to keep focused. If he concentrated, then he might be able to use the Forest to his advantage so they could escape the gnomes. He was only ever able to do it a few times before…

Lev let out a frightened bark when the swarm of gnomes appeared in front of them. Thinking fast and following a tug in his gut, Fang led them to the left, then a sharp right. It was too late. The gnomes completely surrounded them.

They were creatures of the earth, a humanoid monster made of mud and clay only four hands tall. Pebbles were embedded in their skin. Grass was plastered on them like war paint. Diamond eyes glared at them with fierce hatred. Their mouths weren't visible unless they were open. But every single gnome surrounding them had their mouths open, baring needle sharp teeth.

The gnomes stood frozen around them savoring their victorious hunt before the kill. Fur bristling, Fang's nose twitched, taking in everything around them. Quinn pulled a nasty snarl, a warning rumbling behind her teeth. Thaddeus looked at him expectantly. Muscles tense, Lev crouched low to the ground as if preparing for a leap.

A plan quickly formulated in his mind. Eying Thaddeus, a silent message passed between them.

Instantly, Fang sprang. He sailed over the gnomes, which erupted in gnashing and growling. When he landed, he took down many of the little monsters and then bolted through the crowd. Thaddeus burst through the masses just beside him, whilst the other two came up behind.

The gnomes retaliated, running after them and jumping for them. They grasped fistfuls of fur or latched on with their needle teeth. Fang tried to force them off, but they were like leaches. They held fast.

Being the smallest and most limber, Quinn was able to dodge most of the leaping gnomes. Those she couldn't would often miscalculate the jump and either flew over her or smacked into her side.

Thaddeus' tactic was simple enough. When his back was littered with the creatures, he'd roll across the ground to squash them all. But Fang preferred to stay on his feet. Avoiding the gnomes trying to mount him, he made a point of jumping into the air. The force would send them flying.

Lev flailed about, bucking like a bronco. His attempts failed miserably.

The gnawing sound rang in Fang's ears, more aggravating than anything. One of the cursed things snagged hold of his ear. When he shook it off, the stinging proved that it tore.

Bursting through the thicket, the air thinned drastically. It sucked away his breath without warning. Instead of avoiding the spot, he barreled into it. The magic in the air was weak, drained.

Every gnome began to choke and wheeze with every breath. Fang planted his feet on the spot, thankful the other wolves did likewise. Coughing and sputtering like the air was poison, the gnomes stumbled away. In the blink of an eye, every one of them had disappeared into the Forest.

Thankfully, gnomes couldn't live long without magic.

Fang shifted form, wiping the blood from his torn ear. Sniffing the air, he realized where they were, or rather, how far they were from where they needed to be. Anger boiled inside his chest.

● ● ●

"What were you thinking?!" Fang barked at Lev, fuming. He'd barely changed back into a man. "Do you enjoy setting off dangerous detours to chase us in the *opposite* direction of where we're headed, or do accidents just enjoy finding you?"

Lev scrambled to his feet and exclaimed defensively, "Look, I didn't mean to cause trouble! It's not like it caused any serious damage."

"My nose disagrees with you," Quinn mumbled, pinching the bridge of her nose where blood ran down her face from between her eyes.

"No damage!" Fang cried, silver eyes ablaze in frustration. "Because of this little detour, we won't make it to Grimrose until tomorrow!"

"But that's not too bad," Lev insisted. "It's only one day."

"One day is all it takes to lose someone forever." Fang shoved Lev back forcefully, nearly knocking him off balance. Lev backed away hastily, but Fang kept coming at him. "I've been after this girl for *seven* years! It took one moment of unstable magic to cause that mirror to take her to another world. *I was that close!* Now, I'm that close again and *you* had to set off a horde of monsters!"

"Look, I'm sorry, okay?"

"You're sorry?" Fang spat, grabbing him by the collar. "Zoë is turning to gold! *Sorry* isn't enough anymore!"

"It's not my fault your girlfriend is becoming a fortune," Lev snapped.

"SHE'S MY WIFE!"

"That is enough, you two," Thaddeus stepped in just as Fang thrust his fist back to pummel Lev. "What is done is done and there is nothing that will change it."

Fang scowled. He knew Thaddeus was right. They didn't have time for this.

Reluctantly, he released Lev. As soon as he found his footing, Fang punched him in the face. Lev's head snapped back as the impact threw him to the floor. Adrenaline pulsed through Fang's veins, fist still clenched.

Turning away, he growled, "But that still felt good."

*****

Unable to sleep, Red stared up at the stars and wished the pain would go away. It wasn't just her ribs now. She was wrestling with her own thoughts and conflictions so hard that it hurt. Nothing scared her more than revealing her past. With every footstep to Chliobain, the promise she'd made to Jack throbbed behind her temples.

What's more, she'd seen the vial and its contents. It wouldn't last longer than two days, and once it ran out, she herself wouldn't be able to last long. For all they knew, she could get an infection. No amount of sprite dust could fix that.

Time was growing short. The chances of reaching Chliobain, or any help at all, were slim. And she still had a promise to keep.

Everything hurt.

"Red?"

She looked up to find Wendy looking down at her, her silhouette framed by starlight.

"May I join you? I can't sleep."

Nodding in consent, Red wiggled over to make room for her friend. Wendy gratefully laid down beside her.

"Is it the voices?" Red asked softly.

"Voices?"

"Sometimes there are voices that come from the trees, calling your name. I thought that might be why you couldn't sleep."

Wendy shook her head. "No, I haven't heard any voices."

Then you're lucky, Red thought to herself.

"Do you?"

She thought a moment, wondering why her first instinct was to lie. Maybe she could change that a little at a time. Quietly, Red dipped her chin in affirmation. The lie died in her throat.

"Who calls for you?" Wendy asked gently. By her tone, Red knew that she wasn't obligated to answer if she didn't want to.

Red sighed, "Everyone."

"Do you ever hear *her*?"

Her back stiffened, realizing who she meant. All she could do was shake her head, though. If the Forest wanted Red to go into its shadows, then Lupa's voice would never call for her. That was one demon she'd only have to deal with in person, or in her head.

"Are you mad at me for listening to her?"

"No. I'm just glad she didn't... use you."

Wendy lay so quietly that for a moment Red thought she'd fallen asleep. But her brown eyes were still open, shining with reflections of stars and galaxies. There was something more on her mind.

"I'm afraid she might have," Wendy confessed at last. "She told me that she had an investment on you; that she couldn't have you die, but it wasn't time for you to meet yet."

Red let the words roll around in her head. "At least you had a common interest," she said simply. "Lupa is a lone wolf who makes deals with dangerous people. She wouldn't have helped if she didn't gain anything from it."

Wendy let out a sigh, relaxing beside her. The ground felt more comfortable than it should have. Still, Red's mind wouldn't allow her rest.

"Even the stars seem to change wherever we go," Wendy muttered to herself.

Red wondered if she was looking for the star that could lead her home to Neverland. After scanning the sky, Red pointed it out. "Some things never change."

Wendy seemed relieved at that, brown eyes looking longingly at the second star to the right. It was in a different spot, but it still shone bright.

"I used to know someone who knew the stars better than anyone," Red whispered, the words falling one after another. "She told me some of their stories and names, but I can only remember a few."

"Are there any stories you like best?" Wendy asked curiously. She always did love a good story, Red supposed.

Red wetted her lips, thinking and searching the sky. There were two stars that caught her gaze, a black space below them as if something were missing. Hesitantly, she chose them.

"I'm not sure if it's the one I like best," she admitted, "but I know it best.

"There was a family who grew up in a dark part of the forest, a man and his wife and their little girl. They walked in the shadows and lived in the night, but they were happy. But the girl sometimes looked at other children, the ones who lived in the light, and she wondered at the life they led and soon she grew so curious that she tried to venture amongst them. Traces of shadows clung to her like a cloak. The children in light called her out when she came close, pointing out the darkness that clung to her. The children either teased the girl or cowered in fear of her. Quickly, the girl fled back to her parents in the dark. They tried to tell her that people of light could not understand them, so they would ridicule, fear, or ignore them because of it.

"One day, though, the girl was walking alone in the shadows, watching the light and longing for it. Someone soon joined her, a figure who walked easily between light and dark without discrepancy. When the girl asked how she could do the same, the person gave her a box and told her that if she opened it then her family would be able to leave the shadows and become light. The girl took it excitedly. When she found her family, she opened the box as she was told, but instead of turning to people of light, her parents turned to stars and rose to the sky where all stars belong. The girl was left behind, alone. She could now venture into the light undetected, but was never one of them. Instead of becoming light, she only appeared to be it if she wished. But the darkness had seeped into her soul, hidden."

"That's a sad story," Wendy murmured.

"They say she's still trying to reach the stars," Red continued, voice melancholy, "but the shadow inside prevents her from getting there, no matter how hard she tries."

Wendy stared at the sky. "Stars are echoes of the past. It's important to look to them sometimes for guidance, but as long as people reach for them, they never realize the beauty and potential awaiting just in front of them."

Red didn't say anything. Something about her words hit a nerve in her, and she wasn't sure she trusted herself to give a steady response.

"Who told you that story?"

"Her name was Aurore, daughter of King Thrushbeard," Red responded. "But I called her Briar."

"Why?"

"She introduced herself as Briar Rose when we first met..." A smile tugged at her mouth. "That's when I started using the name Red."

Chapter Eleven

A Beginning to Confessions

Water split the path in a rush of the river. It was just the place to refill their canteens and wash the sweat from their skin. Scarlet tendrils merged into the river, the last of the remnants Grimrose had left them.

Red felt weak from her wounds, and the pain had not lessened since yesterday. She feared that her body was becoming tolerant to the sprite dust and soon it wouldn't matter how much they applied, her wounds would worsen. Infection wasn't her only worry. If the sprite dust backfired, she could begin to bleed on the inside.

"Do we cross it?" Alice suggested, drawing her from her worried thoughts.

Groaning, Red stood to stumble across the river. The water came up to her thighs, churning around her legs. Bubbles rose with the rapids. For a moment, she thought she was going to faint. Then Jack was there, catching her around the waist and helping her up out of the river.

She muttered thanks, suddenly drained. He lowered her on the riverbank so she could wait for the others to join. Then he waded back in.

Gathering her strength, Red closed her eyes and concentrated on her breathing. A cool breeze grazed her neck. The magic in the air here was thick and murky. It was like being smothered in wools, strangely lulling.

Water exploded and a cry split the air. Her head snapped up instantly.

All was chaos. Alice scrambled to retrieve her pitchfork from the river, Kai was thrown to the ground on his back, and Wendy clung desperately to Jack's arm. Her heart plummeted. Something had snaked around his ankles and was dragging him under.

Red hastened to her feet, pitching forward to snatch hold of Jack's arm before Wendy was dragged into the waters with him. Together, they pulled as hard as they could. Jack cried out from the strain. Scales like moss emerged from the river, pure muscle tightening. Tears streaking her cheeks despite herself, she used all the strength she could muster.

Water sprayed as Alice plunged into the river beside them and speared the monster with her pitchfork. The creature reared, a serpentine head shooting from the rapids in pain. Jack cried out again, but the scales had slipped their hold. As soon as it gave, Red and Wendy yanked him from the river and onto the bank. Alice speared it again, so deep that she had to wretch her weapon free from the body. Before the serpent could retaliate, Kai snatched hold of Alice's forearm and helped pull her to safety.

The river raged with the monster, but it soon slinked under and vanished. They scrambled far away from it as possible, not even bothering to stand.

Breathing heavily, Red found she was still clutching Jack's arm. Her side throbbed and burned at once. And his back was bleeding, his ankle blotched and swollen. The pain in his eyes was as intense as her own.

"We should never have come here," she muttered in utter exhaustion.

Jack didn't respond, too out of breath for words. Defeated, he lay his head on the dirt.

● ● ●

Neither of them moved when Wendy crawled over and dutifully reapplied the sprite dust to their wounds. Exhaustion crept into her bones.

"Can you assure that the Master isn't here?" Alice spoke up, sitting calmly on the road beside Kai.

Red craned her head back to look at her before straining to sit up. "What?"

"You think we shouldn't have come here," she responded casually. She stared at her hands folded in her lap. "So can you tell me that you know for certain that the Master isn't here? Can you tell me for certain that we won't learn vital information while here?"

Mind spinning, Red said nothing. She couldn't think of any answer that would suffice.

"If you tell me without a doubt that being here is a waste of time, then I can press this button and we can leave this place right now." Alice finally raised her eyes to Red's. She was completely serious. "If you can't... I can't help but feel that wherever this watch takes us, we are taken there for a reason. Maybe I'm wrong, but then we need to be sure. So," Alice lifted her hand to reveal the White Rabbit's pocket watch, "what do you say?"

Red stared at it in silence. That was their ticket out of here, out of this Forest, maybe forever. All she had to do was promise that there was nothing for them here. Temptation itched in her fingertips. Everyone looked at her, waiting for her answer.

The truth was that she didn't know. She couldn't say anything with certainty. The decision was what did she tell the rest of them.

* * *

Swallowing the sour taste in her mouth, Red wrestled to keep her voice even, "We go on to Chliobain. We can reevaluate from there once we recuperate."

Without a word, Alice stowed the watch under her shirt once again.

Just as some of them were beginning to stand, Red stopped them. After Alice's offer, it seemed even more apparent that they were here. And this time, it was her choice. Whatever happened from now on was on her.

She locked eyes with Jack. He seemed to realize what she was about to say.

"Look, I think it's time I explain a few things in case... or before we reach Chliobain," Red stammered, finding this harder than she thought. She'd hidden her secrets most of her life, and she almost didn't know how she was going to tell them. But if they made it to Chliobain, then there was a chance that they'd find out about her one way or another. She'd rather they heard it from her.

That didn't make this any easier.

"First off, it's best not to let anyone know I'm a wolf. There's a lot of oppression against the Pack, and even though I'm not part of it, it won't make a difference. So, if it comes down to it, leave any explaining to me."

She was met with nods all around. Kai even gave a small grunt.

Her throat swelled. "I don't even know how to start."

"The beginning is typically a good place," Jack said softly, giving an encouraging smile.

Taking a deep breath, Red kept her eyes lowered. "Before the Forest, before any of this... *magic* came into play, I was involved in things I'm not entirely proud of. I was a product of my parents... a thief and a mercenary."

The atmosphere shifted as soon as those words left her mouth. She didn't allow herself to dwell on it for too long.

"I had an entirely different set of morals. I didn't care what I'd become or who I hurt to survive. When I came here, I didn't change; I did the only things I could do. And I could do... most anything I was hired to short of selling myself or people." Red had to work at restraining herself from letting everything flow out like a waterfall. "You'll probably hear a few names I've been dubbed with since being here. When I worked alone, I was known as the Scarlet Thief. That's when I met Lupa, and because of the cloak I wore she started calling me Little Red Riding Hood. The cloak would warn me of any monsters or dangers approaching, and I wore it at all times.

"But then I began working with a man called the Woodsman, and I became the Crimson Wraith, a legend I formulated to hide my identity from Fang. I was another monster in the Forest as far as most anyone was concerned. Together, we were trying to find a way out of this Forest, maybe raise enough money to pay a witch to make a portal. But shortly before we... stopped working together, and I was briefly captured by Bluebeard, I changed tactic. I did everything I could to take down Bluebeard and his web of girl-snatchers. A friend of mine, Briar Rose, helped me sometimes. I also aligned myself with gypsies, and often traveled with them for refuge.

"Then it came to a point where Fang was around every corner. I couldn't go around as boldly as I used to, and anyone who was with me was in danger. Not only the Pack wanted me hunted down, but Bluebeard, Lupa, even the Chliobain royals had a price on my head. Then a prince of Grimrose started nosing around, eventually finding me and hired me to help him find and rescue my friend Briar. It turned out she was actually the Princess Aurore of Grimrose, and she'd been cursed by Carabosse. Something about a spinning wheel... Anyway, I helped Ingénu rescue her if he helped keep me safe from the Pack. Shortly after that, when we were returning to Grimrose, that's when Fang found me."

The silence following weighed heavily in the air. It was unbearable. Red struggled but finally looked up to behold their reactions.

No one was looking at her despite their unreadable expressions. Kai's was stony and emotionless, as usual. She wasn't sure how comforting that was, though. Alice's eyes moved from side to side as if her mind were racing a thousand leagues a second. Again, this told her nothing.

It was Wendy and Jack who showed the most emotion as her confession sank in. Complete melancholy carved into Wendy's face, confusion and hurt drawing creases between her eyebrows. Jack's eyes were narrowed and lips pressed together as if he were wrestling with his thoughts.

She couldn't take it anymore. "Somebody say something."

Jack spoke up first, raising his head and looking at her directly, "So which one was the thief and which the mercenary?"

Red blinked. "My mother was the thief, and my father was the mercenary."

"Hmm." He nodded with interest. "And here I was guessing the bad business was that you and your family were assassins."

She scoffed. "Might as well be."

"Why did the Chliobain royals have a price on your head?" Alice asked next. It was obviously not her only question.

Taken back by the responses thus far, Red stumbled in answering, "I... I stole some family relics from them: a few gold chains and an amber ring they claimed was a giant's. They got the stuff back, just not from me."

"Would they recognize you?"

"Even if someone had seen me, they would remember a face I had at fourteen." Red rubbed her hands uncomfortably. "I've changed in more ways than one since I was her."

"What happened to your magic cloak?"

"Lost, as far as I know. I didn't have time to grab it when Fang caught up."

"Why was Lupa searching for you? And who's the Woodsman? Do you think the gypsies would still—"

"I'm sorry," Red interrupted, still baffled, "is that it? Is that all you have to say? No shouts, no accusations? Just... questions?"

"Yes," Kai said casually, raising icy blue eyes to hers. "How long will it take to reach Chliobain?"

Red was too stunned to answer. She wasn't sure what she'd been expecting from them, but certainly not this. Calm acceptance or ignorance, she couldn't be sure, but either way she'd anticipated anything but.

With a sigh, Kai folded his hands and leaned forward on his knees. "Your mother was a thief, your father was a mercenary, and you were as well. My father was a soldier, my mother's a clockmaker, and I was a blacksmith. The only thing that concerns me is who you are now, not who you were then."

"Yeah, what he said," Jack agreed, "minus the blacksmith part. And the parents bit."

"But I... lied to you," Red argued.

"No, you withheld the truth; which isn't entirely different, but even so," Alice shrugged, "I'm not surprised. Like Jack, I was prepared for the worst."

"That's not what I said," Jack mumbled with a smirk.

Alice made a face at him before continuing, "Besides, we all have things we're not proud of. Even after everything we've been through, we're still learning to trust each other. If you think about it, we've only known each other for... a few months? Half a year? I can't calculate it; Neverland messed up my inner clock."

It was as if something had cracked the dam holding back her emotions. Tears pricked Red's eyes. Her throat knotted up with the overwhelming sense of relief. She struggled to hold it all back. Dread still pulsed in her veins. Not everyone had spoken.

Bottle green eyes finally dared to see her. "Wendy?"

She was twisting grass up in her hands silently. But she hadn't spoken or looked up at all since Red first began her confession.

"What are you thinking?" Red asked softly.

Wendy took another moment to answer, eyes still lowered. "I'm not... I don't care about who you were. I'm just… hurt that it took a near death experience, or fear of us finding out from someone else, to drive you to trust us with it. I'm hurt that you couldn't trust us."

Allowing the words to sink in, Red hung her head in acknowledgement. Something like shame or disappointment churned inside. Maybe she should've told them sooner, or under different circumstances, or not at all.

"But you're one of my best friends," Wendy spoke, causing Red to lift her head in surprise. "I understand how hard it might be, after everything you've been through, to trust anyone. So yes, it hurts now, but it'll pass."

This time, she couldn't do anything to hold back the tears. She couldn't discern the emotions that filled her, and she hated that she could barely control it. But she thought she was feeling something like love. It scared and invigorated her. With all her strength, she kept it contained. It still managed to leak out of her eyes and run down her face.

Kai cleared her throat. "Now, about my question…"

Red laughed, wiping her eyes with her thumb. "That's not one with a good answer."

"Try us." Jack shrugged.

"At least three to four days."

The air grew heavy. No one said it, but by the look in everyone's eyes, the facts were obvious. The sprite dust wouldn't last that long. Red wasn't at all sure they could make it.

Jack was able to convince Wendy that it wasn't necessary to check his wounds that night, since the sprite dust would hold until tomorrow. She'd been getting more concerned by the day. But he insisted that the discoloration she'd mentioned was just a side effect from the sprite dust. Of course, she didn't seem too convinced. But Jack waved it off and kept his discomfort to himself.

He stumbled into a crouch beside the fire, head fuzzy and vision blackening temporarily. He shook off the nausea. Thankfully, no one noticed his exhaustion.

When he laid down, his back stung upon contact with the ground. He suppressed a sharp gasp. He had to turn to his side to accommodate for the pain.

Head still aching, the back of his eyes felt pressurized. Jack didn't complain, though. Despite whatever pain and exhaustion, he didn't have a right to. After all, Red was lying over there with a gaping hole in her side. She had more reason to complain and scream that he did, yet she didn't. Or at least, not as much as she should've wanted to.

Jack closed his eyes, certain the headache would leave by tomorrow.

It didn't.

Chapter Twelve

Everything Goes Wrong

"What are we even going to do when we reach Grimrose?" Quinn questioned in the grey of dawn as they readied for another run. "King Thrushbeard would never let the likes of us in, and there was that whole scheme when the girl was welcomed in court. She could have protection from the royal family!"

"Thrushbeard wouldn't take the matter lightly," Lev joined in with concern, "with a small pack of wolves sniffing around his kingdom. Not that the locals were ever friendly with us to begin with, but it could stir up some trouble. You've heard about the hunters; they're getting popular."

Fang raised a hand to stay their concerns. "I know about the hunters, believe me. And the rumors about Thrushbeard allowing the girl into court. But none of it matters, not when it comes to Grimrose. We won't find trouble there."

"Why is that?" Thaddeus asked, tone calm and even.

"The whole kingdom's been turned to stone since the princess' curse was broken."

"Sounds like some of Carabosse's devious voodoo," Lev muttered. "Why haven't we taken advantage of this? A whole kingdom turned to stone for nearly two years—"

"It is not our way to prey on those who cannot defend themselves in any form or fashion," Thaddeus warned coolly without ever raising his voice.

"The whole kingdom's infested with goblins," Fang added. "If we find any trouble, it'll be from them."

*****

"Jack?" Alice persuaded urgently. "Jack, wake up."

He gave a feeble moan, breath raspy. Beads of sweat decorated his skin and his eyes were bloodshot. Concerned, Alice pressed the back of her hand to Jack's forehead, then trailed down to his flushed cheeks just to be sure.

Curious, she checked the wounds on his back. Her heart dropped. The sprite dust was flaking away, not sealing or disintegrating like normal. There was some kind of strange puss coming out, contaminating his blood. It almost... glittered. She lowered his shirt.

Turning away, she beckoned quietly, "Kai. Wendy. Come here."

Wendy crawled over instantly, brow creased, whilst Kai came from his post. Unfortunately, Red also noticed Alice's beckoning. She didn't look so good. Alice didn't want to worry her or cause more stress, but she supposed that no matter what happened, they were all going through it together.

How poetic.

Where did that thought come from?

Shaking her head, she brought herself back to the present. With her friends around her and Jack, Alice informed, "He's burning up. Doesn't look well enough to travel by most any means."

"No," Jack protested weakly. "No, we... we have to... make it to... Whuppie."

"Whuppie?" Alice wrinkled her nose. "Now who's going mad?"

"He's right," Kai put, eying Red as if her health was also questionable. "Who's to say this lone wolf won't turn up again, this time not so friendly. These monsters seem to show up daily. And it won't take long for Fang to discover you're back, if he doesn't know already."

"What do we do?" Wendy questioned. "Red's ribs are exposed, can barely walk on her own—"

"I can walk just fine," Red countered.

Wendy wasn't having any of it. "Stop it. I don't need you to act tough, just honest."

"Now Jack's sick, his back looks infected, and the sprite dust doesn't seem to stick," Alice added. "We don't have much of the stuff as it is."

Kai sighed, eyes narrowed in thought. He turned to Red. "Which way is Chliobain? How long will it take to cut through the Forest?"

"We are not going back in there," Red stated. "It's too dangerous!"

"We are beyond that now. Which way?"

"Southwest, and maybe two days." Red grimaced as if a pain hit her. "But it doesn't matter! Once you think you're lost in there, then the Forest insures that you are. It's a... manipulation trick. The place is alive."

Something about her words hit a switch in Alice's mind. *"Once you think you're lost...* That's it, then. So long as we aren't lost, then we won't be. Because if the Forest makes us lost only when we think we are, then we can't get lost if we don't think we are. That insures that we can't get lost!"

They were all staring at her as if she was speaking a foreign language. Alice rolled her eyes helplessly.

* * *

"If we go in the Forest bound for Chliobain, then as long as we know that we are on the way to Chliobain, we will arrive," she tried again slowly. "Like Red said, it's a manipulation trick."

Kai nodded resolutely. "Sounds like a plan." Red began to protest, but Kai looked her dead in the eye and said, "We're going in with or without your permission. Do you really want to argue with me?"

Red said nothing. She didn't seem to have much strength to.

Turning back to Alice and Wendy, Kai took charge. "I'll take Jack. Alice, how's your shoulder?"

"I can manage," she responded, twisting her arm to find little resistance. The sprite dust seemed to be helping.

"Good. You'll take Red. Wendy," Kai offered the iron skillet, "you're back up."

Wendy shook her head and pulled out her pistol. "You keep that. I have five shots left, and then a very effective threat."

By the time Alice retrieved her pitchfork and helped Red up to her feet, Jack was as awake as he could get. His eyes fluttered, but he at least held some steady consciousness. Kai knelt down beside him, expression gentle but determined.

"Can you stand, *bror*?" Kai questioned softly, earning a weak nod from Jack. Hefting Jack up, he locked eyes with Alice briefly. "Then let's go."

*****

"Fang," Thaddeus reported, face grave. "There is nothing here but statues and dead goblins. She is not here."

Cursing loudly, Fang slammed his fist into the wall. The stone cracked from the impact. "We were so close!" he screamed, frustration boiling.

When the red wolf ran up to meet them, he was still heaving with anger. But that didn't deter the proud grin Quinn wore when she shifted form.

"I found blood," she exclaimed excitedly, "lots of it. Traces of a trail leads from the town to a path through the Forest. And I'm not talking about goblin blood."

Steadying his breathing, Fang scowled. "The girl's wounded?"

Quinn shrugged, admitting, "Could be. I'm not certain it's her, but it's very possible."

"She's not alone," Lev piped up, suddenly appearing beside them. His nose was smudged with oily blood. "She's traveling with a group. I picked up four, maybe five different scents."

"But they have been gone for a few days," Thaddeus put in levelly. "If she is wounded so badly, she may not have survived."

"I refuse to accept that," Fang growled.

Melting into the grey wolf, he placed his nose to the ground and chased after an invisible trail. What Quinn had said earlier was true. The trail led him to a road through the Forest. By the time he realized which way the road led, he'd picked up another scent, one he knew too well.

What was Lupa doing here?

Shifting form, he decided to ponder that peculiarity later.

"They're headed to Chliobain," he announced with certainty.

"Yeah," Lev agreed hastily, "just what I was thinking."

"Sure you were, clog-nose." Quinn rolled her eyes.

Without another word of explanation, Fang reentered the Forest with the others following in pursuit.

*****

They used the last of the sprite dust on Red's ribs, against her protests. But it seemed she'd lost control.

But they weren't lost. They couldn't afford to be lost.

Unfortunately, that didn't mean they were immune to the Forest's dangers. Already, she had to warn them of trolls sleeping not far from where they trekked. They smelled like tree sap and fungus. But she couldn't detect the gnomes until their eerie diamond eyes stared at them from around tree roots. Red muttered a warning not to mess with them.

Worry filled her abdomen. Her senses seemed to be diminishing with her energy. What happened if a more lethal monster came, and she couldn't warn them? The only weapons they had were an iron skillet, a pitchfork, and a pistol with five shots left.

At least they weren't lost.

Despite her protests, Alice had her arm locked around Red's waist to help her stumble along. Though she wouldn't admit it, she was grateful for the crutch. She was fully conscious and could hold herself up, but the pain was constant and her muscles felt shaky. Together, they were able to travel easier.

They followed Kai, who was fully supporting Jack at this point. Dread filled her every heartbeat. Why couldn't she have been the one with the infection? She would've gladly taken it if it spared Jack from it. Why hadn't he mentioned anything? Surely a fever didn't just appear out of nowhere without warning! But she knew that wasn't always true. The worst sicknesses could sneak up and hit without detection. Red had seen it happen before. That's how her grandfather passed away.

She shook her head. Jack was not going to die. Not today, not tomorrow, not anytime soon. They just had to find help.

"Did you hear something?" Wendy questioned from behind them. She held that pistol with too much precision, a sign that this was far from the first time she'd held a firearm.

Red took a breath and tuned in to their surroundings. But there was nothing. Everything was quiet. That was the problem.

She shook her head. "I don't—"

Then the wind changed and she caught their scent too late.

Men stepped from the shadows and surrounded them instantly. They were silent, grim around the eyes with half their faces covered with scarves. Many wore hats with rims low over brows. An assortment of weapons was aimed and ready. They could skewer them at any moment.

And Wendy's pistol was aimed right for the leader's long pointed nose.

Wiry limbs, long ebony hair, and devilish eyes, the man laughed like a mad Frenchman. "*Qu'avons-nous là?*"

Red's skin crawled. She knew that voice, but never in this situation.

"What did he say?" Alice whispered to Red.

"Ah, English born," the man said, arms held out flamboyantly. Thick eyebrows cast dark shadows over his eyes. "But then, wolves speak English."

"So does most everyone in this Forest," Red muttered under her breath. "English, French, German, some Russian and Kongo…"

The man waved his hand as if her voice were annoying flies buzzing around his face. "Yes, yes! I can understand the point. But mine still stands."

"Leave us alone," Wendy warned, her stance poised. "You're acting far too smug for a man with a gun in your face."

"I have had worse things in my face."

The man pulled down his scarf to scratch his chin. Seeing his whole face confirmed it. Red knew him. He used to have a Vandyke beard and a gold hoop through his ear. But for some reason, he didn't recognize her.

Before she could think of any way to react, he turned to his fellows. "Seems we have intruders on our hands! They think they can… bully their way through, but I think they need a mirror."

"They're a sorry lot," agreed the form beside him with a hat pulled low over his face.

His voice shot through Red's body like lightning. Bottle green eyes blazed. Without warning, she wrenched out of Alice's hold, heart beating out of her chest, charging straight for him. *"You backstabbing TROLL!"* she cried and rammed into him, throwing him to the ground.

As soon as he landed, Red pinned him down and socked him in the face. Again. And again. And again.

Hands grabbed her by the hair and arms, forcing her off the traitor. She wrestled against them, but her strength was spent. Heaven knew that she wasn't going to let them think they got the better of her, though.

Some men helped the liar to his feet. His hat was gone, his scarf hung down his neck, and his mouth and nose were bloodied. Maybe next time she could swell up his eye.

The wiry man grinned mischievously, holding Wendy's pistol in his hands. He must've disarmed her while Red was attacking her old nemesis. "Looks as if this feisty beast knows you, Jimmy."

"It'd seem so." Jim scowled, wiping the blood from his nose. He didn't bother to look at her before he punched her in the stomach. The wind rushed out of her, pain exploding in her abdomen. Red gasped for breath.

When he pulled away, tawny eyes locked with hers. Recognition sparked. The air charged between them.

Then Kai sent a blow right in Jim's eye, sending everyone in a frenzy again.

"Get away from her!" he warned, prepping for another punch.

Regaining his balance, Jim reached up to touch the cut by his eye. He raised one thick straight eyebrow and passed a hand down his long face. Instantly, he snatched the rod strapped to his thigh and swung it into Kai's face with a sharp *thwack!* The blow threw Kai to the ground.

The men around them roared with laughter as Kai shook his head in pain and bewilderment. Wendy ran to his aid, crouching beside him to be sure he was alright. Jack took two steps forward before losing his balance, and Alice managed to catch him before he fell.

"Nice one, Woodsman," the wiry man praised, stepping over Kai with a skip. "Do you recognize this girl?"

Jim looked at Red. Every emotion churned inside her; mostly rage. Then his eyes narrowed.

"Hard to tell," Jim grunted, turning away. "Never was too good with faces."

Her chest tightened. "You know perfectly well who I am," Red spat. "As do you, *Clopin Trouillefou.*"

"Now, dearie," Clopin warned, "it's dangerous business making assumptions like that."

In a swoop, he grasped her chin and got right up to her face. Red's neck stiffened. He jerked her head from side to side intently in his inspection. Scowling, he looked directly in her eyes. She was afraid of what he might see.

"*C'est impossible,*" Clopin muttered under his breath.

"Do you recognize me, yet?" she hissed.

He sneered, revealing missing molars. "I find it difficult to trust my eyes. Things are never what they seem." Releasing her, Clopin stepped back and announced, "Take off a few years and this one could look exactly like the famed Crimson Wraith!"

"That's because I am!" Red cried, aggravated.

Jim's face was stone, but Clopin wheeled on her with murder in his eyes. "You may look like her, but who's to say you're not just the mask over the monster?"

A lump formed in her throat. Helplessly, Red lowered her gaze. How could she oppose such a statement? Instantly, she regretted her hesitance. It came across like a confession to the gypsy man.

"I thought not," he laughed, turning away. "They're shapeshifters! Or some other monster of the Forest."

* * *

Breath quickening, mind racing, Red played the one card she swore she'd never take. "If I'm not Red, then how would I know about your sister…"

That murderous look returned instantly. *"What do you know of my sister?"*

"I know about all of you and the entire operation because I was part of it!"

Nostrils flaring, Clopin pulled a knife and snapped it against her throat. "I'm getting tired of your voice, shapeshifter."

"Take me to her," Red pressed. "She'll know me. If I'm Red—which I am—then she'll know me."

"What if I just kill you?"

"Then you'll never know how much I know, and who I could've told about your little side-business. How many people have no idea it's you and your gypsy family who are responsible for all their troubles? Lupa? Bluebeard?" She lowered her voice threateningly, "Are you willing to risk it, if you're so certain I'm not Red?"

Silence stretched on the edge of a knife. Loathing toiled behind Clopin's black eyes. She had him.

Reluctantly pulling the knife away, Clopin ordered to his men, "Search them. Take anything of value."

"And the intruders?" Jim questioned, unable to look Red in the eye.

"Bring them with us," he responded simply. "We can't have them leaking information."

The gypsies moved forward obediently, searching the five of them for anything lethal or pricey. Iron skillet and pitchfork were taken immediately. Wendy's bag was snatched, and Kai's face darkened when they took the ring around his neck. Neither Jack nor Red held anything of importance.

As soon as Clopin pulled away from Alice with a new prize, it hit her like a rock and the dread set in.

"What is this?" Clopin crooned as he relieved her of the White Rabbit's pocket watch.

"No, please!" Alice begged, grabbing for it without luck. "That's mine!"

"Not anymore," he chanted, flipping it open. He raised an eyebrow. "Strange watch. Looks expensive, though. We should fetch a pretty penny for it. Huh, what does this do?"

All five of them shouted instantaneously, "*NO!*"

Clopin pressed the diamond button.

Red's heart skipped a beat.

Nothing happened.

Alice stared blankly at the watch, earning a smirk from the wiry man. "Why all the excitement? It's just a pocket watch."

Jack huffed, "You're lucky Long Ears isn't here."

Chapter Thirteen

Fragile Bonds

Frustration and dread throbbed with every footfall through the Forest. Red had never before been dragged to the gypsy camp by the hair like this. After everything she'd done for them, and now they were led away like prisoners. No, worse than that; like they were enemies.

Her wound burned. Every rub and bump threatened to snap the sprite dust clean off. She didn't know how long it would hold before it began to bleed again. They had nothing else to help them. Honestly, she should've been dead by now. With Jack's fever and infection, Alice with a bullet hole slowly healing, and Kai's leg having never fully healed from all the torture it's been through; the gypsies were right to perceive them as a sorry lot. It was a miracle they'd made it this far.

Clopin led the group, every step plummeting to a stomp. He threw a glare at her every chance he got, as if to remind her how much he wanted to slit her throat. It baffled her! At the very least, Red used to consider Clopin a man she could trust. Now, he didn't believe a word that came from her mouth. His claim that she was a shapeshifter didn't surprise her, though his distrust hurt more than she'd expected. But Clopin was never a trusting man. And he always had murder in his eyes that made even his friends think him dangerous.

She wished that he'd kept his Vandyke beard, though. It used to offset his sharp features and beaky nose. With it, you could imagine that the devilish flamboyance was just an act, a mask he put on to appease audiences at carnivals. But now, it was clear there was no mask. He really was on the brink of insanity.

Maybe he and Alice would get along.

All in all, she could forgive Clopin later for his distrust. She should've expected it from him, especially after over two years.

The bulk of her hatred and anger rested on the traitor who wouldn't even give her the curtesy of acknowledging her presence. She'd hoped many years ago that she would never have to see Jim again after what he did to her. Of course, she should have known she wouldn't be so lucky.

What's more, Jim knew exactly who she was. He wasn't superstitious, not like Clopin. The blood on his face was enough to prove she hadn't forgotten what he'd done to her. And his grim avoidance of her was enough to prove he remembered, too.

How did he get back? She never would've expected to see the Woodsman back in the Forest. But alas, she didn't care. Nothing would give her more satisfaction than to pummel him again. Unfortunately, the gypsies weren't too keen on allowing her that pleasure.

The air's density lightened. A smart location for a hideout. Little magic meant less chance of unwanted intruders, monster and spell alike. This was where the gypsy camp was, she could sense it.

Sure enough, within the next two minutes they broke into a clearing where twelve large caravans formed a wall encircling it. Hammocks had been strung up between them. Horses and oxen grazed nearby. As for the people themselves, Red was shocked at the minimal numbers of people here. Last she'd seen of them, the gypsies had hundreds in their ever-growing family. Now, she couldn't see even eighty.

Did they split off in groups? Had there been an epidemic? Was there a new sweep of persecution? Did certain villains find out who was actually joining the gypsies? Each scenario was worse than the last.

When a group of children ran up to check out the new prisoners, the men formed a tighter circle around Red and her friends to keep the curious ones at bay. They were of every shape and color. Hardly any appeared like the original French gypsies who came to the Enchanted Forest so many years ago. The gypsies' family had grown beyond just race and blood here.

Stumbling through camp, Red caught a glimpse of ginger hair protruding from a hammock. Her heart skipped a beat. But when she checked once more, she couldn't find the person again. Perhaps now she was seeing ghosts instead of simply hearing them.

When they'd reached the farthest caravan, Clopin sent several of the men away. Only the five prisoners, Jim, two other men, and himself were allowed to enter. Red was forced into the caravan with Clopin as her escort. Gripping her arm tightly, his fingernails dug into her skin. She didn't flinch. At least Jim wasn't the one touching her.

Getting everyone inside was a tight squeeze. Jack was permitted to sit on the wicker chair due to his obvious health… or lack thereof. One man stayed close, a warning hand on Wendy's shoulder. When Kai's brawny escort tried to hold his arm, he shook it off and contented himself with remaining as still as humanly possible. Jim oversaw Alice. Not that she proved difficult in the least. Gaze downcast, she was lost in thought. Red realized that she must've been pondering the incident with the pocket watch. Why hadn't it worked?

But Red had more pressing matters to concern herself with at the moment.

Light inside the caravan flickered from lamps and filtered through colorful drapes in the back. Cinnamon and myrrh scented the air. The walls were elaborately carved, beams pleasantly gilded, and the floor covered with intricate rugs. Curtains hung from the ceiling to divide the caravan in half, now drawn to one side with a loose rope.

A bleat pierced the silence, making Red almost jump in surprise. Trotting from behind the curtain, a small goat appeared and leaped into Jack's lap without hesitation. Maybe he was too sick and tired to acknowledge the creature, but he didn't comment on it. The goat was content to curl up in his lap and fall asleep, the bell around its neck tinkling with every movement.

The goat hadn't been the only one behind the curtain.

"*Qui avez-vous apporter avec vous, Clopin?*" questioned a woman's voice from the other side of the caravan.

"*Ce sont des intrus,*" Clopin replied with a sneer. "*Celui-là prétend être le Fantôme Cramoisi.*"

There was a huff before the woman said in accented English, "The Crimson Wraith has not been seen in years. Many claim she is dead, or retreated to darker shadows of the Forest. But those are ideas from those who still think she was a monster, not a girl. Not Red." A breath hung in the silence.

"Fang still looks for her, so we can only assume that she is dead or returned at last to her home. Either way, she would never come back here."

"That's what I thought," Clopin answered darkly in Red's ear like a threat.

"Then why do you bring them here?"

His fingers grasped her arm tight enough to leave a bruise. "She knew we'd returned, and she knew you were alive. Who knows who she could've told about us."

Silence fell dark and heavy.

Red frowned at Clopin's words. What did he mean? Returned… returned from where? And who was supposed to be dead? When she'd made her threats, she'd intended to scare Clopin into thinking she'd told Lupa or Bluebeard about smuggling their would-be victims into the gypsy family. She'd threatened to have exposed them for who they were. She'd never expected it'd be an even worse threat to know of their presence and existence. That had never been the issue before.

"Would you see if she is who she claims?" Clopin requested.

"Fears change just as pleasures do. Time changes most everything eventually."

"You knew her better than most of us. What we do with them, I leave it up to you."

Again, the silence stretched on for forever. Uncertainty grew in Red's gut. There was one scenario she had never considered when she'd resorted to keep the Wolf a secret: the gypsies' sight. Ever since the gypsies had first come into the Forest, they gained certain magical abilities enabling them to each have a unique inner sight. Before, her cloak had been enough to shield herself from their powers. Now, her secrets could be revealed before she'd intended if she wasn't careful.

A slender hand grasped the edge of the curtain as the gypsy woman revealed herself at last. Tall and graceful, her thick raven hair was pulled back by an emerald and gold headscarf. Eyes of smoke and shadow shone sharply in her olive face. Expression grave, she didn't show a lick of recognition when she saw Red.

Not a word passed between them. With their eyes locked, Red felt her head grow fuzzy. She hated her vulnerability. But she couldn't stop it. A hole had been carved into her walls without her permission, and now the gypsy could peer through.

At last, the woman broke her stare. "She fears the wolf, but so do many."

"Esmeralda," Red spoke up, growing tired and weak with every denial brought upon her. "After everything, this is how our friendship pans out? We have traveled so far, from the Forest to Grimrose where I saw the one place we might've made refuge *cursed*. The only reason we were even going to Chliobain was because of our injuries, and the only reason we cut through the Forest again is because of the fatality of them. And now... Now people I dared to call *friends* don't trust my face or words. It's true, I haven't seen the gypsies in a few years. Things change, as you say, and they have. But why this? Why should we lose another friend to the winds?"

"A friend, you say?" Esmeralda questioned steadily. "If my brother is right, you are no friend. You mock me with your imitation."

"Then at least listen to reason, which you know but somehow ignore," Red changed tactic desperately. "Even a shapeshifter wouldn't hold its face as long as this. And a witch wouldn't know what I do. A common thief wouldn't have the guts to look you in the eye, much less the knowledge I'd already spoken of. We both know I'm no *common* thief."

The look on Esmeralda's face was unreadable.

Wetting her lips, Red took a step forward despite Clopin's firm hold. "You told me this once, and I'm asking you now: *do not even the fugitives deserve sanctuary?*"

It was as if the frosty iron that held her together was shaken, the ice melted. Eyes shining, Esmeralda took in a sharp breath.

"You believe her?" Clopin asked incredulously.

Esmeralda's strong voice came in a rush, "We spoke of it alone."

Relief flooded through her and Red let out a breath she didn't know she was holding. Every muscle quaked in exhaustion. She was so tired.

"Release them," she heard Esmeralda's calm, commanding voice. "They are to be given sanctuary with us."

At last, Clopin released her. Red hadn't realized she was kneeling until her friend knelt before her, holding her by the shoulder to look into her face.

"Tell me what you need," Esmeralda whispered.

"Medical attention." That was Wendy who commanded so boldly.

"For whom? Do not leave anything out."

"Red is severely wounded, Jack has fever, and Alice and Kai have old injuries that need tending."

"I do not," Kai protested under his breath.

"Oh, don't start with that; I've seen you limping all through this realm."

A smile tugged the corner of Esmeralda's mouth. "We will do all that we can. Later, we can talk."

Chapter Fourteen

Final Questions

"Have you come for another answer?" Carabosse questioned without turning from her chores. "Or are you just here to gloat?"

Lupa stopped a few meters away. "Am I interrupting?"

Carabosse followed her gaze and arched an eyebrow. At her feet lay a woman sprawled on the ground grotesquely, back wrenched backwards, eyes rolled back, spit and blood dribbling from her mouth. Her stomach was severely swollen. There was no questioning her pregnancy.

"There is nothing to interrupt." Carabosse waved it off casually, watching with fascination at the squirming human. "In fact, you may enjoy watching. I am cleansing her of imperfection."

"Imperfection?" Lupa echoed, gold eyes glittering. "You sensed it before the child had even drawn breath?"

"Life is easier to smite before it gains the voice to protest."

"And you are certain of its imperfection?"

Carabosse chuckled. "Does it matter?"

The woman gargled, the veins in her neck standing out. Lupa licked her lips.

"My apologies for taking this one from you," Carabosse admitted, "but I haven't had this pleasure in a while. I enjoy getting my hands dirty occasionally."

Reflective eyes gleaming, she continued her spell. There was a lot of blood. It shone in the surrounding stone cracks and ran down in streams from the woman squirming on the floor. Screams pierced the air. Then it was done. The woman drained in a puddle of bodily fluids. When she woke, she was in such shock that all she could do was shake and cry and groan like an animal.

Carabosse looked over her until the woman noticed her presence. "You are cleansed, child. Because of the sacrifice you made, I will bestow upon you a gift. Never again will you have to risk this pain."

Hand hovering over a deflated stomach, the woman cried anew. It was all mucus, tears, and saliva. She didn't understand, or couldn't understand now.

Placing a hand on the woman's head, Carabosse uttered a final spell. In an explosion of shadow, the woman disappeared. The only evidence of her being there was the puddle of bodily fluids inking over the ground.

In a flourish, Carabosse turned from the scene and focused on her guest. "You did not come to witness my pleasures. Why have you come? Do you have another question for answering?"

Lupa smiled, turning to wander the room as she collected her thoughts. Carabosse always wondered at the wolves and their constant desire to move. This one certainly felt the need to circle the vicinities when readying to pose a question. It was as if the very phrasing of her questions was of the upmost importance.

"I have heard tales of a potion that gives the illusion of immediate death," she began, gold eyes scanning the empty air as if searching for the right words. "It is lethal, if

* * *

concocted correctly, or can trap the soul in its own mind until death or resurrection. But rumor has it that it can be transfigured to kill its victim, but trap the last breath in solid form so as to obtain it."

"You wish to know how to make such a potion?" Carabosse asked to clarify.

"Yes, that is my question."

Tapping a talon against the side of her nose, Carabosse stood in thought. Such a potion was unnecessary in her eyes, as she always thought potions seemed a weak way to go about magic. They were effective but cowardly. They were an excuse to avoid taking ownership of your actions. No, Carabosse was many shades of darkness, but she was no coward. She would watch her victims writhe at her feet as she broke their bodies with only her words. She would sink up to her elbows in blood without flinching. She would curse a child before a crowd of thousands. But a potion was to work in secret. No fingerprints detected, no need to watch the destruction, no facing the innocent hatred and fear. It was cowardly.

But Lupa needed an answer.

"Such a potion can only be taken willingly," Carabosse began, bringing to her mind's eye a recipe from an old friend's book of potions. It was yellowed and smudged, but she could still manage to decipher it. The wolf, of course, could not see the pages. But Carabosse read it as if from thin air. "You'd need a shadow's remnants, a lightning strike, crystalized water, and gold blood. Add this to any poison, and you'll get the results you seek."

Lupa inclined her head thoughtfully.

"How you manage to obtain these ingredients is another question entirely," Carabosse continued with a laugh.

"You need not concern yourself with that, great one," Lupa leered mysteriously. "I know many who hold my common interests. Their allegiances lie with me..."

She paused, lost in thought. Carabosse wondered at her words. Lupa was typically very careful about the information she leaked. She'd always assumed it was a means of the wolf's survival. But was her web of contacts more intricate than she'd anticipated? How much power did Lupa actually hold?

Perhaps Carabosse had underestimated Lupa.

"I have come to the realization," she said at last, "that I do not know your intentions for obtaining Little Red."

Carabosse raised an eyebrow, seeing an easy end to her debt. "Is that a question?"

Hesitating a moment, Lupa inclined her head. "Yes, that is my final question."

"Very well." She shrugged absently. "Insurance."

Lupa waited expectantly for her to continue. One could almost smell the wolf's anticipation. Chuckling eerily, Carabosse reveled in it.

"The girl is to insure my reign for the rest of existence," she continued, spreading her arms out for dramatic effect. "Once she is in my grasp, I will never worry about rebels and wizards, prophesies and imperfects."

"You wish to latch your survival to a girl? Be bound to her?"

"I am bound to no one. She is the key to my everlasting!" Carabosse laughed, the sound echoing off the

* * *

walls, causing Diablo to fly in a frenzy. "I serve no one. I am the most powerful being in all the realms!"

To her amazement, a smile stole upon Lupa's face. "For now."

Chapter Fifteen

Recuperating

Her name was Drina, she was a healer, and she was only one woman.

This was why as soon as Kai was cleared from the healing tent, dressed in new clothes and his ring returned, he insisted on helping both Wendy and the old woman with the others. They were the only two with experience, and the only two not chained to a sickbed. Grimly, Drina accepted their help.

She didn't talk much, and there was a large language barrier to break through. Kai was bilingual, not trilingual. And Wendy knew very little French. All in all, they made a great team.

With his left leg and foot entirely wrapped in herbs and pastes he didn't recognize or understand, all bound under tightly wrapped bandages, Kai did Drina's every command. He fetched water, collected ingredients from her infinite stores, and helped dress wounds. Mostly, he tended to Jack whilst Wendy helped with the girls. Drina was very particular about modesty.

Red was constantly in and out of consciousness. The old gypsy woman was often with her, boiling concoctions and chanting spells. Her healing was a mixture of magic and medicine. Sometimes, Kai wished he could understand what she was saying, or wished he could be more involved with tending to all his friends. But Red's situation was delicate. From what he gathered from Wendy, Drina had to speed up the regeneration of Red's flesh and muscle tissue, which was a tedious process.

Alice was the easy one. Late that first evening, she was left with nothing but circular scars on either side of her shoulder. Kai figured it had more to do with force of will on Alice's part. Being on the mend already, she was awake for most of the healing process, and thus had the voice to complain about how much she hated being cooped up like a chicken—her exact words, of course. Drina even had to slap her upside the head to get her to stop clucking like one.

As for Jack, it didn't matter how many potions they forced down his throat or pastes they spread over his wounds or spells Drina murmured over his head, none of it did anything. In fact, his fever got worse. Though his back didn't bleed, the strange puss still formulated. The wounds wouldn't seal. Before the night was over, he was moved to a caravan.

Drina said something about the wounds, saying in broken English that there was something that disagreed with Jack's body and caused the infection. By the next day, she'd come up with a theory that it was the air. Raw magic was infecting Jack.

Dutifully, Kai sat mopping his face. The wet rag did nothing to help cool Jack's brow. Nor did the wet sponge dabbed on his cracked lips and the water trickled down his throat seem to do anything. Jack's breath still came raspy. His skin remained impossibly hot. His body shivered under the many woolen blankets strewn over him to force a break in fever. The worst were his eyes, when they were open. Puffy, bloodshot, and yellow glazed. The infection was worse than he'd ever seen before.

When Drina entered the caravan, grim faced as always, she carried a variety of different herbs Kai couldn't name. Not that he was ever good at remembering plant names.

"Do you think they'll help?" Kai asked as she sorted them out.

Drina raised seagrass eyes to him and shrugged in response.

Kai turned back to the one he called brother. "Is there anything I can do?"

He hadn't expected an answer, but as Drina crushed some herbs together, she said simply, "Magic."

The word settled in his mind like a stone through water. Of course, that was the answer. The very thing that infected Jack was the very thing that would save him. An idea rooted in his mind.

"Your friend is awake," Drina stated simply. For a moment, Kai thought she'd meant Jack. Then it hit him that it was Red. Giving him another glance, the woman made an insistent shooing motion. Though reluctant to leave, Kai nodded in understanding.

Squeezing Jack's shoulder, Kai swore, "I will fix this, *bror*. Everything will be made right."

With that, he exited the caravan.

The early morning light hit him blindingly. Kai let in a full breath of air, passing a hand over his face as if he could wipe away the stress and worry. His thumb ran down the scar on his jaw, a habit he practiced more than ever now.

Wendy approached him instantly, face drawn from working late into the night for two days now. Kai supposed he must've had dark circles under his eyes, too, though she'd worked a day more than him.

"How is he?" she asked, brown eyes big and pleading.

Kai hesitated, but broke the news they both already knew, "He's the same."

Wendy's face dropped. "He hasn't changed even a little?"

Kai shook his head solemnly. He'd never been one to give false hope, and he knew Wendy wouldn't want it even if he offered. But at the look on her face, he wished he could offer some sort of comfort. The truth was that Jack was going to get worse before there was a possibility of him getting better. There was no comfort in that.

Wendy tried to pull a smile, looking on the bright side as usual. "Red's doing better, at least. There's barely a scar left."

"Drina said she woke up," Kai offered, earning a truly wide grin from her. That made him feel better.

She grasped his hand. "Then we should go see her!"

As she turned to run off, Kai called after her, "I need to take care of something first. I'll see you after."

But Wendy was gone before he could get the last of his words out.

Rolling up the sleeves of his loose emerald shirt, Kai turned to weave through the caravans. He couldn't wait on the sidelines anymore, watching his brother slowly die. He was tired of waiting and hoping, all the while feeling completely helpless. There was only one thing he could do now. Kai slipped off to find a way to fix the problem.

* * *

The past two days came by in a blur of confinement, worry, and pain. Healing hurt more than Red thought she could bear. The little old woman that was healing her remained steadily calm throughout the entire process. It was the complete opposite of Red's behavior. With fitful sleep full of horrible nightmares, and torturous sensations when awake, she was anything but calm.

When she woke the third morning, the tent was strangely still. Nothing hurt anymore. Throwing aside the blanket covering her, Red examined her body—noting that strength had returned to her limbs. She ignored the old scars, the ones long settled in her skin. Feeling along her ribs, she found nothing but slight discoloration where her wound had been. She sighed in relief.

After dressing in the clothes laid out for her—a loose beige blouse, a long fern skirt hitched up at one hip, brown leggings and laced up boots—she finger-brushed her coarse hair and stepped outside. Pine filled her nostrils as she inhaled deeply. A cool breeze ruffled her hair. For a moment, she almost forgot where she was.

Then she was tackled.

"Red!" Wendy exclaimed, arms tightly hugging her. Red returned the embrace with a laugh. She couldn't help but notice the dark circles under Wendy's eyes even as she smiled in excitement. There was no mistaking the signs of worry. Heaven knows she'd experienced her fair share of it.

"I'm so glad you're awake," Wendy breathed, pulling back. "And you're feeling better?"

Red nodded, instinctively touching her ribs. "Barely a scar is left."

She in turn nodded, the stress of the past few days sounding in the back of her voice. "That's how Alice was— is. Drina still has Kai wearing some kind of ointments on his leg, but he isn't limping anymore. They're around here somewhere."

"And Jack?" Red asked anxiously.

Wendy took too long to answer. Swallowing, she shook her head, voice butchered with unshed tears. "His wounds are infected. He still has fever, but he's... he's not doing well. If anything, he's worse than before. Last night Kai said he coughed up blood."

Red clenched her jaw, forcing down the overwhelming concern. If only she'd tended to Jack's wounds better in Neverland. This was her fault, it had to be.

Clearing her throat, Red asked, "So Kai's been taking care of him?"

"Gerda's father was a doctor back in Anders. Kai used to help with house calls sometimes," Wendy explained. "He and I have been busy helping Drina with you all."

With a small smile, Red squeezed her friend's shoulder gratefully. "I appreciate everything you've done."

"Of course! I wasn't just going to sit around and wait helplessly." She hesitated. "Though a nap does sound heavenly right now."

"And food," Red admitted, the gnawing in her stomach agitating.

Wendy agreed, probably thankful for the distraction and reprieve. Curly brown hair tied up on her head with a lilac and azure headscarf, she was wearing a cream shirt similar to Red's though wrinkled, too big, and rolled up at the sleeves. Boots came up to bloomers held up by a braided belt. Red wondered if they had difficulty finding clothes her size.

As Wendy led her to a place to get some breakfast, she added, "Oh, and I think there's an old friend of yours who wants to see you."

"I don't think I can handle anymore meeting with old friends," Red grumbled.

Wendy raised an eyebrow. The spot they approached was swarmed with children, playing and grabbing for extra morsels. An elderly man with weathered skin and drooping eyes passed a plate to each of them piled high with rice and beans. The abundance of harvested food indicated recent trading. It wouldn't be surprising if they'd returned from preforming a carnival at Chliobain.

"You know, when you were telling us about the Woodsman, I don't recall anything that would predict the warm welcome you gave each other," Wendy prodded between mouthfuls.

Heat crept up her neck.

"Were you two close?"

Stomach tightening, Red did her best to compose herself. "Not as close as I used to think." *But close enough to hurt*, she thought bitterly.

"I take it things didn't end well."

She shrugged. "We were supposed to escape this place together. But he blind sighted me; made me feel safe and then gave me up to the wolves when I least expected it. I thought, *hoped*, that was the last I'd ever see of him."

Wendy was silent, probably trying to read between the lines. After a few more bites, she spoke so casually Red almost couldn't believe she'd said it. "Let me know when you see him again, and I'll help hold him down if you want to beat him up again."

Red laughed so hard she nearly spat out her rice. Guilt crept in soon, though. How could she be laughing? Jack was still sick, and by what Wendy had mentioned, he didn't seem to be getting any better. She hated being unable to control things she couldn't be in control of.

"There she is," Wendy stated, drawing her from her thoughts.

Unsure who she meant, Red turned to follow her gaze. She shook her head. Surely she couldn't be here. Of all the places... But even from this distance, Red recognized the ginger hair and large frame of her old friend.

Pale blue eyes looked their way. "Red?" the woman questioned, still on the other side of the clearing. But then she dropped whatever she was doing, hiked up her skirts, and ran straight for her. "Red!"

Red stood just in time for a smothering, overjoyed embrace. "Briar," she gasped in surprise.

Though two years had passed, Briar had hardly changed. Freckles dotted her oval face where the sun kissed her skin. Shorter by a head, she hadn't grown much at all. Gypsy skirts and a fringed sash fit her well, though her blouse wasn't originally made to house big bosomed women. Briar didn't show any discomfort at the amount of cleavage shown.

Pulling away, Briar observed her at closer quarters. Red could only imagine how much she'd changed, especially after the mess of Clopin not recognizing her. By the way Briar's eyes searched her face, perhaps Clopin's reaction wasn't entirely misplaced.

* * *

"I can hardly believe it's you!" Briar exclaimed. "Thank goodness for your eyes... but even they seem darker. Maybe it's the lighting? But your hair is so long, and I swear you've grown taller."

"I can't believe you're here," Red guffawed. "I thought you were in Grimrose, cursed."

Her face fell. "No, Ingénu and I didn't find out about Grimrose until we arrived after we couldn't find you. It was a side effect. Once my curse was broken, Carabosse set off one that turned everyone in Grimrose to stone." Her voice dropped to a grumble, "I almost wish that I stayed trapped in my own body if it meant sparing them."

Red didn't respond. Of course, she would never have allowed that to happen, not after everything she and Ingénu had done to find Briar. There was always a way to break curses, or at least that's what Briar used to tell her.

"Is Ingénu here?" Red questioned, looking around the camp to see if the Grimrose prince was anywhere to be found.

"He's here somewhere," Briar answered with a wave of her hand. "It's hard to keep tabs on my husband these days."

Wendy offered, "He went out with the hunting party this morning."

"That's where he is!" Briar pointed at Wendy. "And I'm still mad at you."

"What? Why?"

Red shook her head. "Wait... *Husband*?"

"Yes and yes," Briar answered both in turn. "We were married here with the gypsies after they returned. Can you imagine Clopin preforming a wedding ceremony?

Thankfully, being a royal, I have the power to appoint people with certain positions, according to Ingénu. So now Grimrose has a new wedding master. They don't know it yet, of course.

"And I'm mad at *you* for not confirming the rumors when I asked you, and for keeping me from seeing for myself!"

"To be fair, I was only following Red and Drina's orders."

"Is that true?"

Red nodded, realizing the difficult situation Wendy had probably found herself in. After all, she couldn't confirm Briar's identity or intentions with Red unconscious for two days. She was grateful that Wendy was trying to protect her. Just in case.

"Fine," Briar relented, "then I guess we can be friends."

Wendy smiled and shrugged.

Red grasped her old friend's hands. "I'm so happy for the two of you."

"Wendy and I, or Ingénu and I?"

"Both."

Briar laughed. "I'm just glad we found the gypsies so soon. We weren't expecting to find them at all after they'd disappeared."

"Clopin mentioned something about that," Red voiced. "What happened? Where did they go?"

"I suppose you were gone for that, but surely you could guess it."

Raising an eyebrow, Red didn't answer. The gypsies constantly traveled from place to place. Why would this journey be any different? Was this the reason why their numbers were so diminished?

Briar's smile dropped. "Oh, I guess not. They went back home; France. Paris. Whatever that realm is called."

Red's heart leapt. How long had she spent trying to find a way out of this Forest, trying to buy or steal or work a way out of here? And the gypsies made it.

"Why would they come back?" Red asked, trying to repress the fact that if she'd had a choice, she never would've returned to the Forest.

"Not everyone did," Briar answered, looking around as if there were intruders eavesdropping. "And technically, they're not supposed to be back. Rumors travel around, of course, which helped Ingénu and I find them. As for Esmeralda, she's supposed to be dead."

"Dead," she echoed.

"Don't ask me why or how. Best to let that rumor spread or Clopin will have your tongue pulled from your throat."

Frowning, Red looked over to Esmeralda's caravan where the goat grazed in front of it. The more she learned about the changes since she'd been gone, the more confused she became. Everything was so complicated.

Briar asked when the hunting party would be back. Wendy explained they would return at dusk, bringing Clopin, Ingénu, and Jim with them. Though Red pulled a smile to express her excitement at seeing her friend again, and even the possibility that Clopin would stop treating her like a stranger; her skin crawled at the prospect of meeting Jim again. There was no avoiding their meeting again.

At least she had until dusk to decide if she would kill him or not.

Of course, as soon as Alice saw him leave the caravan with that hard-set jaw and clenched fists, she followed him. Something about it made her curiosity peak. Weaving through the gypsy camp just along the outskirts of the Forest, Alice wondered what was wrong. Obviously, something about Jack or Wendy had set him off. He wouldn't even go to see Red now that she was better. Granted, neither was Alice.

Maybe this had to do with Jack's condition. She wondered when he would be getting better.

If he would get better.

She shook her head. Where did that thought come from?

Calmly and without warning, Kai turned to face his tail. Icy eyes looked at her under a raised eyebrow. Alice stared right back, straightening her spine. Had his eyes always been so brown in the center? She'd never noticed it before.

"Why are you following me?" Kai asked, voice low and strained from the stress of the past few days.

Alice shrugged. "I wanted to see what you were up to." She looked over his shoulder to the caravan he'd been heading for. "What do you want with Esmeralda?"

His expression didn't change, but somehow he seemed grimmer. Even before he explained himself, the look confirmed her presumptions. With a sigh, Kai relented, "Jack isn't doing well."

"How bad is he?"

"I'm not in the mood for an interrogation."

"It was only one question!"

"Alice, it's never one question with you."

She huffed and crossed her arms. "Just tell me. How bad is he?"

Looking over his shoulder at the caravan impatiently, he sighed and amused her, "His back won't heal, the infection is getting worse, and his fever…" Rubbing his scar agitatedly, he gave the caravan another glance. "I need to talk to Esmeralda."

"Alone?"

That word seemed to get to him. He wouldn't look at her now.

Without another word, Alice stomped ahead of him and rapped on the caravan door. Kai started after her, calling something but she didn't hear him. She just knocked. That little goat trotted over and started chewing on Kai's pantleg.

The door opened a crack, hesitating. Smoky eyes focused on Alice and narrowed suspiciously. Hinges groaned as Esmeralda opened it wide enough to see her fully. "What brings you here?"

Stepping back, Alice looked at Kai expectantly.

Kai sighed, but didn't waste time with unnecessary remarks. "Jack is sick. Is there anything—a spell or plant— we can use to heal him?"

With a nod of approval, Alice turned to Esmeralda. The goat clambered up to the gypsy's feet instantly, bleating until Esmeralda scooped him up in her arms.

"Drina has told me of your friend's condition," Esmeralda informed. "He is not responding well to her medicines and treatments. I know of no plants specifically, nor spells. But magic is dangerous here. Even if it wasn't, Drina says his body would reject outside magic."

Alice felt her heart drop. "So nothing can be done?"

Smoky eyes looked between Alice and Kai, expression unreadable. With a sigh, she adjusted the goat under her arm. "I may know someone who could help find something for your friend."

Kai perked up, asking the questions before Alice could, "Who? Where can I find them?"

"*We*," Alice corrected under her breath. She wasn't going to let him do this alone. Nothing good ever seemed to happen when they went about things alone.

"Her name is Kezia. I will take you to her." Esmeralda pulled back to grab her headscarf. "She sees clearer than most."

Chapter Sixteen

Blind Sight

As soon as Kai saw Kezia, he pulled Esmeralda aside and growled, "What is this, a joke?"

Alice was already sitting beside the girl who was to help them save Jack. Sitting cross-legged on the opposite side of the caravan, Kezia had long dark hair pulled back into a tangerine headscarf. Her sunshine dress glowed against her olive skin. When the light hit her eyes, they shone in a pale murky fog.

She was eight years old.

She was completely blind.

Sensing an embitterment, the goat wiggled out of Esmeralda's arms and scampered over to the young gypsy. Esmeralda was unfazed by Kai's harsh glare.

Agitated, Kai hissed, "I thought you were taking us to help."

"I have."

"She's a kid! How is this supposed to help Jack?"

Calmly, she repeated the phrase she'd used before, "She sees clearer than most."

"*She is blind!*"

"I know she's blind!" Her eyes were like storm clouds now, ferocious and churning. "Kezia was born blind, and will always be blind until heaven welcomes her. That doesn't mean she cannot see."

"Do you think I'm a fool? That is exactly what it means!" Kai was on the verge of breaking his whisper with frustration. "If you're blind, you cannot see."

"With your eyes, perhaps, but not with your soul."

"I don't have time for riddles."

"Be patient, and you'll understand," she cautioned. "Whether curse or blessing, when my people and I came to the Forest, we obtained a special *inner* sight unique to each individual. When anyone joins our family, they also inherit this sight. Some see clearer than others, and it can develop with age. Some even have difficulty harnessing it. Kezia sees better than most her age, and her control over it has proven difficult but manageable."

Kai only allowed a moment for the information to sink in, glancing at the young girl with the goat in her lap. "What can Kezia see, then?"

Esmeralda followed his gaze. "She sees most everything. The past, the present, and various forms of the future. It's a terrible burden to know so much, but she bears her sight better than I."

Frowning at her words, Kai turned to the gypsy, examining her face. The storm in her eyes had calmed. Softening his voice, Kai asked, "What do you see?"

Esmeralda refused to look at him.

Commotion tore his attention away as Alice cried out, collapsing into a pile of baskets. Kezia had her arms reached out as if to catch her, but couldn't. Her expression was of shock and concern.

"Sorry!" she exclaimed, small hands still outstretched.

Kai rushed to Alice's side, but she waved him off. "It's alright. I'm fine! I was just... startled."

The girl lowered her arms, seeming to feel better knowing Alice wasn't upset. The goat bleated for attention. Scratching him behind the ears, Kezia gave the creature a kiss on the snout much to his satisfaction.

Kai frowned at Alice despite her assurances that she was fine. Eyes wide, face white as a sheet, she looked like she'd seen a ghost. He wondered what happened, resorting to ask her later. Clearly, she wasn't going to tell him anything now.

Facing Kezia again, Kai knelt in front of her. He still found it difficult to ask this child for help. Nuzzling the goat, she looked the image of innocence. Kezia reminded him of another young girl he'd been under the mercy of. She had liked animals, too.

The goat responded to his presence by lifting his head expectantly, the bell around his neck jingling. This drew Kezia's attention. She turned her face in his general direction. "Hello."

Finding himself smiling at her casual greeting, Kai said, "Hello."

White eyes locked on his, a chill shocking down his spine as if she could see right through him: what he was, what he is, and what he will be. For a moment, he wondered what she saw. But then he realized he didn't want to know. Such a knowledge would ruin him.

Finally, Kezia cocked her head. She spoke English well, her accent flowing in delicately. "What's your name?"

"Don't you already know?"

"Papa says it's still polite to ask."

Kai grinned, finding how easy it was to like this girl. "Kai."

The blind girl smiled broadly, revealing the uneven pearls of the prime age for losing teeth. Kai was convinced it was the most beautiful thing he'd ever seen.

"I'm Kezia," she greeted happily. "Do you need help?"

He nodded, then remembered she couldn't see him. "Yes."

"What's wrong?"

Kai hesitated, unsure if he could burden her with his troubles. But Jack was dying, and Kezia seemed genuinely open for so young. Alice sat next to him, her face still pale. Her presence somehow encouraged him to go on.

"Our friend is sick and his wounds are infected. His body is rejecting magic, and medicines are not helping," he explained gently but filled with growing urgency. "Is there anything that can heal him?"

Kezia screwed up her face in thought, pale eyes drifting. Petting the goat soothed it back down to snuggle in her lap. She was silent for a long time.

Kai didn't have to turn to know Esmeralda stood behind him like a sentry.

At last, Kezia spoke up. "There's a rare creature called an *abada*, similar to a unicorn except with two horns and it's much smaller. The horn of an abada has healing properties that can cure anything, even your friend."

"Are you saying we, what, *poach* it?" Alice questioned disgustedly.

Frantically, Kezia shook her head. "No! An abada is too fast to hunt, anyway. But there are horns that have been harvested from the dead."

Eagerness filled his chest. "Where can I find it?"

"Where can *we* find it?" Alice corrected, eyeing Kai.

Scrunching her face again, Kezia searched the air for answers. It wasn't long before she gave a small whimper and buried her face in the goat's side. "An evil place. I don't want to look inside!"

Kai blinked, unsure what to make of it. He wanted to assure Kezia that she didn't have to look, but he needed to know. Jack's life was at stake.

"The Bell Ringer knows where it is," Kezia added, muttering into the goat's fur.

"What does Quasi have to do with..." Esmeralda started confusedly, then her voice dragged off. Her face fell in horror. "You can't mean that God forsaken place."

"What is it?" Kai questioned, finding those smoky eyes churning once again.

But Esmeralda answered him passively before she spoke again to Kezia, "Bluebeard's fortress. I can't ask him to go back there. And if Carabosse or Lupa catch wind of his existence... It is better he stays here while the world thinks him dead."

Tilting her face up, Kezia said gently, "Don't worry, he doesn't have to go. Just ask him about the treasury. That's where the abada horn will be."

With a nod, Esmeralda seemed to shed the sudden worry from her shoulders.

Growing anxious, Kai started to rise. "Then we should go talk to this Bell Ringer."

But Esmeralda stopped him with a hand on his arm. He almost ignored her, but for the look in her face. Something about it told him they weren't finished gleaning information from Kezia.

Alice leaned forward. "How many should go?"

"Six," Kezia replied after only a moment's thought.

"*Six?*"

"Who will go?" Esmeralda spoke quiet but serious.

She thought a moment, as if running different scenarios through her mind. Kezia scratched the goat under his chin, lifting her face to Esmeralda. "You will go. You know the place enough to find the treasury when the Bell Ringer describes it to you."

Grimly, Esmeralda nodded, stormy eyes hidden in shadow.

"The Woodsman should go as well. If he doesn't..." Kezia squeezed her eyes and hid her face in the goat's neck, as if she saw a terrible future should the Woodsman not attend the journey. But she looked up to bravely continue, "The Crimson Wraith will go; she'll find something she's been looking for. You'll need a Pathfinder and a Lie Detector." Reaching out, Kezia touched Kai's leg lightly. "And you. You'll take the last spot on this journey."

A flood of relief washed over him at those words. Not that it would've stopped him from going anyway. But something about Kezia's suggestions rang as something close to prophesy. She'd chosen the best way to get the best solution. Or at least, that's what he hoped.

Then Alice spoke up, confused, disappointed, "What about me and Wendy? Jack is our friend, too. We want to help; we're not incapable."

Turning to her, Kezia gently placed her hand on Alice's knee. Alice flinched at the touch, but if the girl noticed then she didn't show it. Foggy eyes searched the air before her. "The Lost Girl has another journey to prepare for, and you... you are the only one who may find the right questions to ask." She leaned forward as if telling a secret. "I have a feeling you'll be visiting me a lot more than you think soon."

Alice sat back, silently accepting this. Her shoulders still sagged, though, and she stared at her hands with a frown.

Kai wondered about the others who were to join the adventure with them. Everyone in this Forest seemed to have so many strange titles. The Bell Ringer, Pathfinder, and Lie Detector were a mystery. But the Woodsman he knew, though he didn't much care for. The bruise at his temple was still sensitive from their meeting. He could put up with the Woodsman if it meant helping Jack. However, Red wouldn't be too happy about such company.

Jerking back, Kezia screamed. Muscles tensed and her body shook, breathing tight and heavy. Her eyes squeezed shut in terror. The goat wiggled out from her stiff grip and scampered away with a bleat.

Impulsively, Kai took hold of Kezia's hands despite Esmeralda's belated warning. Burning fire lit behind his eyeballs as his body pressurized. His vision changed, and suddenly he saw as Kezia did:

He stood on rough, murky ice, cracked everywhere like spider webs. Cold bit into his skin. His very bones shook from it. But his hands were strangely warm and sticky. Looking down, he found his palms wet with crimson blood. It stained the floor, frozen in scarlet pools. Ice and blood...

Kai cried out and stumbled back, shoulders crashing against the caravan wall. Muscles quavered. His skin felt clammy. He heaved like he was drowning just moments before.

"Kai!"

Alice was suddenly there by his side, keeping him from falling. He wanted to tell her that he was alright, but the chill lingered. Words failed him.

Sobbing, tears streamed down Kezia's face. Kai felt the urge to comfort her despite the fear still coursing through his veins.

Esmeralda knelt next to the hysterical girl, careful not to touch her. "Go outside," she beckoned, giving them one look. "I will meet with you in a moment."

With a curt nod, Alice pulled his arm over her shoulder to help him out the door. But before she could lead him away, Kai looked back at Kezia. Fear and despair contorted her face. Tears made her milky eyes swim. What horrible images did she continue to see?

But despite this, the scared girl mumbled one thing over and over again, "I'm so sorry. I'm so sorry…"

He nearly fell to the ground, his legs still shaking. But Alice was there, holding him firm to the spot. She was much stronger than she looked.

"Are you alright?" Alice questioned, voice firm. "Did you see something?"

Shock waning, Kai only nodded.

"What did you see? Kai?"

"Blood," he said at last, passing a hand over his face. "Blood and ice."

Alice didn't press for more details, brow lined with concern and thought.

Rubbing his scar raw, Kai shook the last of the chill away. It wasn't just what he'd seen that unnerved him. It was what he felt that haunted him. Cold, shock, despair, fear, cold... He didn't like it.

Forcing himself to calm, he examined Alice. Her face was regaining color. But that ghostly look from before...

"You saw something, too, didn't you?" he guessed.

She looked away briefly, gaze lingering on the trees. "I touched her arm," Alice's voice came strained, hesitant. "The vision was from a few weeks ago. I saw my father sitting by the fireplace, a bottle on the table beside him. He held a glass in one hand, and an old toy of mine—a stuffed rabbit—in the other." Blue eyes fell to her feet. "He was staring at it like he used to look at me, with something between sadness and disappointment. I almost didn't catch it when he spoke... 'Happy Birthday, Alice.'"

Kai didn't know how to respond. "I didn't know it was your birthday."

Alice huffed a laugh, looking up to reveal her eyes has grown glassy. "Neither did I. I'm a year older and nothing changed. No one noticed, not even me."

"Your father noticed."

"He did," she admitted, then looked him dead in the eye, "until he downed his drink and threw both glass and toy into the fire in one of his drunken rages... The last thing I saw was the rabbit burning."

Somehow an inkling of guilt creeped into his gut. Alice's family was such a broken one—a dead mother, a drunken father, a runaway sister. Kai couldn't imagine living with a father like Alice's. The memory of his father was of a good man, a loving husband, a diligent soldier. He taught Kai to track and hunt, to live off the land. When they would walk back home from hunting trips, his mother and grandmother would always be waiting for them. Always. His mother would greet them with rough kisses and cheese pies, while his grandmother was ready with fresh new stories to relay. His father took it all in as if it was the last time he would step through the door.

Kai was fourteen when they got the notice. Winter stung the air. That walk home from work was the longest in his life. His mother was covered in snowflakes and wood shavings. His grandmother clutched the notice in her papery hand. Winter always stole the ones he loved.

"I'm sorry," Kai said softly.

Alice shook her head. "Father's always been that way, at least as long as I've known him." Then she laughed at some irony. "It seems madness is inherent."

"You're not mad."

"Are you sure about that?"

"You're not mad," he repeated, "not in the way he is."

She smiled appreciatively. "I suppose. Even so, sometimes I feel…" But she didn't finish her thought. She looked back at the caravan, checking. "But that's not all. I felt things, too. Time. Age. Jack's older now, too."

Kai smirked. "He'll be glad to hear it. You'll have to tell him when he wakes up."

Those words hung in the air with growing tension. Alice locked eyes with him, the thought between them clear.

But Kai wasn't going to take *if* for an answer. Jack would wake up. He was going to make sure of it.

The caravan door opened and Esmeralda stepped out, face dark and headscarf fallen around her shoulders. Before either of them could ask about Kezia, she assured, "She will be fine soon, at least as much as she can be. She has not had a vision that bad in a while. I'll send for her father soon." Esmeralda turned to Kai. "You must get Red and meet with me as soon as possible to talk to the Bell Ringer. It may be wise not to inform her of the Woodsman's role in this journey yet. I suspect it won't sit well with her."

Kai nodded in agreement before turning to do her bidding. Alice was right at his heals for a while. As they walked, Kai asked of her, "While I'm gone, promise me you'll look after Jack."

"As long as you promise that you and Red will come back safe."

Hesitating briefly, Kai grunted in consent, unsure if he'd be able to keep his end of the bargain. How many promises could he make without knowing if he could keep them? No one knew what the future had in store, except for perhaps one blind gypsy girl.

As Alice walked off, Kai called after her, "Alice!"

She turned to walk backwards, the sunlight shining off her blonde hair in a way that reminded him of Gerda. But her hair was lemon; Gerda's was honey. It was the only similarity between them.

"Happy not-birthday," he wished brightly, offering a smile. Then he frowned, unsure if he said it correctly. "Right?"

She grinned with a laugh that was entirely Alice. "Close enough. Thanks, Kai."

Then she was gone, but Gerda stayed close as she always did.

Kai went off to find his friend.

They stepped deeper into the Forest, far enough away from camp to not be overheard, but close enough to find their way back. As soon as they'd reached that point, Briar wheeled on her, hands on her hips. "Spit it out," she ordered, entirely unlike a princess. Such things were not inherent.

Confused but suddenly defensive, Red asked the obvious, "Spit what out?"

"Don't be cute. Whatever it is you're not telling me!" Briar huffed. "After growing up with *Mère* and Aimée, I know when someone's hiding something."

"I'm not hiding anything!"

Briar raised her eyebrows.

Red felt flustered. "At least not more than usual."

"Come on, Red. I know you're hiding something from the others, and I understand holding back! The gypsies can be a little intimidating at times. But Red, it's me! What is it?"

Sunlight filtered in through the leaves overhead, casting beams around them. A blue-skinned sprite buzzed up to snatch a strand of Briar's ginger hair, but she didn't even flinch. Light blue eyes glued on Red expectantly, stubborn and unyielding. That glare was another unroyal habit she'd probably never outgrow.

Realizing Red wasn't ready to reveal the Wolf yet, if ever, she scrambled for something to say. "It's nothing; I promise. I don't know what you're talking about."

Briar cocked her head and frowned. Now she waved off the sprite when it came back for more hair. "You're different. That much is obvious. But we've been through this before. If there's something wrong, how am I supposed to help if you don't tell me? You're my best friend, or at least the closest thing I've ever had to one. If you need to get something off your chest, I don't judge, and I'm a great listener!"

Red couldn't help but smile, kicking her feet at the fallen leaves. "I know."

"Then tell me!" Briar pleaded. Before she allowed time for a response, her expression changed amusedly. "Is it a boy?"

Heat rushed up her neck, but Red shook her head instantly. "No, of course not!"

"Uh huh."

"Don't look at me like that!"

"Don't think I didn't notice how you showed up with *two* handsome young men in tow. And then there's the matter with Jim…"

"I don't want to talk about Jim. And as for…" She shook her head, pulling herself together. "It's not a boy."

Briar sighed, as if disappointed that this wasn't an issue of romance. "Fine, if it's not a boy, then what? Is it Fang?"

At the sound of his name, Red looked away toward the Forest around her. She wasn't sure if it was due to a fear of finding Fang or a fear of Briar seeing the memory in her eyes. Briar took it as the former.

"So, it is about him," Briar acknowledged, hands falling to her sides. Softly, she assured, "You needn't fear him. I won't let him touch you."

Forcing a smile, Red imagined Briar taking on Fang, the short heavyset girl against a wolf. She didn't know who would win in that scenario. Appreciatively, she said, "I know."

But Briar's expression was dead serious, eyes darkening. "No, I mean it. I didn't succeed in breaking my own curse, but it paid off at least somewhat when it was broken. Now the power of starlight is mine."

"Briar, I..."

"I can ensure that Fang can't touch you," she went on. In horror, Red realized that her eyes were blackening and brightening. Pools of darkness leaked into the whites of her eyes. But they weren't brightening, but speckling into swirling constellations until they became the night sky. "No wolf will ever hurt you, I promise."

Dread seized her instantly. Before Red could stop her, Briar raised her hands. Palms shone in silver and gold light. Pressure tightened inside Red's skull instantly, forcing a cry in shock and pain. Her heart raced to impossible speeds. Claws dug through her insides, teeth gnawed her esophagus. She gasped for air, lungs burning and squeezing. Snarling growls surrounded her, echoing in her head, reverberating in her throat. It was as if the Wolf were wrestling to escape. She wasn't in control.

The pressure drained, dwindling the pain to numbing sensation. Noise faded. The Wolf settled back in. Red heaved, catching her breath, realizing she'd fallen to her knees. It took all her strength to look up at Briar who stood before her. Her hands no longer glowed, eyes returned to a summer sky. But she frowned with an indistinguishable emotion of either anger or fear.

"It should've worked." Stumbling back, Briar muttered in confusion, "The spell should've worked. No wolf would ever be able to touch you. It *should've* worked, unless…"

Red's heart dropped. It was too late. "I can explain!"

"Are you one of them?"

The dreaded question hung there like a noose. Red could see it swing, summoning her, ready.

"Are you one of them?" Briar repeated, voice cracking with betrayal. "A wolf? One of the Pack?"

"No, I'm not part of the Pack," Red said quietly, looking up at the noose tightening around her neck with one word, "but…"

With a wet huff, Briar turned away. But Red could imagine the angry tears, the betrayed look in her eyes. Remorse filled her chest. There was no turning back now.

"But there is a Wolf, now, inside," Red continued just above a whisper.

Briar took a deep breath. "How?"

Flashes of memory flicked through her mind, images of teeth and blood and the full moon. She swallowed the lump in her throat. "The night Ingénu and I got you back, when I disappeared. When he chased me down, I don't think Fang realized…"

There was a sniff. "And the others? Your friends, are they wolves, too?"

Red shook her head. "No. I met them in an asylum of sorts—except we weren't the crazy ones—back home." The last word came out awkward and unnatural. The world where she was born, it didn't feel like home. Did she even have a home?

Briar turned to face her now, revealing a face not even flushed much less tear streaked. If anything, she looked more concerned than angry. But she had to be, at least a little. "So, that's where you've been all these years?"

Red nodded. "Yes, mostly."

"Mostly?"

"Before ending up here, the others and I ventured to Wonderland and Neverland."

"I thought those were only fairytales." Briar's eyebrows shot up in amusement. "What were you doing there?"

Slowly and cautiously, Red tried to explain their discovery and hunt for someone who was presumably responsible for their greatest and worst experiences in the realms. When she spoke of their assumption that this Master was trying to take over the realms, Briar's face grew grave.

"Carabosse."

Red's green eyes snapped up. "What?"

"Carabosse," Briar repeated, more sure than before. "She is the most powerful person in all the realms. There is nothing she craves more than power and control."

Red let that settle in. She'd considered before if Carabosse could be this mysterious Master, but Briar's words enlightened the possibility. Silently, however, Red decided to keep the hypothesis to herself. Jack was still sick, and if she could do anything to help him, then that was her first priority. The Master could wait until then, or rot in hell.

Briar shook her head as if waking from a dream. "Where were you bit?"

Silently, Red brushed away her hair and pulled down her blouse's neckline to expose the pale scars at the base of her neck. It burned where the magic in the air touched her damaged skin. Briar blanched as if seeing it made it real.

"I'm so sorry, Red," she whispered.

Covering the bitten flesh, Red pretended like it didn't matter that she was one of *them*. One of her greatest fears found a way to weave itself permanently in her soul. But it did matter. When she felt the urges during a full moon to lose control. When she felt ghost pains of Fang's teeth sinking into her shoulder. When she looked at herself, *every time* she looked at herself. She was one of them. She was a monster, physically and internally, more so now than before.

Then another thought penetrated all other concerns. She couldn't control the Wolf, or Carabosse, or Fang. She needed to help Jack. That was one thing she might have control of, if only a little.

And when Kai came to get her, Red was ready to do anything.

Chapter Seventeen

The Bell Ringer

As Kai led her to meet Esmeralda, he explained the situation with Jack and his poor condition, the abada horn and where it lay. Red's fists clenched at the mention of Bluebeard. But perhaps this trip would prove fruitful on many levels. Last time she faced the bride thief, she'd been a girl. Now, she was a monster. She could bring him down forever.

As for Kai, he looked worse since last Red saw him. Dark circles lined his eyes. His face was pale and sullen. Veins stuck out in his neck from its stiffness, and the scar running down his jaw was stark white. Distant eyes signaled a preoccupied mind. Something in his stance frightened her. It wasn't Kai himself, but rather what he might do. Then again, wasn't that what Red feared in herself?

Approaching the caravan with a rounded green roof and an orange horse painted on the door, Red questioned, "Why would Esmeralda want to meet here?"

Before Kai could respond, the door swung open to reveal the woman herself. She was stoic, acknowledging the both of them with a small smile.

"Come in," she beckoned, stepping back into the caravan.

Stepping up the ledge, Red heard Kai mutter behind her, "Kezia told us who could help, a Bell Ringer."

She froze halfway through the doorway, heart skipping a beat. She'd only known one man who was dubbed such a title. *Quasimodo.*

Entering the caravan with Kai in suit, she shut the door behind them. At first, she could only see Esmeralda in the dimly lit room. But a dark shadow fell over the far side of the caravan, and from it came heavy breaths and the scent of oak, maple, and bronze. Even after so many years, the smell of those bronze bells couldn't wash away.

Kai kept a wary focus on the shadows where the Bell Ringer sat hiding in wait. But Red felt no nervousness.

"Red?"

When Kai stepped back in shock at the unexpected voice, she almost smiled in amusement. The Bell Ringer spoke with a voice she could only describe as angelic: light and powerful, soft but intense, strong yet sincere, deep and silent. So many opposites blended together to make a beautiful tune.

Red leaned forward. "Quasi, we need to talk to you."

She sensed his hesitation with having a stranger in the room. Despite Quasimodo's good heart, first impressions rarely went well. Only Esmeralda was known to never flinched in repulsion. Once there was a time when Red herself feared him. Quasi could be a dangerous man, if he wished, though he was often gentle.

"Kai is a friend," Red assured as Esmeralda in turn held out a hand for Quasi to let him know all was well.

Slowly, cautiously, a hand three times the size of Kai's came forth from the shadows with fingers as stout as a birch tree branch. His right hand looked like a child's compared to the left despite its normal size. The skin on his right arm was riddled with burn scars webbing up to his neck. A massive shoulder caused him to hunch over. Broad chest, small waist, and kneeling legs.

Deformation continued up his face with a swollen brow and twisted nose. He had scraggly brown hair and large teeth in his lopsided smile. Even the color of his irises were different: one the shade of the cool autumn sky, the other as dark as pine needles.

Quasimodo was a man of opposites, but whereas his voice and heart was deemed exquisite, his appearance was anything but.

Looking up at Kai, Quasi seemed saddened and concerned by his reaction. Red could tell Kai was trying his best to hide it, but such shock was difficult to conceal. Quasi lowered his eyes, used to this response.

"We will meet with the others later," Esmeralda spoke to the whole group. "But I believe it best to keep our journey between us for now."

Red nodded. "The less chance of word getting out, the better."

"What do you wish to know?" Quasi asked curiously, looking at Esmeralda with such love in his eyes. This man would do anything for her.

Esmeralda held his hand, kneeling to look him in the eye. "We're going back to Bluebeard's fortress."

He scowled at that, as if the very name of the place made him want to tear it to the ground.

"Kezia said you would know where the treasury is," Esmeralda continued gently.

Red frowned at this. Why would Quasi know where to find Bluebeard's treasury? No one knew where to find it, and anyone who did was killed or a member of his bride trafficking ring. When did the Bell Ringer find out about it?

"Why would you go back there?" Quasi asked his friend in concern, holding her hand with both of his.

Go back? Red thought. *But when would she... Does this have to do with why Esmeralda is supposed to be dead?*

"We have to find something to heal their friend," Esmeralda explained, "an abada horn in Bluebeard's treasury."

"And if you face *him*?"

"We'll make sure he never hurts anyone ever again," Kai spoke up with deep promise.

Multicolored eyes looked to him in surprise. But Kai didn't look away, which shocked him even more. Quasi nodded appreciatively, this promise exciting him. Turning away, he lit a lamp to light up the caravan in a warm glow. Wood shavings littered the floor around carved figures assembled in a magnificent scene. Red had seen Notre Dame Cathedral once when she was a little girl. The likeness before her was incredible, tall towers and delicate arches and saints watching from the walls. Figurines stood scattered around a miniature village in Paris. There were two that caught her eye, both at the steps of Notre Dame. One stood tall, a yellow haired knight, looking out at the village. The other was broken, smashed to pieces, the remnants of a judge.

But Quasi ignored the scene, shuffling to a trunk and shifting through it until he found what he sought. Pulling out a much smaller sculpture of a building with tall spires, he held it up for them to see. Red's throat tightened in recognition. Bluebeard's fortress.

● ● ●

"The reason no one has found the treasury," Quasi explained, "is because the entrance is hidden where no one would dare look."

He cracked open the building to reveal its insides. Though it didn't include all rooms in the fortress, it explained enough. Quasi pointed to a door beneath the grand staircase.

"This is the entrance to the crypt where he throws his murdered wives. On the other side of that room is a door poorly concealed. That's the treasury." He shut the fortress with a click. "No one ever searches beyond the corpses."

"How do you know this?" Red asked, still piecing things together.

As Quasi stowed the sculpture away again, he spoke, "I was there. When the gypsies were held hostage and Bluebeard was readying for a new bride, it was the only place I could hide. But when I tried to escape, I was trapped in. And I had to wait until..."

But Red didn't need to hear the rest of the statement even if he did finish it. She knew of Bluebeard's methods. When his voice trailed, she guessed, "Until he disposed of his old wife."

Silently, Quasi nodded. Shame lined his eyes.

When your freedom depends on the death of an innocent, it haunts you forever, Red thought empathetically. *Even if you couldn't save them anyway.*

Blue and green eyes looked up at Kai, asking for assurance. "You'll stop him?"

Working his jaw, Kai nodded. "He'll get what he deserves."

Red's gut clenched, not with repulsion but anticipation. She itched to put an end to Bluebeard herself. He would never touch another girl again.

Placing a hand on Quasi's large shoulder, Esmeralda kissed him on the forehead. "*Merci, mon ami.*"

Quasimodo put his scarred hand over hers. "*Être sécure, mon amie.*"

With that, they left him alone with his wood carvings and flickering lamps. When all three stepped out of the caravan, Red turned to shoot a question at Esmeralda, but the look on her face stopped it dead in her throat. She concealed it quickly, but Red couldn't deny what she'd seen. Fear. It had churned in her smoky eyes. Red couldn't bring herself to ask about the gypsies' encounter with Bluebeard.

Checking the sun, Esmeralda spoke, "I will make preparations. If we are swift, and the rest of our party comes in quickly, we will leave at dusk."

"What do we do, then?" Red asked, anticipating dusk with a new fervor.

She looked between the two of them. "Rest. Say your goodbyes should the worst happen. You and I both know that, for some of us, it may be a one-way trip."

They parted ways, and Red went to see Jack.

She fell asleep holding his hand.

Dusk was well on its way when the hunting party returned. Red recognized three of the men: Clopin, Jim, and Ingénu. Jim snuck away with a sack of game slung over his back, daring to give her a quick glance before he disappeared. Her blood chilled at the sight of him. But she wasn't going to give him the satisfaction of earning a reaction from her other than boiling steel. For now, she could avoid him. At least the Forest didn't whisper to her anymore. It wouldn't use a ghost she could readily confront.

With a laugh, Briar ran past Red to greet her husband joyously. Ingénu met her with equal gladness and kissed her without shame. Red understood their happy relief. One never knew when the Forest could swallow up a loved one forever. Every welcome was a happy one.

Clopin clicked his heels as he passed the couple, wiggling thick eyebrows to send nearby children into laughing fits. Red smiled. That was the Clopin she knew and remembered. Dangerous, yes, but a born entertainer with a heart for children.

When he passed her, he saluted with a smirk before his sister pulled him aside. There was no warm greeting or shamed apology, but normality. It was as if their confrontation never happened. She found comfort in that.

"Is it really you? My criminal for hire turned sister in arms?"

Lighting up instantly, Red turned to the prince. "Just a friend."

Ingénu clasped her forearm, taking her by surprise when he pulled her into a hug. "Never *just* a friend, Red." When he pulled back, he didn't look her over as his wife had done. Instead, he clasped her shoulder with a grin, as if she truly were a long lost companion. "After all this time, I thought you dead. But I should have known! You were never so easily killed."

Despite his current circumstances, Ingénu still looked like royalty. Even when they'd first met, when he tried to keep his title secret, Red could smell the highborn class a mile away. Hickory brown locks were neatly combed and trimmed. Broad shoulders, tall build, face unblemished save for a mole on his temple and jaw. Deep russet eyes gleamed under a strong brow. True, his skin had darkened from being outdoors, and calluses roughened his hands. But Ingénu stuck out among commoners just as much as Briar did among royalty.

With a raised eyebrow, Red regarded the raised scars emerging from under his wool shirt that stretched up to his neck. "Seems to have healed up nicely."

He instinctively touched his chest where the scars continued, hidden. "Even wounds from a dragon heal eventually. Thank you, my friend."

Wind and fire spurred behind her eyes. Remembering facing that great beast came easily. Blazing heat radiated from the dragon like a giant furnace. Claws like scimitars split open the prince's chest before he could drive his own sword into the dragon's heart. It was one of many adventures and trials they faced together to find the Sleeping Beauty. But Red had to work diligently to keep Ingénu's wounds from festering.

"If only you weren't leaving so soon," Briar said to Red with a teasing pout as she stepped up next to her husband. Though Esmeralda didn't want the news of their journey to spread, of course somehow the whole camp knew about it.

Two and a half heads shorter than Ingénu, Briar linked her arm through his. It was good to see them together after all they'd been through. "We have so much to catch up on, the three of us."

Red locked eyes with Briar, a knowing look passing between them. They'd talked before about whether to tell Ingénu her secret. Though Red was hesitant, Briar was adamant that she and her husband did not keep secrets from each other. Reluctantly, Red relented.

I won't even see his reaction, she thought to herself, looking at Ingénu. She wasn't sure if that was good or bad, or even if it was easier. She'd have to wait until she returned to find out.

Of course, Ingénu had no idea what was going on.

"You are leaving?" he asked with a frown.

Briar patted his arm. "Not for long, I pray."

Briefly, Red explained the situation to him, about Jack and the journey for the abada horn. At the name of Bluebeard, Ingénu's usually smiling face darkened. Grimrose was not immune to the bride trafficking, though most of the danger awaited on the paths through the Forest. Many knights and soldiers were trained to find any of Bluebeard's men that ventured past the kingdom's walls. Unfortunately, as Ingénu once explained, he sometimes had to turn in his own fellow soldiers who took personal pleasures whilst helping in Bluebeard's revels secretly. The thought disgusted her. Poison could infiltrate most any system, it seemed, even the noble ones.

By the time she'd finished, Kai joined them with two packs and an assortment of weaponry. Red realized how quickly their journey was approaching. With the pack, she was given a short bow, quiver of arrows, and a falchion that she strapped to her belt. Kai himself bore a broadsword and two strong daggers.

"So, you are to embark on this journey as well?" Ingénu asked seriously but not unkindly.

Kai nodded. "I am."

Ingénu shook his hand firmly as if they hadn't just met. "Then God be with you both."

Kai smiled in gratitude.

At the sight of Esmeralda approaching them, followed by two other figures, Ingénu pulled Red into an embrace of farewell. His smile was hopeful, as if he expected them to be back by the morning. She wished she had that faith.

Briar clasped her arms around Red and squeezed her tightly. "Be back soon."

"Take care of yourself," Red wished in turn.

Pulling away, Briar then turned and surprised Kai with a hug of his own. Red smiled at his shock. When the ginger princess stood on tiptoes to whisper in his ear, Red heard, "Look after her."

She pretended not to hear.

The couple was gone before Esmeralda reached them. Her followers were a lot younger than Red expected, children really, both small and thin. The girl was nearly thirteen with wavy dark blonde hair cut half way up her neck and light brown eyes that shone in her thin face. Shorter by a head, the boy had the same eyes and tousled hair though cut closer to his ears. He couldn't be older than ten.

"These two are accompanying us," Esmeralda introduced, "Gretel and Hansel."

Gretel held a shy, reserved nature revealed in her posture. Her brother on the other hand couldn't keep still as he excitedly bounced from one foot to the other.

Red raised her eyebrow at Esmeralda in silent question.

"Since they joined us, Gretel is able to see paths," Esmeralda explained casually, nodding to the girl as a blush crawled up her face. "She'll find the way to the fortress. As for Hansel..."

"I can see lies," the boy piped up, grinning toothily.

Gretel rolled her eyes. "Which is why he's so good at telling them."

"They're inseparable," Esmeralda went on.

Kai seemed to understand better than Red did, muttering, "The Pathfinder and Lie Detector."

Shaking her head, Red decided not to question any further. She supposed she'd been doing worse things at Gretel's age than going on a dangerous expedition. As for Hansel, Alice and Wendy had both undergone their own adventures at his age.

Never underestimate children, Red reminded herself. *They can experience the same horrors as the rest of us without knowing any different.*

"Wait!" cried a running Wendy as she rammed into Kai in an instant bear hug. The impact caused some brown curls to slip and fall over her face. "Come back soon," she told them both as she moved onto Red, wrapping her arms around her tightly.

When Alice came up close behind, her expression looked somewhere between forlorn and cheerful, an impossible combination yet somehow Alice achieved it. She came up and gave Red a short hug without hesitation, which shocked her. Red didn't think Alice and she had ever hugged before.

"Be safe," Alice said to them both after she pulled away and gave Kai a matching embrace. "Keep each other safe. And get back, soon."

"We will," Kai assured.

Red didn't understand how easily he could make such promises.

As they prepared to set off, Red caught a whiff of someone that made her spine snap straight and skin crawl. She didn't even have to look to know who was filling the final spot on their trip.

Sharply, she grabbed Esmeralda by the arm and stepped close, fuming. "What is *he* doing here?"

Esmeralda didn't flinch. "The Woodsman is to join us to the fortress."

Red almost laughed, unamused. "You can't be serious."

"Kezia said that Jim was to be of the six who go. Therefore, he will come."

Red scowled, completely aghast that this should happen. Why hadn't anyone told her? They were probably afraid she wouldn't come.

Another time, perhaps, or a different me, she thought. *But now is not that time, not with Jack's life on the line.*

Still, she couldn't bring herself to look at Jim.

"Whatever embitterment you have, set it aside," Esmeralda advised. "I will not allow outright conflict within our group."

Red looked away briefly, unable to keep the ice from her tone, "Fine, but don't expect me to be the one who saves his neck should we run into danger."

"As you wish."

Releasing the gypsy, Red faced one of the caravans where Wendy ducked in with an armload of herbs. She muttered a last goodbye to Jack, wishing with all her heart that they would be back in time to save him. Sighing, Red turned away and joined Kai.

Six figures left the gypsy camp and entered the dense Forest as dusk fell in all its glorious beauty.

Chapter Eighteen

Run as Fast as You Can

Jack couldn't tell which was dream and which was reality.

All of it blended together into a haze, confusing his already muddled brain. Memories and visions pulled him in and out of each other as if through thick jelly with jarring force.

He was a boy, small for his age but with a big personality. Back at the orphanage in England, he played with Jill and Harry amongst the other orphan kids in the field. Harry eyed him with a mischievous smirk. In one swoop, he snatched a doll away from his sister. Jill cried out in protest, but Harry held the toy just out of reach.

"Catch it, Jack!" Harry shouted, hurtling the doll his way.

Jack caught it with a laugh, spinning around and made a run for it with Jill right after him. He kept running.

Faster.

Faster.

Jill's cries disappeared, replaced by thunderous hooves and raging moans. Panic seized him. The doll in his hands crumbled to powder. Even as his legs raced under him, he couldn't gain any distance. The rolling hills around him melted way into a familiar valley where his parents worked. He skidded to a halt. Something went wrong, and suddenly a stampede swept across the valley.

Jack screamed, but they didn't hear him. Their cries rang in his ears as his parents were trampled underfoot.

Terror pulsing through him, he turned and sprinted off. The thunder returned behind him, rumbling and toiling, trembling the earth. He dared to look back. The herd was after him now, taking on demonic proportions. Bleeding scarlet eyes, yellow foaming mouths, and they snorted billowing smoke. Jack ran hard, desperately trying to escape. It was no use.

Just as they caught up to him, the scene changed. Jack was running through the Welsh woods, laughing. Harry and Jill were with him, but he was faster. They were all older now, but not really. Not yet.

Suddenly, they came upon a strange sight that caused them all to stop in their tracks. A beanstalk stretched high above their heads, the top far beyond sight.

"I've never seen a beanstalk so high," Jill gaped in awe, "or thick."

She was so beautiful now, eyes bluer than the sky, hair like dark chocolate. Jack didn't know where the thought came from.

"Wonder where it goes?" Harry pondered, placing a hand on the stalk. The branching vines made for a perfect ladder.

"Let's find out," Jack said without thinking.

He started climbing, the vines indeed forming perfect hand and foot holds. Harry followed instantly, Jill scrambling after them.

Just as quickly as Jack was climbing up, he started hustling down. Sweat beaded his skin, pain compressing his chest. He was alone. The beanstalk shook violently. Tears slid down his face in streams. Screams echoed in his ears, terrible screams. His foot slipped and he fell into instant freefall. Leaves and small vines whipped his back as he plummeted. Then there was nothing but open air.

He landed on cold stone flat on his back. Air rushed out of his lungs. Someone was suddenly there standing over him.

"Go, Jack!" Harry cried, panic alit in his blue eyes. "Go, now!"

Jack stood to go, finding himself in a courtyard much too large. But Harry turned back with sword in hand.

"What are you doing?" Jack called after his friend.

"I'm not leaving without her!" Harry proclaimed.

"She's gone, Harry!" he shouted, throat tight. "Jill's dead!"

"You don't know that!"

Without fully comprehending it, Jack was running again, always running. Loud rumbles followed behind, shaking the ground.

"*Jaaaaaack*," a gruff voice called after him in two long notes. A flash of blue and brown eyes flicked across his vision. "You can't run forever, Jacky. You can't run."

A piercing scream made him whip around and he saw her on the ground. Jill. There was blood everywhere. Her face was hidden under her dark hair, her body sprawled out on her stomach. But Jack didn't go to her. He knew, somehow, he knew... Jill was gone.

"Jill," Jack yelled, desperate. "*Jill!*"

His vision blurred. There was a face over him, hazy at the edges. Blue eyes.

"Jill," he whispered.

His throat was dry and his skin felt grimy. His whole body shivered uncontrollably, but he felt so unbelievably hot. Pain throbbed behind his temples.

"Jill," he mumbled again.

But it wasn't Jill. Blonde hair. Jill had dark hair.

Another face appeared. Dark hair. Brown eyes. Not Jill.

Then Jack was running again.

Running.

Running.

Running...

*****

There was no path to lead them where they were going. Only Gretel knew where they were headed, her eyes seeing a road Red couldn't perceive. But at least this meant they weren't lost. The Forest couldn't manipulate them, not even in the dark.

Hansel trotted close to his sister's side mostly, but often grew tired of keeping her company. He'd scamper around the others in search of something interesting. It was like trying to control a curious puppy.

Wings ruffled the air. Instantly, Red drew her bow and fired into the dark. With a cry in pain, a raven fell to the ground in a puff of feathers.

As she retrieved her arrow, Esmeralda spoke impressively, "You've improved. Your reflexes have tripled since last we met."

"I improved much during my journeys with Ingénu," Red said passively. She didn't comment more on the subject, stowing the bird's carcass for later.

The Wolf inside bristled, sensing peril.

Before she could further investigate her instincts, Gretel held up a hand and came to a halt. "Wait. The path shows danger."

"We're in the bloody Forest, love," Jim muttered. "'Course it does."

"I can't tell what it is," Gretel continued, closing her eyes. "But it's getting close. Their path is getting shorter."

Steadying her breathing, Red stilled herself to let her senses flourish. Snuffling breaths. Heavy footsteps barreling towards them. But when she smelled them, her heart skipped a beat.

"Tree sap and fungus," she muttered, opening her eyes. Without explanation, she caught the others' attention. "We have to run."

It didn't take much persuasion, especially when a guttural sound like cracking wood filled the air. All but Kai recognized the hunting cry of a troll.

Esmeralda turned to Gretel urgently. "Which way."

Face paled, the girl grabbed Hansel's hand and sped deeper into the Forest. They ran after her, Red trailing behind just in case.

It wasn't long before Red wasn't the only one who could hear the clumsy galumphing of their pursuers. Branches split as massive bodies stampeded between trees. The Forest did nothing to stop them.

There was no outrunning the trolls, even without the two children who led them.

Jim voiced it first to Esmeralda, "They'll be upon us soon enough. We've got better chances fighting them."

Grinding her teeth, Red hated to admit that he was right. Even so, she didn't like the odds. They weren't better by much, especially if she was to keep the Wolf under wraps.

One shout from Esmeralda caused Gretel and Hansel to skid to an instant halt. The boy drew a short blade, too enthusiastic for someone about to face a bad of trolls. Kai drew up next beside them, catching his breath. The rest weren't far behind.

Looking straight at Red, Kai questioned lowly, "How many?"

"Four," she responded, finding no need to catch her breath, "all adults."

"Better spread out, then," Jim suggested, having overheard. "Best to attack from all sides. We're less of a target that way."

"I can work some illusions," Gretel suggested meekly. "The magic is strong here. It can keep the trolls focused on the wrong—"

In an explosion of leaves, dirt, and splinters, the beasts were upon them. Massive bodies towered over them, their bulk as thick as boulders. With arms thicker than tree trunks and legs stubby, they were like small mountains and mudslides all at once. Jaws stuck out in an underbite. Uneven square teeth filled their maws. Skin cracked like tree bark, eyes murky as a swamp.

All four charged and the group scattered.

Instantly, Red fired an arrow into a troll's eye. It screamed, the sound shaking the trees. Before she could set another arrow, the troll swung its arm and struck her in the side to send her flying. She landed hard, the wind knocked out of her. The blinded troll jerked around aimlessly. The others had to keep on their toes.

With a strong swoop, Kai severed another creature's thigh. He dashed under it to avoid the outburst and stabbed it on the opposite side. The troll doubled over, screaming. Nonstop, Kai leaped against a tree, using the momentum to push off and spring towards the troll with his sword raised. The beast sent a blow for him, colliding into its target. Its arm only passed through an image.

The troll turned just as the real Kai flew from the other side and brought his blade down into its neck. Dark blood sprayed him. It gave a gargling scream before the troll collapsed.

Pulling free his weapon, Kai turned to thank Gretel who stood close by. Her hands fiddled with the air as she worked her illusions.

Esmeralda held two double edged scimitars, movements like the dances she performed. Her blades sliced a troll's skin rapidly. It reacted extravagantly to catch her, but she was too sly as she dodged its outbursts.

With an axe in each hand, Jim came up to plant one weapon in the troll's chest and the other in an open wound at its knee. The troll retaliated by diving for him, sending Jim rolling. One of his axes was still in its chest.

Using the distraction to her advantage, Esmeralda leaped over the creature's arm onto its hunched back. She straddled the beast and drove both scimitars between the shoulder blades. She held on tight as the troll went down.

Gretel worked tirelessly at keeping the partially blinded troll distracted with images of her brother, face paled with the strain. The real Hansel crawled under the creature's belly stealthily. Gretel shouted at him angrily. But Hansel didn't listen, thrusting his short sword into its abdomen. The troll cried out, growing dizzy.

Gretel screamed, her illusions sputtering out of focus. Hansel was practically paralyzed as the troll began to collapse, but he was trying to retrieve his stuck blade.

Taking careful aim, Red shot another arrow into the troll's other eye. The troll reared, revealing the boy underneath enough for Kai to bolt, grab him, and roll out away from the massive raging feet. Quickly, Red fitted another arrow to shoot it in the throat. It screamed again, gargled.

"Will this thing die already!" Red shouted, drawing her falchion.

Esmeralda beat her to it, raising her blade to sink it deep into the troll's jaw as it fell. It died instantly.

"You alright, kid?" Kai asked, crawling to his knees.

Hansel nodded rapidly, eyes wide. His sister rushed up to him, enfolding her brother in a squeeze.

"You're okay? Are you hurt?" Gretel rambled anxiously. "Curses, Hansel! You could've been killed!"

"I'm fine, Gretel." Hansel rolled his eyes.

A massive fist slammed into the ground just beside Red, reminding her with a start about the fourth troll. A cloud of dirt flew into the air. She barely missed another blow, whipping around to shove an arrow into the troll's armpit. It flung its arm at her, sending her shuffling back. A cry like a toppling forest vibrated in its throat.

A shot split the air and a hole drove itself through the troll's brow. Blood sprayed her face. The troll fell, its head hitting the ground right at Red's feet.

Breathing heavily, adrenaline pumping, she turned to see who fired the shot. Jim stood there with raised pistol, the smoking barrel aimed at her nose. They stood like that, frozen, eyes locked. Then Jim lowered the gun.

"My last bullet," he said grimly. "Those're hard to come by in this Forest, my…" He dropped his gaze, but she knew exactly how that sentence was supposed to end.

Heat flared up her neck. "I didn't ask for your help. I can handle myself."

"Didn't look that way. But next time a troll's about to kill you, I'll be sure to remember that."

She clenched her fists, steeling the Wolf inside ready to attack. But Kai placed a hand on her shoulder to hold her back. She regarded it momentarily then shook it off, stepping closer to Jim.

"I am *not* yours," Red sneered, "especially not your love."

"Sorry," Jim said lowly, unfazed. "Force of habit."

"Next time, bite your tongue."

"Or what? You'll do it for me? I didn't think you were interested in that anymore."

Fuming, she clenched her teeth. If she even tried to retaliate, she knew she'd lose control and the Wolf would take over. Turning away was the hardest thing she'd done all day. She marched after the others.

They weren't to sleep until dawn, but Hansel couldn't last that long. The Woodsman carried him as he drifted in and out of a nap. He sang a melancholy tune to ease the boy. It developed words, sweeping over the group calmly:

"The Forest is dark, dearie, The Forest is dark;

● ● ●
170

The moment you think that you're lost in the woods, then you are.

Do not lose your way, dearie, Do not lose your way;
The monsters are lurking not far from the path should you stray.

Things aren't what they seem, dearie, Things aren't what they seem;
Kind grins are bared teeth; Please don't answer the calls from the trees.

Do not pay them heed, dearie, Do not pay them heed;
Hear footsteps behind you, beware but don't fret, they're just checking.

The air is alive, dearie, The air is alive;
To help and to hinder, but it's how some learned to survive.

These woods are too old, dearie, These woods are too old;
Watch for crimson wraiths, keep your strength and wits close should you go.

Deep in the Forest."

Even when Hansel squirmed out of his arms, the Woodsman continued his song. But Kai could tell that it made Red tense rather than calmed. He recognized some of the lines in the song, tips that Red herself had used when warning of the Forest's dangers. Perhaps it was a song that the Woodsman taught her when they worked together. Or at least when they were supposedly civil to each other.

Hansel perked up beside Kai curiously. "How'd she know there'd be four of them?"

"Who?"

"The Crimson Wraith. You asked her earlier. How'd she know there'd be four trolls?"

Kai shrugged. "I don't know."

The boy's brown eyes glimmered, a smirk stealing the corner of his mouth. Kai felt his gut tighten, realizing his mistake. Hansel saw the lie. But the kid said nothing, turning to run to his sister's call.

They made camp at dawn. The Woodsman was still singing when he took first watch.

*****

At the sound, Fang looked up from where he lay. Arctic and red wolf lay side by side, Quinn's head atop Lev's. Thaddeus was curled up nearby, his bushy grey tail over his nose.

He heard it again: trees rustling, twig snapping beyond the undergrowth. They were made on purpose. Someone wanted his attention. Fang rose to his paws, carefully trotting into the dark shadows.

He entered a small clearing, silver rays of moonlight filling the area. A Mongolian wolf sat in the middle of it all, her nose pointed to the moon above. Fang swiftly changed form, approaching the wolf cautiously.

"What are you doing here, Lupa?" he questioned deeply.

Gold eyes turned to him easily. They never changed as Lupa shifted shape. She smirked, rising to her feet.

"Come now, Fang," Lupa cooed, flashing her pointed teeth. "You act as if you were not happy to see me."

Fang said nothing. It was unlike Lupa to pay him a visit so close to a full moon. She usually obtained bloodthirst in anticipation and terrorized any unsuspecting humans near and far. Of course, the highlight of this was the night of the full moon. Fang did not approve of her pleasures in forcing others to become wolves, not to mention her slaughtering habits. She wasn't of the Pack. But Lupa was his aunt, and she had her moments. After all, it was Lupa who suggested Fang as bounty hunter for Carabosse. It made him uncomfortable to know how close Lupa kept with such company as the sorceress.

Her eyes glittered. "I have recently discovered that the dark sorceress is not on our side."

"Our side?" Fang questioned. Though they were family, he never considered himself to be on the same side as his aunt.

"She does not follow our grand plan."

"You mean *your* grand plan?"

Lupa ignored his comment. "Carabosse's intentions with Little Red are—"

"Not my problem," he interrupted, concealing his annoyance with this. "The girl is to save Zoë. It's not my concern what happens to her after. She's just a girl."

"She is so much more than just a girl," Lupa's voice was smooth like honey but dripped with poison. "Things have changed, Fang. When you have Little Red, take her directly to me. Bring her friends, as well. You and the Pack shall be rewarded greatly."

"No, Lupa!"

She looked more amused than surprised at his statement. But it didn't stop him.

"Things haven't changed," he continued. "I will find the girl, and when I do, I will give her to Carabosse who *will* honor our agreement by healing Zoë. These plans you have are not mine, and I will not endanger my Pack by roping them into this mess."

"You are making a mistake," Lupa crooned, lips curling. "I have told you before how pointless it is to love Midas' daughter. She is not a wolf, and unless you take advantage of the full moon—"

"No."

She pouted. "Now, Fang. I know I'm the *Big Bad Wolf*, but you do not need to treat me like it."

His jaw tightened. "We're done here."

As he turned to leave, Lupa called, "You are going the wrong way. You will not find her where you are going."

Fang stopped, turning silver eyes back towards her. He didn't bother asking how she knew such things.

"As of right now, Little Red is on her way to Bluebeard's Fortress," Lupa continued, twisting a long caramel curl between her fingers. "If you are swift, you will find her there."

"Bluebeard's Fortress? But I thought..."

"Yes. Nevertheless, that is where she is going."

"Why there?"

Lupa shrugged. "I only act like I know everything."

He shook his head, trying to work out why the girl would try to go to that foul place. But when he looked back, Lupa was gone. She had an easy bond with the Forest, able to manipulate it to her will. In a matter of hours, she could go anywhere she wanted in the Forest.

The night was still young, and Lupa was probably on the hunt for innocents to destroy. He would have to keep an eye out in a few days, after the moon. Fang made it his business to let the new wolves of Lupa's victims feel welcome into the Pack. Quinn had joined as a small child after a full moon brought Lupa along. The Pack had adopted her as they did all wolves.

Never did the Pack turn on their own kind.

Never.

Chapter Nineteen

Swing and Burn

When no one in their right mind would willingly go searching for someplace, there was no need for sentries.

Or at least, that's what Red kept telling herself.

According to Gretel, they were closing in on the fortress quickly. They held their breath with every step, the very air charging with impending danger. Swords were drawn. Red had an arrow nocked and ready. No one was going to take them by surprise.

Gretel came to a stop, crouched low behind wild undergrowth. "It's just beyond this hedge," she whispered.

A chill ran down Red's spine. She tried to prepare herself, taking a deep breath. Only once had she been to this place and faced Bluebeard himself. She'd been captured and held with seven other girls in the fortress, waiting in solitude until Bluebeard arrived to claim his next bride.

Guilt pulsed in her veins remembering those girls. They had planned to escape together, the seven of them. But something went wrong. Another wedding came along, and when Bluebeard came to take the second girl of the original eight, they made a break for it. But they were only a distraction. One girl stayed behind to help Red sneak out the window with a promise to return and save them.

The girl was chosen as the next bride because of it.

Later Red found out what became of them. Every day after she'd escaped, Bluebeard married one of the girls in the evening and murdered them the next morning. Red never went back for those girls. She couldn't save them.

Since then, the Crimson Wraith became the bane of the bride trafficking.

Now she was ready to rip the man to shreds once and for all. In fact, she longed for it with a hunger that almost scared her.

Hansel wrinkled his nose. "It stinks."

"What's the plan?" Kai asked, voice hushed.

Esmeralda's face had significantly paled. She looked deadly. "We might be able to enter through a window around the south side. That's where he keeps the girls."

"He must bar his windows, now," Red insisted, recalling how she'd escaped.

Esmeralda shook her head. "If anyone escapes, he simply replaces them. His current wife is the only one he keeps a firm eye on."

"Does he have servants?" Gretel asked meekly, wringing her hands.

Hansel spoke up, "Greedy men always have servants."

"We might be able to use the servant's entrance."

"Or we could walk through the front door," Jim announced from the hedge.

Esmeralda raised an eyebrow at him. "Do you suggest pretending to be part of his crew with new captives?"

"No, I mean we just walk through the front door." Jim pushed aside the hedge's brittle branches. "Something tells me we won't find much resistance."

Red frowned, stepping forward to take a look. The fortress stood tall, blackened, and broken. Spires that once pierced the sky were toppled into itself. Debris surrounded it, littering the ground in a messy obstacle course. The structure was completely unstable, covered in ash.

Numbly, Red stepped forward into the clearing. No one stopped her, not her traveling companions, not Bluebeard or his men. She walked through weeds and ashes straight up to the door. It opened at her touch with a groan. Birds flew into the air and out a gaping hole in the ceiling.

Bodies lay grotesquely scattered throughout the space, skin melted to their bones. Most lay curled on the ground as if waiting to let death take them. Some were hardly recognizable. Others were unfortunate victims to scavengers and insects. A vulture didn't even acknowledge Red's presence as she walked past.

Compelled by a force she couldn't acknowledge to its entirety, Red turned to the rickety staircase and climbed without hesitation. Crusty blackened carpet crunched under her feet, sending up puffs of grey. Pieces of the stair fell under her weight.

The room wasn't hard to find. Red stopped in the open doorway, stomach tightening. There he was, collapsed against the foot of his tattered bed. Scraggly burnt blue hair stuck out in all directions. Rich nightclothes were in tatters. Both eyes were charred to nothing in his skull. He was another few bird meals away from being nothing more than a nasty skeleton. Another body lay in the remains of the mattress.

Red couldn't tell what she felt. It wasn't supposed to be this way. He wasn't supposed to die this way, in a housefire stumbling out of bed. She could imagine that he was already half unconscious by the time he fell out of sleep with his unfortunate wife, full from a lavish meal, feeling no pain. This wasn't justice.

Grinding her teeth, Red grabbed him by the throat and dragged the corpse away. The floor threatened to cave under her as she stomped back down the hall. A flock of birds scattered at the noise. Without hesitation, she ripped off a rope wrapped around the remains of heavy curtains.

She didn't break pace. She didn't think. She just acted.

Reaching the banister, Red strung up a noose, pulled it tight, and pushed Bluebeard's corpse off the edge. His neck broke with a snap. The others entered the room below, but she just stood there and watched him swing like a criminal.

Maybe this was the justice she demanded.

She felt nothing.

*****

"Why are we going *there?*" Quinn asked with a scowl. "That's west of here."

"It's where the girl will be," Fang said sharply.

"But the trail leads south to Chliobain."

"How do you know?" Lev added, taking Quinn's side as usual. "Is it a feeling? An instinct? How do you know she'll be at the old kidnapper's place?"

Fang caught Thaddeus' eyes on him. The older man gave him a look expressing that he too wished to know of where such information came from.

But Fang hesitated, eyeing Quinn skeptically. He wasn't sure how she would respond to him following the word of Lupa. She always avoided the lone wolf. Fang didn't blame her. Quinn had never trusted Lupa, ever since the night when she got the scar on her forearm. The stark white marks of a wolf bite.

They still looked at him expectantly.

Clenching his jaw, Fang confessed, "Lupa told me."

Quinn froze, her breath cut short. He instantly regretted his words.

Lev put a hand on her shoulder, unsure what else to do. Quinn fingered the scars on her left forearm as if she felt the sting again.

Thaddeus leaned in closer to Fang, the crow's feet deep next to his eyes. "Are you sure Lupa tells the truth? She is not always trustworthy."

"She's not trustworthy," Fang admitted, voice low, "but Lupa never lies."

"Perhaps. But she must have other intentions. I would never put it past the lone wolf to hide portions of the truth when it best suits her."

Fang sighed, clenching his fist. "I don't doubt it. Nonetheless, we're following this lead. Chliobain is a fortified kingdom, and no one there takes kindly to the Pack. And the girl is resourceful. If there's a chance of finding her outside such a populated area, I'm going to take it."

Thaddeus let out a long sigh through the nose. His eyes didn't harden. "I admit, I hope this is true. We will follow you. Better a charred crypt than a prejudiced kingdom known for its giant killing queen."

Fang nodded thankfully. He rubbed the dragon cuff around his wrist, hoping to have it removed soon. He looked down at his hands. There was a tattoo around his left ring finger, reminding him what he was fighting for.

Thaddeus turned to Quinn and patted her shoulder. "Are you well, cub?"

She stuck out her chin and nodded resolutely. Her face was pale, but her eyes gleamed with determination.

"Good. Then let's go," Fang grunted, looking up. "It's not far."

*****

Red was still standing there when Kai came to get her. He didn't say anything, just stood with her as if to let her know she wasn't alone. She felt empty.

"I don't remember their names," Red said at last, so soft she wasn't sure he could hear her. "But I remember their faces."

It was true on a number of levels, but Kai seemed to somehow understand what she meant now. "You're not responsible for what happened to them."

"Maybe not," she lied. "But he is."

They stood staring at the hanging corpse below them for a moment more before Red finally turned to follow Kai back down the staircase. The rest of the group was waiting for them. Gretel held her brother close, but he peaked at the destruction despite her attempts to keep him from looking. Esmeralda looked straight up at Bluebeard grimly. Light glittered on her raven hair. She said nothing.

Jim rammed into the door below the grand staircase. Dust cascaded down on his head. But the door stood steadfast, locked.

Kai stepped forward to help figure out how to break down the door, the two men taking turns slamming into it. No matter what they did, it didn't give. Red was about to step up to knock it off its hinges despite the risk of exposing her unnatural strength when Esmeralda walked right past them and retrieved a key hidden in the mouth of a nearby statue smeared with soot. Both Jim and Kai looked more than a little annoyed. Esmeralda ignored them, unlocking the door and stepping away. She dropped the key in the ashes as if it burned.

Now, no one wanted to open the door. Gretel volunteered to stand guard, obviously hating the idea of witnessing a sight worse than the scene they stood in. Despite his protests, the others agreed that Hansel should stay with her.

Jim shoved open the door with his shoulder, the hinges creaking. The stench hit first. It was unlike any other scent in the universe, decay and murder. Swirling darkness awaited them. Instantly, they covered their noses and mouths with scarves and rags, though it didn't help much. Each of them fashioned a torch to hold aloft.

Grimly, they descended the staircase into the dark crypt. Red didn't want to look, but it was inevitable. The entire room was covered with bodies, undisturbed by the fire. The first layer was the worst, the newest and freshest victims. They looked the most human. She suppressed the urge to vomit as they stepped over Bluebeard's wives who had been tossed down the stairs like vermin. The firelight flickered over piles of them, mangled and broken.

Something cracked under her foot, soft and brittle. Red squeezed her eyes shut. Her hand shook.

Someone took her hand and her eyes shot open. Kai's fingers were cool and reassuring. Squeezing it tight, Red let him lead her on. Jim's tawny eyes looked back at her in concern. She didn't have the energy to reprimand him for it.

Esmeralda led them through the best possible path over the bodies. As they grew older, the piles grew neater, corpses laid shoulder to shoulder with some organization. It was as if over time, as Bluebeard grew in his obsession, his disregard for the women rose also. It showed in the way the bodies were strewn.

By the time they'd crossed the room, the corpses were close to mere skeletons lying face up with hands folded over their breastbones. Just when Red didn't think it could get any worse, the light flickered to the wall ahead of them. Human remains hung along the wall displayed by large iron meat hooks stuck through their spines. Thin tufts of hair hung over their skulls, clothes nothing but tattered rags. Rings gleamed in the firelight from each of their left hands. These had to be the oldest of the lot, Bluebeard's first wives. None of the other girls wore wedding rings.

Red didn't even notice the door until Esmeralda opened it. Dust stirred at the sudden air exposure. Though musty, the air was a little cleaner on the other side. Without a word, they ducked into the treasury.

Heavy wooden chests lined the walls, some open wide like overstuffed mouths. Polished statues stood like sentries guarding the treasures. Everything else was littered in small piles, neater than those in the room behind them. Red couldn't imagine how Quasimodo survived in such a place.

They split up, scouring the premises for what they'd come for.

Red caught Jim lining his pockets with whatever he could fit in them. When she frowned at him, he shrugged, "No one else is using it."

"You'd steal from a place like this?"

"Why not? We've stolen from dead devils before."

Red huffed, but Esmeralda spoke up, "Take what you will. Just remember, whatever you take you have to carry yourself."

Jim didn't seem to mind that scenario too much, filling his pack strategically.

After rifling through stacks of treasure, Kai announced his find in solemn victory. The abada horn was long, curved, and twisted. Polished in a gleaming bronze, Kai cradled it carefully. They regrouped, readying themselves to brave through the crypt again. Both Esmeralda and Jim had bulging packs.

It was no easier going through the tomb a second time. Esmeralda almost tripped and pitched toward a group of decaying flesh when Red caught her arm to stop her. They treaded more carefully now. When they emerged at last, Red could still see the bodies every time she closed her eyes. The burnt figures here didn't hold a candle to the horrors below.

Hansel made a face at the horn Kai held so tightly. "Is that it? We came all this way for a fancy spike?"

"*Ja*," Kai grunted, headed for the door.

Jim pulled a small smile, crouching before the two young ones. "I found these," he said gently, taking out two small treasures from his pocket. "Thought you might like them."

To Gretel was given a simple necklace inlayed with a smooth white stone, and to Hansel was given a small marble duck. Both took their treasures thankfully. Jim ruffled Hansel's hair before he stood. Red didn't know what to make of it.

As they left the remains of Bluebeard's fortress, Hansel grumbled, "I still can't believe we came all this way for a fancy spike."

"Hush, Hansel!" Gretel scolded, grabbing his hand.

"At least we got to fight trolls."

"Would you stop complaining!"

Red was the last to leave, looking back to the nightmare in their wake. Bluebeard still hung there swinging. She burned the sight in her memory. Then she turned and slammed the doors shut behind her.

Chapter Twenty

Found

Wendy felt Jack's forehead, sighing in disappointment upon the heat her fingers detected. His eyes fluttered open slightly, bloodshot. But she knew that he wasn't awake. This was happening more and more now. He'd mutter things, phrases, names... most too slurred to understand. It worried her.

This kind of thing would happen sometimes when she sat with a Lost Boy who was on his last breath. Memories would emerge to haunt them. It would slip through their lips and shine in their eyes. Much like Jack was doing now.

Drina stomped across the caravan and shoved a drink into Alice's hands unexpectedly. "Drink."

Alice seemed stunned, but took it without question. Wendy suppressed a smile at the older woman's abruptness. Though she tried to hide it, Alice's sudden headaches were obvious. Wendy wondered if it was due to Alice or Remus' side of things, and if it was the Hatter, she wasn't sure if Drina's concoction would work.

"I keep wondering what she meant by it," Alice voiced after downing the foul beverage.

Wendy sighed, wiping the sweat off her brow and pushing away the curls that fell in her face. "I do, too. I wish this fortune teller explained a little more about this journey I'm supposed to go on sometime."

"She's not a fortune teller exactly," Alice responded quietly, staring at Jack's twitching features. "But she said I might find the right questions. The thing is, I don't know what I'm supposed to ask."

"Well I'm sure you'll figure it out," Wendy assured, wringing out a wet rang. "If anyone can think of the right questions, it's you."

Before she could start bathing Jack's neck, the door burst open. Clopin's head poked in. Drina was thrown into a frenzy of French profanity at the intruder. But the man ignored her, stating simply, "We're leaving."

Alice stood instantly. "What do you mean?"

"Jack isn't healthy enough to be moved," Wendy added. "And the others aren't back yet."

"The boy will be fine. He can stay in here," Clopin insisted darkly. "As for the others, Gretel will be able to find us again."

He ducked back out of the caravan but Alice stormed after him. Hustling to her feet, Wendy following at her heels.

"You can't be serious," Alice shouted after him. "What makes you suddenly want to pack up and leave?"

"Because, dearie," Clopin turned on his heels to face them once more, arms swinging dramatically, "there's been a wolf attack nearby. Lupa paid a wandering peddler a visit last night. We found the scene not twelve kilometers from here."

"So?"

"We cannot afford to have that devil at our doorstep," Clopin hissed. "If Lupa heard wind of the people we house, she'll have all of our throats."

Wendy felt a chill at the thought of the gold eyed woman who visited her not long ago. She didn't want to face her again, either.

"Where do you expect us to go?" Alice persisted.

"Chliobain." It was Ingénu who answered, coming from behind to join them. "Aurore and I still have connections with the royal family, and the gypsies have always been welcome there." He placed a hand on Wendy's shoulder, russet eyes kind. "We may be able to find supplies there to help your friend."

"Yes, yes, yes!" Clopin waved his hand. "The details don't matter. Point is we're moving as soon as the horses are hitched."

*****

Red followed Esmeralda to a glade on the edge of the premises as the others rested nearby. The day's events lay heavy on them all. Without explanation, Esmeralda took the wildflowers into her hands as they walked. But when she entered a glade of crosses, Red stopped short.

"What is this place?" she asked in a whisper.

Esmeralda knelt before a centermost figure with the name *Phoebus* carved across the wood. "A memorial," her friend answered.

The gathered flowers in her hands lay limply in her lap. The petals' bright colors glowed radiantly. Moss and sprite dust covered some of the crosses, of which Esmeralda calmly brushed off. A sprite zipped over to pluck a flower and steal off with it. Gingerly, the gypsy arranged the flowers around the crosses.

She pulled out an intricate gold cross from her pack, an item retrieved from Bluebeard's treasury. "It was the worst possible place to turn up after we came back from Paris," Esmeralda said quietly, steadily. "We just finished the memorial when what was left of our family was raided. I was taken with two other girls, both younger than I. Both escaped, thankfully. But then the wedding came along, and I..." Her voice broke briefly. She rubbed the jeweled cross with her thumb. "Quasi saved me just in time. He took me back to the caravans, and we drove away as quickly as we could."

Red swallowed the lump in her throat. "But why pretend to be dead? You said it yourself, Bluebeard didn't care about escaped girls."

"But he did care about his current wife," Esmeralda put quickly. Slowly, she pressed her lips to the cross as if to seek comfort.

Red couldn't imagine many hells worse than being Bluebeard's wife.

Then Esmeralda pulled something else from her pack. "I found this down there. I don't know how it got there, but I believe it ought to be returned to its rightful owner."

Waves of crimson fabric cascaded out of the sack. Red's breath caught in her throat. Esmeralda lifted the cloak towards her for her to take it. Her fingers tingled at its touch, clutching it tightly to her. She thought the cloak was long lost. It felt comforting to hold it again.

She lifted her head to thank her friend, but stopped. Esmeralda wasn't looking at her anymore. Different words came to Red's tongue.

"Why did you come back?" Red asked gently. "Paris?"

Breathing back the shaking tears threatening to rise, Esmeralda touched the name on the erect cross before her lovingly. "After so many years, we finally found a way back home. But when we got there... it wasn't home anymore. It was an entirely different world years after everything we'd undergone. Nothing was familiar except for one story kept alive due to the man I long ago left behind." Now she began to cry. "We escaped Paris years ago after a prejudiced tyrant nearly burned me at the stake. Somehow, we ended up here, leaving Phoebus, *mon amour*, alone. When we returned, I found out what became of him. He never stopped looking for me, for any of us. He made sure no one forgot our story, not until his dying days."

The chain wrapped around her hands, the cross gleaming in the sunlight. Esmeralda covered her face. Her sobs fell against the memorial like pebbles.

Silently, Red left her friend surrounded by flowers and crosses. She needed to be alone.

The crimson cloak weighed heavy in her hands. She reveled in its closeness. As soon as she would put it on, it would warn her of danger and monsters, shield her from the gypsies' sight. It would make things easier.

Circling the outskirts of the fortress so as not to risk getting swallowed up by the Forest, Red took a deep breath to shed the stress of Bluebeard's memory. She wouldn't soon forget his horrors. But now, she needn't fear him. If his bride trafficking ring still existed, it was in disarray and would soon disintegrate. She could tell Ingénu of what's happened here so he could spread the word and abolish the remnants of the ring. There was hope now.

She set aside her bow and quiver for a moment. Gripping the fabric, she threw the cloak over her shoulders. It felt like cool water draping down her spine. Red sighed, allowing herself this comfort.

In a split second, the fabric burned against her skin. The hair on the back of her neck shot up.

Danger.

It was too late.

Red whipped around just as a flash of grey sailed straight for her. The wolf collided and she crashed to the floor, air rushing out of her lungs. His paw pressed to her throat, his teeth bared. Fear pulsed through her. The fabric itched irritatingly to urge her against the danger. She struggled to breathe and fight the shock.

The grip on her throat elongated into firm fingers rather than claws. The weight on her diaphragm changed to secure her as his legs grew. Fang glared down at her, silver eyes shining in victory.

"I've got you now," Fang growled.

Something clicked, triggering her fight for survival.

Red thrust her knee up to smash against his spine. His body reacted instantly due to her unexpected strength, flinging back in a painful arch. Her breath returned to her quickly. Without hesitation, Red punched him in the ribs twice. The grip in his legs gave and she rolled out from under him.

She pitched forward to grab for her bow and quiver. Hands grasped her ankles and dragged her away. Flinging her arm out, the weapon was just beyond her fingers. Just as she remembered her falchion, Fang tore it from her belt and threw it into the trees. Wiggling to free herself from his hold, Red's fingers found the sharp edge of stone. Latching tight to the rock, she twisted around and swung. The rock smashed against the side of Fang's head. He cried out, forced to release her.

She scrambled to her feet and dove for the bow and arrows, but Fang morphed and lunged. They were sent rolling.

Instinct took over. The Wolf snapped at him, digging her claws in his grey hide. Fang's muscles tensed in surprise. Catching him off guard, the Wolf threw him away with strong legs and spun toward her fallen weapon.

Paws turned to hands. Red drew her bow and aimed it at the kneeling bounty hunter.

Fang furrowed his brow in utter shock. Silver moon eyes stared up at her in disbelief. Red's chest heaved, but she held her stance.

"You're one of us?" Fang whispered, mirroring the very question Briar had formed just yesterday.

Her string was pulled taunt, ready to shoot him in the eye. Rage boiled. "You *made* me. You turned me into one of *you!*" she spat the last word out as if it were poison. Tears threatened to emerge in anger, but she kept them back with clenched teeth.

Fang's shoulders slumped, gaze falling to his open hands as if they bore a hideous brand. Red's muscles shook with anger. Was he sorry for what he did, or was he just asking for sympathy?

"Who do you work for?" she barked. "Who wants me?"

Fang just stared at his hands.

"Answer me!" she cried. "Who's your client?"

"My client?" His voice sounded far away. Silver eyes met hers, a strange cloud behind his pupils. "Carabosse."

Her chest pressurized, stomach tightening. She remembered what Briar had said about the possibility of the sorceress being the Master they sought. And the White Rabbit told her that the one who hired Fang must be this same person.

So, it's Carabosse…

"Why?" she pushed. "Why does she want me?"

"I don't know."

"You've hunted me for seven years and you don't know why?"

"I'm a bounty hunter. So long as I get my payment, I don't ask questions."

"What payment is worth this?"

"A cure," he said numbly, rubbing a tattoo around the finger on his left hand, "for someone I love who is suffering a fate she doesn't deserve."

"Why should I believe you?"

"I have no reason to lie."

Her arrow pointed right at his pupil. Red wanted to kill him, put an end to everything. Why shouldn't she? He'd ruined everything, turned her into a freak and a monster. It would be so easy, release the arrow, watch him bleed. But something stayed her fingers.

Tightening her jaw, Red lowered her bow. "Go. Get out of here. Leave me alone."

Fang's brow knitted together, disbelieving. Slowly, he stood and cautiously backed away. He turned back though, as if he remembered something he'd lost.

"If I had known, I never would have…" his voice trailed off.

Red waited. She noticed the cloak didn't burn anymore.

"I'm sorry," his tone was filled with remorse. "I'm so, so sorry."

Red narrowed her eyes. This man, this beast she'd come to fear and despise, who hunted her for years suddenly appeared as frail as glass. His entire being melted away, leaving behind only regret. She recognized the feeling. Fang was horrified with himself.

He looked away briefly, thinking over his next words. "Come with me," Fang offered.

Red stepped back, her stomach hollow.

But his eyes lit up slightly, hopefully. A new plead entered his demeanor. "The Pack, we can give you a home, a family. We can help you learn how to use the Wolf, help you understand its power. We'll accept you as one of our own in a way no one else can."

"You expect me to forget everything you and your family have done?"

Fang sighed shamefully, but his sincerity shone in his eyes. "I cannot express how sorry I am for what I put you through. But don't blame my family for my mistakes."

"What's changed?" she asked, but she knew the answer.

"We *always* look out for our own."

Despite everything, Red couldn't help but ponder his offer. Uncertainty twisted with hope in her chest. Was it really true? Could she be happy surrounded by others like her, people who understood and accepted her? She could have a family again. Maybe she could learn to harness and accept this Wolf inside her.

Perhaps...

"*Red!*"

She and Fang looked back where the voice came from in the distance. Red turned back to the man willing to give her everything she'd ever wanted. She took a step toward him. The cloak didn't warn of any danger.

"*Red!*"

She recognized the voice now. Kai. With his voice came a picture of four friends, people who she hadn't known for long yet accepted her completely for both the Wolf and her dark past without personal understanding. Maybe she didn't need understanding to be loved.

Her mind was made up.

"Thank you, Fang," she met his silver eyes, "but I have all the family I need."

He nodded solemnly. "If you ever change your mind, you know where to find me. I won't hunt you anymore, Red. The Pack never turns on its own kind."

With that, he shifted into the grey wolf and disappeared into the Forest. Red sighed, retrieving her weapons before she returned to the others.

*****

Caravans rolling, the horses and oxen trudged on through the Forest as if the trees were no obstacle. Alice and Wendy sat on the step of their cart, feet dangling off the side, trying not to fall off with the bumps in the ground. Alice held the pocket watch in her hand.

"What do you think is wrong with it?" Wendy asked.

Alice shrugged, pulling her racing mind to the present. "I don't know. Maybe it's this place, maybe it's just Clopin, or maybe it doesn't want us to leave yet. I don't know." She brushed her thumb over the silver. "It's cold."

Wendy felt for herself. There was a strange vibration beneath their fingertips. Alice pursed her lips thoughtfully, stowing the pocket watch under her shirt.

"I can tell when your gears are turning especially fast," Wendy voiced, cocking her head. "What's on your mind?"

"I feel like we're losing focus," Alice admitted.

"What do you mean?"

She frowned. "I mean, what did we learn about the Master back in Neverland really? That it's not Hook. That they're gathering forces. But we knew that already!"

"But if it's like Red suggested that one time, if it's Carabosse…"

"But what if it's not Carabosse? What if we're asking the wrong questions?" Alice sighed. "I feel like we keep asking the wrong questions and get distracted along the way."

"To be fair, we were separated back in Neverland and most of us were fighting for our memories."

"True. But now?" Alice shook her head, feeling the pocket watch swing against her chest. "We have to remember why we're here. Or at least… figure that out."

"*Comment est ton probléme?*" Clopin's French exclaimed, jarring them with his sharpness. Alice half expected he was yelling at them. "Get back in your caravan!"

He appeared before them, waving his arms at the cart across from them. A distorted face was sticking out of the window, the wind ruffling through his brown hair. Alice could only guess who this must be. It was as if the Bell Ringer had stepped out from one of her father's books to look down at the fanatic man in surprise. Quasimodo.

"*Es-tu fou?* You could be seen!" Clopin scolded, running up under the traveling caravan's window. "Esmeralda would have my head if that happened!"

Quasimodo's face fell in disappointment, but he nodded consent, turning back inside and drawing the curtains. Clopin shook his head exasperatedly, walking off to check on the other carts. A swarm of giggling kids avoided his long-legged gate.

Wendy sighed. "I feel bad for him. Being forced to hide in the shadows, not even allowed to stick his face in the sunshine. It's awful. Why is he forced to live like this?"

"Well, because he's..." Alice struggled to find the right word. "He's... different."

"Why should that matter? He's not so different from us. Why would it matter if he has a hump on his back or scars on his arms?"

Alice didn't know how to respond to that.

A grumbling voice behind them answered for her, "Because of Carabosse."

The girls turned and Alice nearly fell off the cart in surprise. Clopin stood behind them, dark eyes looking down on them. How did he get there? Clopin ignored the question in her eyes, kneeling between them to talk face to face.

"It's because of Carabosse that he has to hide, and others like him," Clopin's voice was foreboding. "A prophesy was told long ago that she would meet her doom by the hand of an *imperfect*. Ever since then, the sorceress has been obsessed with destroying the disfigured, anointing Lupa with the task of slaying any in the Forest."

"They persecute the disfigured because of some prophesy?" Alice questioned with a deep frown.

Clopin lowered his voice to a deep growl, "There are many who will stop at nothing to escape their destiny. Carabosse cannot be defeated by anything or anyone but this prophesized *imperfect*. To secure her own revenge if ever a thing should occur, she set a curse upon herself that whoever shall kill her shall meet death with her. Yet they say that this curse sealed her fate."

"So, every disfigured person is killed except for Quasimodo?"

He smirked. "What makes you say that?"

Alice scowled, unsure how much she liked his secretive tone. Instead of questioning, she waited for him to continue explaining in his own way.

As she expected, Clopin shifted his weight and leaned forward, clearly enjoying the thrill of telling them his stories. "How much do you really know about the Crimson Wraith?"

"Only what she's told us."

"Do you know why we let her stay with us? It certainly wasn't out of the *goodness of our hearts*," he sang. "Or why Lupa had it out for her for so long? The Crimson Wraith didn't just save girls from the bride-trafficking ring, or scare those sick demons out of their wits. She saved the unwanted." He waved a hand before them, at the gypsies and the caravans. "Many people wouldn't be here today if the Crimson Wraith didn't exist. A monster, some called her. But in the shadows, only said in whispers, she was an angel in red."

So, she is a hero, Alice thought to herself. *She just doesn't see it.*

Wendy frowned in concern. "So, anyone here could end Carabosse, and die because of it?"

Clopin shrugged. "Perhaps, perhaps not. Either way, Quasimodo cannot be seen. His disfigurement cannot be hidden. If Lupa or Carabosse were to find out of his existence..." He drew a finger across his throat.

Alice didn't know what to make of him.

Suddenly, his face brightened. "But we won't have to worry about that! Chliobain is a kingdom where no evil sorceress is welcome. We should be there in two days' time."

With that, Clopin jumped over their heads and rolled on the floor, leaping to his feet and walking off. His words remained, hanging heavy in the air.

"Two days," Wendy whispered with new worry. "Jack doesn't have two days."

Alice stared behind them where more trees were left behind, each step taking them farther away from where they began. Maybe if she looked hard enough, Red and Kai would appear with the abada horn.

"They'd better hurry."

Chapter Twenty-One

Facing Shadows

The dragon cuff felt heavier than ever before.

Fang stared at his hands, contemplating it all in his mind. How could he have been so careless? What he'd done... He once swore that he would never pass on the wolf in the way Lupa did, or Fenrir who led before him had. But that night, he'd been desperate. How did he not notice the full moon?

Because I didn't care.

He wasn't looking at the moon. He was only focused on the girl, on Red. But now, because of him, she was a wolf.

This changed everything.

"Now, what?" Quinn questioned, piercing through his thoughts.

Fang huffed, his mind clearer than it'd been in years. "We're done."

"Done?" Lev inquired with an ugly frown. "Why?"

"Because she's a wolf."

"So?"

Thaddeus glared at Lev disapprovingly. "The Pack *never* turns on our own kind."

Lev shied back, obviously taking this as a warning.

Thaddeus turned to Fang. "It is not your fault."

Quinn placed a hand on his arm. "You didn't know..."

Fang shook her hand off, standing with a sigh. "But it is my fault. I'm responsible; there's no getting around it. And if she ever comes to the Pack for refuge or family, we are to accept her without question. Make sure everyone understands."

With that, he started off away from them. He heard Quinn stand to follow, but Thaddeus stopped her knowingly.

"Where are you going?" she called.

"To face the consequences of my mistake," Fang responded without looking back. "I'm going to Carabosse."

"She won't take it well," Lev put.

"It doesn't matter. I'll find another way to heal Zoë," Fang stated, ignoring the impossibility of achieving this in the time his wife had left. "I'm going to make this right."

*****

"You're back!"

The girl hadn't even turned to Alice when she approached, but Kezia smiled broadly. Alice trotted behind the reading caravan where Kezia was perched. Instead of Esmeralda's goat, a cat lay in her lap.

"Mind if I join you?" Alice asked.

"*Oui!*"

With a running start, Alice jumped onto the ledge beside the girl. She flinched when her arm brushed Kezia's, but thankfully no visions came at the touch. At least Kezia didn't notice her reaction.

The cat purred pleasantly, twitching its whiskers. Alice reached over to scratch it between its brown and black ears. One green eye opened slightly to look up at her, the other apparently sealed shut from an old wound. Closing it again, the cat contented itself to the attention.

"How's your friend?" Kezia asked kindly.

Alice sighed, thinking back on when she last left Wendy with Jack. "If the others don't return soon, Wendy says that he could either be forever internally scarred by the infection, or he won't survive. It's an impossible situation."

"It's a good thing you thrive in impossible situations."

A laugh flew from her mouth. She wondered how much Kezia knew about her. Did the girl only know what she saw, or did it go deeper than that?

"I can't answer all of your questions," Kezia admitted apologetically, bowing her head. "But I can help lead you down the right path to discovering them yourself."

Alice nodded. She figured it wouldn't be so easy and straightforward. The White Queen, Celeste, had tried to tell her things about the Master back in Wonderland, but either she didn't know much or she couldn't tell them much.

"I don't suppose you can tell me who the Queen of Hearts' and Captain Hook's Master is?"

Kezia shivered and shook her head. Whether that meant she couldn't say or didn't want to see the answer, Alice couldn't tell. Then Kezia spoke with her eyes squeezed shut, "Someone you won't expect."

With a sigh, Alice decided to voice a stream of questions to see if any could be answered, "Where is the Master? Who are their followers? What are they planning? How do we stop them?"

Kezia shook her head. "You're asking the wrong questions."

Alice frowned. Nothing could be more direct than what she'd asked. It was all they were here for, all they were trying to figure out throughout this journey. How could they be wrong?

Sensing her confusion, Kezia scratched the cat's back and tilted her chin toward Alice. "Many of the answers you seek have been made known between the five of you already. You just need to know what to look for." She paused as if debating how big of a hint to disclose. "Why do you forget where you came from?"

Rolling this around in her head, Alice tried to think of where all they'd been before now. She assumed that the Master would have something to do with one of their respective realms: Enchanted Forest, Realm of the Snow Queen, Neverland, Giant Country, or Wonderland. But Kezia asked where she came from.

"Do you mean England?" Alice questioned, then realized she didn't know where Red and Jack were born, and Kai was from Sweden. "Or, I suppose, that world in general?"

Kezia giggled as if this were a guessing game. "You are close."

Then it occurred to her, so obvious she almost shouted it. "The Facility." She frowned. "What does that insane asylum have to do with this?"

"You see the Facility as an insane asylum." Kezia leaned close as if confessing a dark secret. "What if you're wrong?"

A whole flood of questions rushed into her mind so quickly it made her temples throb. But Alice couldn't distinguish them. It was just one swarm of confusion. But for the first time, she felt like she was about to make headway on why they were here. At the same time, was she on the brink of destroying everything she thought she knew?

Sensing her mind racing, Kezia held out her hand. "What do you want to see?"

"Take me back there," Alice found herself saying with strong assurance. "Take me back to the Facility."

Kezia nodded. Alice hesitated slightly at her outstretched hand. The cat looked up at her with its one eye.

You wanted answers, didn't you? the cat seemed to be saying.

With a deep breath, Alice clasped Kezia's hand. Her vision changed, but this time, she was ready:

Dark halls. Three rooms with heavy iron doors. One had deep claw marks in the walls. Another had ticks down the bedposts to keep track of the days. The last she recognized instantly as the room where she and Wendy stayed.

Her vision zeroed in on the tunnel entry behind the bed. Then everything went fast as she rushed through the tunnel and into the space connecting all their rooms. It was completely empty.

Halls flashed past in a blur, revealing quiet rooms with no inmates. There was the interrogation rooms, the courtroom where the two men and one woman had passed judgement on her, the circular space where Anne Christiansen gathered them up for escape. Then the lift, broken and unmoving. Lights that used to glow eerily down the passages were dark now.

She went up and up and up until she was outside, looking at the door to the Facility, barred shut, abandoned.

Alice sucked out of the vision uncomfortably, still gripping Kezia's hand. Blinking, she tried to make sense of what she'd seen.

What happened to the Facility? Where did everyone go? Where did the tunnels come from? Why did they only connect Alice, Wendy, Jack, Kai, and Red's rooms? Was the Facility what she used to think it was?

Was it all a trap?

Then it hit her.

"Why us?" Alice questioned aloud, following the string of thoughts that came with those words. "Why would someone want the five of us? We're from different places, went to different worlds under different circumstances and ages and times. The only thing we have in common is the Facility. But if even our placement within the Facility was predestined... What do we have in common? Why does the Master want us?"

Kezia kissed the cat on its brow, receiving a lick on the nose. "I think you're asking the right questions."

This time Alice didn't hesitate when she took the girl's hand. The scenes flashed by, only confusing her more.

Wendy. She stood on the edge of a cliff, the wind tossing her brown curls and pulling a blue ribbon from her hair. A boy, Peter Pan, swooped by beneath her. They both looked so young. Taking a deep breath without closing her eyes, Wendy jumped. She was falling, falling, falling... Peter dove beside her, ready to catch her. Then with a laugh of triumph, Wendy flew.

Red. Running, running, running through the Forest. Someone was chasing her. Everything else went so fast. The wolf caught her, wrestled her down. Red screamed as the beast bit her shoulder. She bled freely. Fang pinned her to the ground. The moon looked down cold and full.

Kai. He didn't have his scar. He snuck around a wall of ice with a strange object in hand. Instantly he faced a figure covered in crystalized shards like a second skin. Before the figure could strike, Kai lunged forward and threw the icepick-like weapon at a mesmerizing mirror hanging on the wall. Glass exploded. The Snow Queen screamed. Kai's jaw bled and healed in one instant.

Jack. Or at least, one could only assume. He was so dirty and bloody he was nearly unrecognizable. Body shaking, chest heaving. He cracked a broken smile, daring the darkness to do its worst. A gigantic hand emerged from the swirling shadows and held his head back. Jack screamed in hysteric terror. Light gleamed against mismatched eyes. Waves of liquid gold descended upon him, flowing into every available opening.

Alice. She saw herself in the Queen of Hearts' dungeons, Remus standing in front of her. He muttered something. Alice held his beating heart in her palm. All at once, she plunged her hand into his chest and they both screamed as their heartbeats meshed and their souls fused. Then it was over.

The scenes resonated in her mind even after Kezia released her. What did they mean?

Kezia shivered, having seen the same as Alice. But before Alice could try and make sense of everything, the girl said, "Everything else is up to the five of you. Ask them. For what lies ahead, you need to trust each other with everything."

"What lies ahead?"

"Too many futures," she muttered weakly. Sniffing back her sudden timidity, Kezia faced Alice and offered a kind smile. "Can I show you one last thing? I think you need it."

The emotions flooded through her strongly this time, emotions that weren't all hers.

He sat in the room with the White Rabbit, both busy with their own separate projects. White was surrounded by potions and strange ingredients. Remus tossed a flamingo feathered hat onto his friend's head jokingly, laughing. White ignored him. But the Mad Hatter returned to work quickly, fingers flying over his needles and threads. Piles of leather armor formulated beside him. Then he froze, stirred. Eyes like endless blue skies met hers. The air charged. He smiled madly, whispered her name: Alice.

The vision changed.

A woman with dark blonde hair and blue eyes walked down a busy street, beautiful and put together. Her husband met her outside their brick house in the city, kissing her fondly, tickling her nose with his mustache. She grinned, holding her purse tightly to her. With a wink, they entered the house. A little girl sat on the floor with a toy elephant and some doll clothes. She greeted her parents with hugs and kisses. With a mischievous smile, the woman pulled a kitten out of her purse and handed it to the overjoyed girl. The woman spoke the child's name lovingly: Alice.

Tears streamed down her cheeks when Alice was pulled from the vision. It had been so long since she'd seen Remus... and even longer since she'd seen her sister. She didn't even realize how relieving it was to see Lorna, to see that she was alive and well. It hurt. It hurt so much that somehow Lorna could move on from her and live so happily. But she was glad. The Liddell sisters would probably never see each other again. At least they were happy with the lives they'd chosen.

But it would always hurt.

"Thank you," Alice muttered, squeezing Kezia's hand gratefully.

The girl smiled broadly, wiping away stray tears of her own. Alice took a deep breath and slipped off the moving caravan with a brief goodbye. When a final question emerged, she turned back to trot after the cart.

"I forgot to ask one more thing," she called, prepared to board the perch again. "Could you show me Anne Christiansen?"

"Anne Christiansen?" Kezia asked curiously, blind eyes wandering. Her words stopped Alice in her tracks. "Anne Christiansen does not exist."

*****

"They're moving."

"What?" Esmeralda questioned with a scowl.

"They've left," Gretel restated, narrowing her eyes. "They're path is lengthening. I think they're headed for Chliobain."

"Why?" Jim asked.

"I don't know."

"She can see *paths*," Hansel said matter-of-factly, "not read *minds*."

"How much farther are they?" Kai asked.

"Twice as far as last time. But it grows every moment."

Worry churned in Red's abdomen. Last she'd seen Jack, she wasn't sure if he'd last the night, much less two days or more. If she were alone, then perhaps she'd be able to reach the caravans with the Wolf. But this was the Forest. If anything went wrong, she could completely lose track of them.

Perhaps they could manipulate the Forest into helping them, or into shortening the path. But they would have more chances of reaching the caravans in time on their own than in bending the Forest to their will. They needed something different.

She looked at Gretel.

"How does your sight work?" Red questioned, stepping closer to the girl.

She tucked a short yellow lock behind her ear. "I'm still figuring it all out. But I can see a path to anything. It looks like breadcrumbs."

"Do you have to know what the destination is exactly?"

"Not necessarily, I don't think."

Red's mind raced. "Then try finding a path for a faster way through the Forest. There has to be a way, magic or beast."

Gretel frowned, eyes searching the Forest around them. A cool steady rain pattered down on them. Red tucked her cloak tighter around her. If there was any danger in where the girl led them, then she would be warned.

Hesitantly, Gretel started forward, Hansel following faithfully beside her. The others pursued without a word wherever the breadcrumbs led them.

First came the wraiths.

The cloak warned with a slow burn that increased with every step. Red cautioned the others. Weapons were drawn and ready.

When she heard the wet stretch of muscle, she knew they were surrounded by smiling wraiths that lurked just beyond the trees. The rain had masked their scent. One emerged, its hooded face sweeping up to Jim's. Instinctively, Jim swung his axe up to behead the monster. Kai caught his arm. Jim glared at him. But the wraith leaned closer, smile stretching.

"It's just checking," Kai said lowly.

Without a word, they backed away together. The wraith followed a few steps then stopped. Gretel kept forward, undisturbed. Hansel looked around in interest. The further the group travelled, the cooler the cloak got.

Next were the lucky piggies. They buzzed in a large flock around an overgrowth of honeysuckle and blueberries, unperturbed by the rain. They looked like hedgehogs with round wings sprouting from their backs. A smaller one of them followed Hansel and nibbled at his ear. Ripping off some honeysuckle, Hansel fed the lucky piggy over his shoulder. It didn't leave after that.

Then Gretel stopped where the trees were shrouded in mist. She shook her head and looked around. They'd reached the end of their trail of breadcrumbs.

"Nothing's here," Jim announced, waving a hand through the mist in front of him.

Red narrowed her eyes. She didn't trust the fact that she couldn't see anything but mist and shadow. It smelled of pine, cool rain, and mint. Suspiciously, she stepped forward with her hand outstretched. Fingers connected with shadow. She didn't flinch.

Slowly, the snout pushed against her palm with a huff of mist. An onyx needle pierced through the darkness as the rest of the animal emerged. Fog clung to the ebony unicorn, the front half fully visible now.

Red heard the others step back behind her in surprise, except for Gretel and Hansel. They stepped forward to the second unicorn protruding beside hers.

Stroking the unicorn's muzzle, Red marveled at the beast's beauty. Its mane cascaded down its neck like tangible shadow. Deep eyes reminded her of Briar's when she'd tried to cast her spell, dark and starry. She wondered if it sensed the Wolf. If it did, it didn't shy. Instead, it seemed to welcome her with those black eyes and cool touch.

More unicorns seemed to formulate from the mist and shadows around them, more than they needed.

Red glided to her unicorn's side and, carefully, pulled herself up on its back. The others approached the beasts, but she already had a fistful of the watery mane to hold tight. Thoughts of her urgency, of Jack, of the Forest flying by and rain pelting her face filled her mind. Responding to them, the unicorn moved. It was like riding a breeze and wrestling a hurricane all at once. The others were soon with her, surrounded by a herd of onyx unicorns.

Her heart pounded in anticipation. She was on her way to Jack.

Chapter Twenty-Two

Tables Turn

"Ah, bounty hunter. I assume you bear good news."

Fang said nothing as he approached the sorceress' throne, his eyes lowered.

"You are empty handed. Have you come across dilemmas?"

"You could say that," he muttered. Standing up straight, Fang forced himself to look her in the eye. "I cannot do what you require of me."

The corner of Carabosse's mouth twitched. "Excuse me?"

"I cannot give you the girl."

"If you are doubting your abilities…"

"No, I have no problem finding her."

"Then what is the issue?"

"The issue is that Red is a Wolf, and I will no longer be hunting her," he snapped. His words rang in the air. Diablo ruffled his feathers uncomfortably, the only thing that moved. Bolstering his courage, Fang finalized, "Everything's changed. We're done."

"Done?"

The word echoed through the large room. Carabosse's face darkened, glowering down at him with reflective eyes. Torch lights dimmed to hardly more than a flicker, turning viridescent. The floor vibrated under foot.

Carabosse stood, a dark cloud forming around her head, shadows clinging to her eyelashes. "You do not have the right, the *privilege* to say when you're done," she thundered with lightning on her lips. "I say when you're done! If you *ever* thought you had a say in the matter, you are beyond misled."

The air charged drastically. Taking in a calming breath, she closed her eyes. The darkness faded around her and the floor stilled. She sat back in her gothic throne of bone, studying Fang with her cold eyes, evaluating.

"And what of your precious Zoë?" Carabosse spoke in a quieter tone that was just as deadly. "Your actions will seal her fate."

"That is no longer your concern," Fang growled. "I will find another way."

Carabosse's reptilian eyes shone devilishly. A malicious smile stole across her face. "And what if she were to be in my possession?"

His heart dropped. Fists clenched. But the sorceress only raised an eyebrow in victory. She had him now. He felt like a puppet, and Carabosse knew exactly which strings to pull.

With a snap of her fingers, a figure materialized by her side. There stood Zoë, frozen in shock. A lump formed in Fang's throat. The gold infection had spread, shooting down one leg completely and stretching up her left forearm. It webbed from her spine and dusted her eyes. Most of her hair was solid gold strands now.

"Fabien," she cried, her voice strained as if the gold were choking the words from her.

"Zoë!" he screamed, rushing to her.

Just as he reached her, she vanished. Fang collapsed and slid across the floor, having fallen right where his wife had been. He glared up at Carabosse, fierce eyes ablaze like boiling silver.

"If you hurt her, I swear I'll—"

"You'll what? Kill me?" Carabosse chuckled, stroking her precious raven down his backbone. "You may be many things, bounty hunter, but you are not my supposed dispatcher."

Fang's jaw clenched. How could he have been so foolish? He should've known better than to trust the demonic witch. The dragon cuff burned into his wrist, searing into his skin. He didn't cry out, though. He wasn't about to give that satisfaction.

"Bring me the girl within the week, or I will hunt every wolf in this Forest and slaughter them like dogs," Carabosse continued calmly, holding just the right strings to bend him to her will. "And I'd hurry if I were you. Zoë won't last much longer."

*****

Wendy sat on the edge of Jack's caravan when the ginger princess joined her without even asking for permission. But she didn't mind. Wendy liked her, though she didn't know whether to call her Briar Rose or Aurore. It seemed like a safe bet just to call her by her birth name.

The rain fell lightly in front of them, dripping off the lip of the roof. Aurore adjusted her blouse and straightened her skirt, swinging her legs over the ledge like a child. Wendy did the same.

"Can I ask you something?" Aurore said right off the bat.

Wendy nodded.

"I know about Red," she began, lowering her voice. "She told me before she left. And I just want to know…" She struggled over her words before asking outright, "Is she alright?"

"What do you mean?"

"I mean, with being a wolf. Does it, has it… *changed* her?"

Wendy let the fact that Aurore knew about the Wolf settle first before she answered, "I don't know. I didn't know she was a Wolf for a while, but I've never known her before it."

"But besides that," Aurore continued, waving it off like it was of small consequence, "do you think she's changed?"

She thought a moment, remembering the steely girl she met in the Facility, so long ago it seemed. Red hardly spoke to them at first. But then a hard day hit, and they didn't see Red for two nights. When next Wendy saw her, Red was broken and hurting, curled in Jack's arms. He, for one, looked completely thrown that she even let him so near. Now, Wendy realized it must have been after a full moon.

"Yes," Wendy finally said. "I think she's changed. She's stronger now, in more ways than one."

Aurore nodded in silent thankfulness. She looked back at the leagues they left behind, kicking her feet in the rain and mud splashed up from the caravan wheels.

"What's Chliobain like?" Wendy asked.

Aurore shrugged, twisting her hair. "I haven't been in many years, and I once swore never to go there again. See, I was raised there,"

"I thought you were the Princess of Grimrose?"

"I didn't find out about that until I was eighteen. Before then, I was something of a daughter to a wretchedly awful bottom-feeder of a woman and shared her with a lying brat of a sister—pardon my nastiness, but it takes everything in me to remember to love them, and part of that is a love for speaking ill truths of them." Aurore puffed out her cheeks with a huff. "Don't get me wrong, they were both beautiful and in a sense clever, or they *are*, if they're alive still."

"What happened?"

"*Mère* heard of a few lords in need of lovely wives, decided to play at being a little younger than she was. Aimée was young enough, skinny enough, and the favorite between us besides. So..." Aurore twisted her hair again into knots. "A traveling merchant was given a pretty penny to take me far away to Sol-Måne. Instead, he abandoned me in the Forest."

The caravan tripped over tree roots, jolting them and showering them with fresh rain and thick mud. Aurore laughed when Wendy got a splash of it in the face. Wiping it off, Wendy spat out the foul stuff.

"Is that when you met Red?" she asked.

"No, not even close," Aurore laughed. She wasn't twisting her hair anymore. "I wandered long, but a shepherdess found me. She took me in, taught me to work with my hands, showed me the stars and told me their stories. She rekindled a love for life and God that dear *Mère* butchered out of me. That's what a mother is supposed to be."

She grew quiet, hands folded in her lap, eyes on the ground moving past them. Her words turned soft like butter. "Once, she took me to the village where plenty of disgusting pretty teens decided to have a go at me for being fat. I can't help my weight much, you see. But I wasn't always this confident with it. *But* I could snap my tongue right back at them even then. Afterwards, the shepherdess pulled me aside and told me true that just because I'm fat doesn't mean I'm ugly. People can be born pretty but we make ourselves beautiful." Aurore paused and looked up at the leaking sky. "I hope Euna is that kind of mother, or at least something close."

Thunder seemed to rumble in the distance. The Forest shivered. Wendy narrowed her eyes at the land they left behind. Aurore leaned forward as well.

"What's that?"

Her heart skipped a beat. Somehow, she knew before she could even fully make out the forms. "It's them!" Wendy cried, slipping off the cart with feet splashing in the mud. She shouted it while running through the caravans. Almost slipping in the mud, she shouted it again, "They're back! Stop the carts! Stop the carts!"

"What's with all the shouting?" Clopin snapped, sticking his head out around the side of a cart. "You're acting like a hyperactive gnome. What do you mean *stop the bloody carts?*"

"They're here," she explained, panting, trotting forward. "Red, Kai, and Esmeralda; they're back!"

Black eyes widened then crinkled with a smirk. Clopin leapt off the caravan in a flurry, stamping around the carts bellowing, "*Arrêtez!* Stop the bloody carts!"

Red sat by his side, taking Jack's hand in hers. Drina shaved off layers of the abada horn to sprinkle in a broth. Easier to go down his throat.

Carefully, once the broth was prepared, Drina lifted Jack's head and poured it into his mouth. It was so ordinary looking that Red almost doubted its power. Briefly, Drina explained that it would take time for the horn to eat out the infection.

Twining her fingers through his, Red leaned forward. Her voice was strained at first, forcing a small smile. "Hey, Jack. Can you hear me?"

He gave no answer.

"I suppose it's my fault. I did a rotten job of those stitches," she laughed uneasily, but the truth of it hurt. "The abada horn will work, though. You'll be up in no time."

There was still no response.

Red brushed the hair away from Jack's clammy forehead. "You've got to wake up, Jack. You have a schedule to keep, stuff to do, remember? We'll be done soon. Then we can do the things we talked about. I'll help you get your friend back; Harry, wasn't it? We'll go to Giant Country and get him back, easy. Then we'll go to the orphanage, the one you talked about, and you can see your old pals."

She could barely see his chest rise and fall.

"Maybe I'll introduce you to my Grandmother, if things haven't changed since…" She shook her head against the thought of how the world might be an entirely different place since she'd left it. "Never mind. She'd like you. She might not act like it, but I'm sure she will." A tear fell on his pale purpled hand. "Please wake up."

* * *

Hesitantly, Red leaned over and kissed him on the forehead. She pulled back slowly, unsure why she did it.

His grip tightened slightly. Her heart leapt. Fingers grasped her hand, his hold firm. His head teetered. Red let out a relieved sigh, taking this as a good sign. Jack would be alright.

"*Shoo!*" Drina waved, suddenly there with more broth. "Off with you! He must heal."

Regretfully, Red relented, releasing Jack's hand and heading for the door. When she turned back, however, she saw Jack's eyes crack open and almost thought he muttered, "*Rubes.*"

Almost.

Outside, the air smelled like the rain that held its breath for another shower soon. Blankets of clouds covered the sky, strangling the last of daylight. The unicorns left a shroud of mist behind them when they left. Perhaps it all would've been beautiful. But they were in the Forest, she felt like death, and an approaching familiar scent made her spine crawl. It completely ruined the moment.

She hoped he wasn't going to talk to her. Of course, she was wrong.

"Rubina," Jim's thick voice was lower than usual.

"Don't call me that."

"You don't want me to call you *Rubina*. You don't want me to call you *my love*. What am I supposed to do, call you by one of your fancy titles or some acronym everyone else seems to dub you?"

With a sigh, Red turned to face him. "What do you want, Jim?"

Tawny eyes lowered as if embarrassed to reveal some sincerity behind his snarky remarks. "I've been thinking a lot..."

"That's dangerous. Must be a strain."

"I've been thinking about what happened back at Lille-Havfrue since you came back."

Her stomach tightened. "Have you now?"

He passed a hand over his long face. "I want to apologize for..."

"For what?"

"For leaving you behind."

Red looked at him from his thick soled boots to his short-cropped hair. She let her rage simmer. "Is that it, then? That's what you're sorry for: leaving me behind."

He threw his hands in the air. "Can't you just take an apology?"

"Of everything that happened, you're *sorry* for leaving me behind? Not for deceiving me, not for leading me on, not for giving me up for a pocket of gold, not for setting every possible predator on me at once and leaving me with *nothing* but a scarlet cloak and one of your blasted axes?!"

"All of it! Alright?"

Red stalked forward, backing him into the Forest. "Tell me, did you know who exactly you were giving me up to, or did you even care once they waved a pretty penny under that fat nose?"

"Tell me you wouldn't have done the same thing if someone offered you a way out of this hell?"

"So, you've gone from apology to defense in about twelve seconds. I'd say that's a new record."

"It's because that's what you do! You can't believe an honest thing presented freely to you until you've driven him mad and shoved a bloody knife up his..." Jim chucked a yell into the air in aggravation.

Red kept on dangerously. "I've got more than enough reason not to trust you again. I guess you did warn me, didn't you? Don't trust anyone, especially you."

"And I meant it when I said it," he confessed in a growl. "But things changed."

"You're right, things did change," she spat. "You gave me up and bought a ticket out of here, only how'd that turn out for you? And I was left under the mercy of my enemies: wolves, soldiers, bounty hunters, thieves. You want to guess who won the scramble?"

"I didn't—"

"Bluebeard." Her words came faster as everything fell from her mouth and set her heart racing. "You took everything away! After everything we did, everything we were. I dared to trust you, to let you get close, and you *left me behind.* You abandoned me to follow a ghost tale your deluded grandfather peppered you with until you believed them."

"You believed them, too."

"Because I wanted a way out of here. And if following you to your hidden treasure island would get me out of this Forest, then fine, I played along until I trusted *you* more than your pretty stories." Red spread her arms. "That's the whole reason why I followed you all the way to Lille-Havfrue! I told you we could stowaway easy on one of those fancy ships with a captain who could travel between realms.

Buy a witch's portal. Anything! Did you plan to lead me like a lamb to slaughter the entire time? Was *all* of it a lie?"

He didn't answer, fists clenched, teeth bared. Red didn't care. She didn't even give him the opportunity to respond.

"Don't you dare think all you did was leave me behind. You betrayed me in more ways than you can ever know."

"I know! And I…" Jim cut himself short, looking somewhere past her right foot, fists clenched, the veins in his jaw pulsing. Then he straightened his back again and looked her in the eye with more self-control than she'd ever seen in him before. "I really am sorry, Rubina."

Her temper cooled slowly with every heavy breath, but she kept her glare hard. She hated his sad eyes that wouldn't look away. She hated his refusal to shout right back at her. It took too much energy to remain angry at a man who wasn't angry right back at her. Energy she did not have.

Narrowing her eyes, she regulated her tone. "What happened to you?"

Jim just stood and stared at her as if he too was tired. It forced her to really look at him for the first time since Lille-Havfrue. He had a new scar by his left eye. The years had changed him some but not much, hardened his features, tightened his muscles. His ears were still big.

"I didn't make it back," Jim said at last. "Over and over and over again, I didn't make it back. I got on a ship, had my own fill of my grandfather's stories of life at sea. Turns out, it's not all it's cracked up to be. Didn't battle pirates and gain glory or hunt down an island full of treasure.

It's all harsh water and tough men. I was always better at being the Woodsman than some seaman."

Red huffed, biting back a smart remark about pickpockets and seadogs.

Jim ignored her. "It never took me home. So I got off at the port kingdom, Belle. I'm sure you've heard of it. That's where Ingénu is from, where his vile brother King Fourbin still rules. When he'd heard wind that the Woodsman was in his city, he was the less than forgiving type."

Without warning, Jim lifted his shirt to reveal lash marks across his ribs and torso. Just as she processed them, he covered himself again.

"I escaped Belle and managed to pass for an actual woodsman for a while. Then I came across these kids…" There it was. That look in his eyes she didn't recognize. "They asked if I had a home or family, and they took me here. Of course, Clopin wanted me to prove my worth. Ingénu vouched for me, said he'd be responsible for me until Clopin was satisfied."

"Is Clopin ever satisfied?" Red raised an eyebrow.

Jim half smiled. "He was after I saved his life from a shapeshifter. Remember how we used to take care of them?"

"Keep them talking until their eyes flicker," Red responded softly. "I remember."

He looked at her as if she was a reminder of a past he'd buried. She could recognize that look anywhere. Perhaps it was that recognition that released her tension and hatred for him.

"I woke up every day regretting one thing," Jim started again, thick eyebrows drawn sorrowfully over tawny eyes. "Leaving you. I'm sorry for it more than anything else."

"I'm not." The words were out of her mouth before she could fully process them. But nothing seemed more true. After everything that came from Jim leaving her behind, it all led her here. She wasn't sorry for that.

Jim sighed, his shoulders relaxing. It was probably the closest thing he'd get to forgiveness. Perhaps it was more than he'd expected.

Red thought back on his words. "When those kids asked about your family, what did you tell them?"

"That I'd left my family a long time ago," Jim confessed, "and they've certainly given up waiting for me."

"You were my family for a time," she said quietly. "You know that, right?"

Jim nodded grimly. "I know. I just wish I'd let you be mine."

A shout of excitement forced her to turn away, back to the caravans where a swarm of gypsy children were roused by the walking miracle. Red felt something release in her chest and bubble to a smile she couldn't control.

Jack. His face was pale and hair messy, but he was awake. He was alright.

The kids crowded around to see him. Hansel was taking the opportunity to proclaim how he'd battled trolls to help save Jack while that lucky piggy buzzed over his head. Several of them called for a celebration, even when it started to rain again.

Laughing, Jack looked up, dark blue eyes locked with Red's. His dimples deepened when his smile stretched. He waved. Red started forward, but Wendy beat her there.

● ● ●

"Jack!" Wendy collided into him and squeezed him tight. Alice was at her heals to embrace her surprised friend.

By the time Red reached the caravans, Kai was there clasping Jack on the back.

"Missed you, too, brother," Jack said with a grin.

Before anyone else could greet him, Red ran up and threw her arms around him. She nearly knocked him over, but she didn't care.

"Slow down, Rubes!" Jack exclaimed, returning her hug. "I'm alright."

"I know." She pulled away and hit him on the shoulder. "Don't do that again!"

He rubbed the sore spot on his shoulder. "You know, it really hurts when you do that."

The children got their way in the end. There was a celebration of sorts. Nothing fancy, but it was happy, which was a nice change of pace. Some musicians struck up a tune, summoning the free spirits to dance under the stars.

Briar danced the best of all of them, not because of any natural talent, but because she danced with her soul. Not everyone saw it that way. Some men muttered amongst themselves in French and snickered. Ingénu turned toward them, but Briar rounded on them first.

"If you say a woman of my size and nature shouldn't be dancing like this, then maybe you need to take a good long look in the mirror and reevaluate your life," she snapped so harshly the oppressors practically cowered.

Immediately, as if in spite, Briar started to dance again like a belly dancer. Grinning at his wife, Ingénu joined her.

Jack was still processing everything by the fire pit. "So, you're saying that we made it to a gypsy camp," he pointed to Red, "You got better." He turned to Kai. "You both set off on an adventure with Esmeralda, the Woodsman, and these two," nodding to Gretel and Hansel, "battling trolls in search of a magic horn to make me better while you two," he turned to Alice and Wendy, "have been taking care of me while the whole lot of us make our way to Whuppie, *all the while* avoiding wolves and an evil witch lady who wants to kill everyone. Is that all?"

"Yes," Red confirmed.

Hansel elbowed Red slightly, whispering, "*You lied.*"

She shushed him.

"And I've slept through all that?" Jack groaned, setting down his second helping of beans and rice. "I missed all the fun!"

"*Fun?*" Gretel scoffed, shaking her head.

Briar plopped down next to Red with a cup of water and an exhilarated expression. She leaned close. "I like this boy." Red shoved her when Briar wiggled her eyebrows.

Jack took a big gulp of goat milk, clearly having obtained his appetite again. "So, what about this special sight thing? How does it work? Do all of you gypsies have it, and what kind of things do you see?"

Esmeralda leaned forward, holding her tankard in both hands. Her gilded cross hung around her neck. "When someone joins our family, they obtain an inner sight unique to each person. Drina sees sickness and disease, Nicu sees the thoughts of animals, Abella sees the invisible, and Ourson sees hidden treasures."

Clopin skipped on over wearing a mask with a pointed nose, dangerously cheerful. "And Yves sees your life's clock tick-tick-ticking away. Kizzy sees every dead person you know shrouding around you with visions of the last time you saw them. And Tyce..." He chuckled, shaking his head as he lowered himself beside his sister. "That boy looks deep into your eyes and sees *exactly* what you want more than anything in this world."

Jack raised his eyebrows, checking over his shoulders as if to find Tyce or Yves behind him. The lucky piggy flew over his head and cooed pleasantly as it bobbed to Hansel.

"What do you see, Clopin?" Jack questioned before shoving bread in his mouth.

Clopin's black eyes gleamed behind his purple and gold mask. A scary smile stretched across his lips. "I see *pleasure.*"

"Pleasure?" Alice stated in disbelief. It was the first time she'd spoken all evening.

"Do not take it lightly, dearie. Pleasure takes many forms. It is not as *innocent* as it may sound." Clopin sneered. "I have seen pleasures that would frighten every one of you out of your skins. It can drive a man mad."

Alice smirked. Clopin narrowed his eyes, but said no more.

"What about you?" Jack nodded to Esmeralda. "What do you see?"

Esmeralda didn't respond immediately. Smoky eyes stared at the drink in her hands. A shiver traveled down Red's spine. Amongst all the sights in this gypsy family, Esmeralda's scared her most.

Finally, Esmeralda spoke with a voice clear as day, "I see fear."

"What kind of fear?" Jack asked, for once with more questions than Alice. "Fear in general, or—"

"I see the fear of all living beings. It takes different forms from creature to creature; as great as the universe barreling in on all sides, or as empty as a void of nothingness everywhere you turn." Esmeralda locked eyes with Jack, picking apart his mind like the pages of a book. Jack's spine stiffened, but he could not look away. "You fear snakes and... cows."

A few strangers snickered. Red glared at them, wondering what they would do if their minor fears were exposed.

"You're afraid of snakes?" Wendy asked curiously. "You didn't run into Kaa back in Neverland, did you?"

Jack scowled. "Ah, yes. I had the unfortunate pleasure of meeting your blasted boa on that island."

"Python."

"Whatever."

But Esmeralda wasn't finished. Her eyes were still locked and reading. "Most of all, you fear of history repeating itself. You fear that your friends will meet their doom and you will have no power to stop it, just like what happened with Harry and Jill." Smoky eyes gleamed and churned. "Your fear takes the form of a giant pouring sand down your throat from an hourglass."

She broke her stare and Jack gulped. He didn't seem all that hungry after all.

"What about those without fear?" Alice asked.

"Everyone fears something," Esmeralda clarified. "Even the most powerful and brave have fear."

"What do you fear?" Kai voiced lowly. "Death?"

"Death is but a gateway to heaven," she responded evenly, staring into the flames before her. "I fear of being trapped, to have my freedom ripped away from me and my people. I fear of being immobilized, unable to do anything about my imprisonment. My fear takes the form of chains."

A scream split through the camp. Caravan doors burst open, and Kezia flew out into the mud crying. Her fists pressed into her eyes as if that would drive away the visions. Esmeralda leaped to her feet and rushed forward, Alice on her heals to help the fallen girl.

"WAR!" the girl cried, cheeks stained with tears. "Blood, and death! Horrible, terrible things!" She sobbed heavily, screaming with every breath.

Alice grasped Kezia's arms to help her up, then let out a cry herself and flew backwards. Standing quickly, Red started toward them. Esmeralda gave a shout of warning, holding out an arm. Even she dared not touch the girl. Wendy helped Alice out of the mud.

"A battle approaches," Kezia sobbed, her words thrown to the wind. "Death awaits. A terrible evil has already been made known." She gasped, tearing her hands from her wide eyes. "The Lost Girl and Giant Slayer must find the Bear Wizard before the Raven Sorceress rises. Free Grimrose from her stone prison. Gypsy and Grimrose then must ride for the Raven Sorceress."

Suddenly, Kezia turned directly toward Red. Blind eyes bore straight through her. Her heart sped a thousandfold.

"Take off your mask," Kezia implored, words directed at her. "The Wolf cannot be trusted, but can be used."

Her eyes rolled to the back of her head and she fell into the mud. That's when Esmeralda rushed forward to retrieve her, holding the Kezia tight. The camp held its breath. Her words hung in the air, vibrating.

"*Qu'est-ce que ça veut dire?*"

"Death awaits…"

"What is she talking about?"

The questions brought rising tension to stir in the mix. Panic was around the bend. Clopin stood on a log and took off his mask, raising his arms for calm.

"*Calmez-vous!*" Clopin demanded with authority. "Do not panic."

"But what could she mean?" Gretel questioned, holding her brother's hand tightly.

"It means exactly what she said it means! None of you are deaf, except for Enzo over there, but he doesn't count." Clopin's black eyes flashed. "War is afoot."

Chapter Twenty-Three

The Lost and the Slayer

"What the devil?!" Clopin sputtered among various other exclamations in French. "Giant Slayers and Lost Girls? It's like the girl has lost her wits. And what's this about a *terrible evil*?" He spun on Red suddenly. "And why did she talk to *you* about some bloody wolf?"

"*Clopin, calmez-vous!*" Esmeralda snapped. "Put your finger away before it's pointed back at you."

He glanced at his accusing gesture as if his finger had caused him great offense against his will. Awkwardly, he lowered his arm and shoved his hand in his pocket.

"We need to pick this apart one phrase at a time," Ingénu suggested, "so we can understand it."

"I do not remember asking your opinion," Clopin voiced, stepping back to look at them. "In fact, I do not remember asking for most any of you to join this discussion."

Red sighed, looking around at the group standing between two caravans: the royal couple, the gypsy siblings, the Facility escapees, and Jim. It was crowded, but necessary. Besides that, this was Esmeralda's idea.

"I agree with Ingénu," Esmeralda spoke. She was still muddy from helping Kezia earlier that evening. "We should break it down to its directions, so we know what to do."

"Excellent." Clopin hopped up to sit cross-legged on the edge of the caravan. "Let's start with the *terrible evil* she talked about after the blood, war, and death bit."

"We already know about that," Alice said, waving her hand like it was unnecessary. "We've been calling it the Master. We've been looking for him or her for some time."

Clopin stared blankly at her. He spread his arms out. "And you only see fit to tell us now?"

"Red told me," Briar spoke up with a shrug.

"Well isn't that fine and dandy!"

"We do not know what this terrible evil is," Ingénu cut in, eyeing Red for assurance, to which she agreed with a nod. "But we can figure out what we do know."

"*The Lost Girl and Giant Slayer must find the Bear Wizard before the Raven Sorceress rises*," Esmeralda recited perfectly.

"They say the queen of Chliobain was a giant killer," Ingénu offered. "Maybe she is the Giant Slayer."

"No." Jack shook his head grimly. His eyes were lowered, his arms folded over his chest. "That'd be me. Haven't heard that name in a long time, but..."

Red frowned at his guarded behavior. He'd never spoken of being the Giant Slayer before.

"I'd be the Lost Girl," Wendy confessed as well. "Kezia has already warned that I'd be going on some journey. I guess this is it."

"What about this Bear Wizard and Raven Sorceress?" Alice asked.

"The sorceress is Carabosse," Briar explained easily. "As for the wizard..."

"Oh, isn't this splendid?!" Clopin clapped his hands mockingly. "Now we'll be fighting against Carabosse, will we? Or did you forget that minor detail at the end?"

"Not alone. Grimrose will help, and Chliobain." Ingénu cocked his head. "Or did you forget that minor detail at the end?"

Clopin sneered. "She didn't say anything about Chliobain. And your kingdom, good prince, is a bit *stiff* at the moment."

"Not for long. She spoke of freeing Grimrose. The wizard will help."

"The wizard hasn't been seen in years! He's abandoned us. How are you going to find him?"

"He hasn't abandoned us!" Briar shot, blood rushing to her face. "He would *never* abandon us. Don't you *ever* speak ill of Isbjørn again. He left to protect us."

"A lot of good that did."

Briar slapped him in the face, succeeding in shutting him up. Clopin was too baffled to do anything.

"All this debating is pointless," Jim groaned. "I'll tell you what's going on. Those two are going to find the wizard, take him to Grimrose and break that curse. The rest of us will find the path and continue to Chliobain, fetch us some troops and supplies, then *all* of us will meet up on the way to Carabosse's fortress. Lots of blood, lots of death, we kill ourselves an evil sorceress; everyone's happy!"

"Except for Carabosse," Jack added. "Which, by the way, I never would've pinned down for a *raven* witch."

"What makes you say that?"

Jack shrugged. "I don't know. Sounds like something between *caribou* and *caboose*."

Jim gave a half smile. Returning to the subject, he voiced, "Only thing I can't place is where the wolf thing comes to play."

Red's gut seized as all eyes turned to her. She stayed composed and shrugged it off. "I don't know. *The Wolf cannot be trusted*, that's pretty straight forward. We can't trust Lupa…"

"Or Fang," Esmeralda added.

Red hesitated. "Fang is part of the Pack. If Kezia meant the Pack, she would've said wolves, or just Fang. But Lupa's a lone wolf. And we know she's a thousand times worse than Fang."

"Who cares what Kezia *would've* said," Clopin grumbled, rubbing his smarting cheek. "No wolf can be trusted, Pack or no."

Clearing her throat, Red continued, "I don't know about how the wolf can be used. Maybe Lupa or Fang is starting to turn against Carabosse."

"And the mask?" Clopin asked suspiciously.

"Figure of speech, perhaps. Maybe there will be a mask I'll have to remove." The lie came easily, slipping from her tongue like honey. "If there is, I'll keep an eye out for it."

Esmeralda held her gaze, unconvinced. Red's heart plummeted, realizing her mistake. She'd let herself fear, and Esmeralda saw it.

Jack helped Wendy mount her steed, though she probably didn't need it. There had been some grumbling already about the absence of the unicorns, but they weren't here, so they'd receive no help from them. Jack shook his head. He'd never seen a unicorn before. His one chance had already left while he was still sleeping.

Kai tightened the straps on their saddlebags. "Stay out of trouble," he advised with a sideways glance at Jack.

"I'm not keen on throwing myself into it," Jack retorted humorously.

Raising an eyebrow, Kai looked up at Wendy with a wink. "Look after him."

She just grinned down at them in response.

As Jack tied off his new leather bracers, Aurore came up to them with a note and directions. Both of which she gave to Wendy. "Give this to Isbjørn," Aurore instructed, passing the sealed letter. "It should help convince him. As far as where to find him, they say he'll always be found east of the sun and west of the moon."

"How do we bloody well do that?" Jack questioned, making a face.

Aurore shrugged. "Figure it out. That's the best I can tell you."

Pocketing the note, Wendy thanked her, though Jack didn't like relying on some riddle to give them directions. There had better not be an eclipse tonight.

"Be sure to stay away from monsters," Red cautioned, helping Jack strap his sword to his belt. "Trolls smell like tree sap and fungus, goblins like mud and sweat. Gnomes won't bother you if you don't pester them. On second thought, stay away from them, too…"

Jack caught her hands in his, holding them close to his chest. "Rubes," he assured, "we'll be fine."

She wouldn't look at him. "I know. But you've just started feeling better, and—"

He squeezed her hands. "We'll be fine. Besides, I've got Wendy! She's the muscle."

The wind whistled past and those bottle green eyes finally looked up at him. He smiled encouragingly. It started to rain.

"It's almost dawn," Esmeralda voiced, stepping up with extra flasks of water that she added to their provisions. "You'd best be going."

Releasing Red's hands, Jack hoisted himself up on his horse. It fidgeted in anticipation, hooves tapping in the mud.

"Wait, Jack," Red stated, reaching up and grabbing his forearm. He turned. She hesitated. "Dragons. If you smell smoke, start running."

He sighed, but pulled a smile. "I'll be sure to keep my schnoz on edge."

Urging her horse forward, Wendy led the way out of the gypsy camp and Jack was forced to join. She didn't take long before making a race out of it, riding west of the moon.

"*I'll be sure to keep my schnoz on edge,*" Wendy mimicked with a laugh.

"Shut up, Wendy!"

"Hey, if I'm the muscle, what does that make you?"

"I've already been damsel in distress once."

"Some damsel you made."

*****

Fang's stomach felt hollow as he approached the whole of the Pack. They were entertaining themselves while waiting for him, as expected. He didn't want to face them. Thaddeus padded up behind him, the scar across his eye gleaming pale in the grey light.

"What happened?" the older man questioned in gruff concern. "What is the meaning of this meeting? Did Carabosse not take it well?"

"No, Thaddeus, she did not take it well," Fang snapped.

The retort caused Thaddeus to draw his eyebrows together in a deep frown. Fang regretted bursting at him. He clenched his fists to hide the fact that his hands were shaking. He'd never felt so angry, so desperate. He hated it.

"I'm sorry," he said lowly, "but she's got Zoë."

Thaddeus glowered, fists clenched for an entirely different reason. "I knew the witch could not to be trusted."

"Now she wants Red or Zoë dies," Fang growled, "one way or another."

"You know the Pack never turns on our own kind unless under grievous circumstances. I know you. There must be something else to make you compromise our ways."

Fang didn't answer, Carabosse's threat pulsing through his veins.

He turned back to the gathered wolves, heart pounding. The clearing was overflowing with them, both human and wolf forms of every species and color. Howls echoes around him in greeting as Fang made his way through the crowd, Thaddeus following. Pups scrambled to get a look at their Alpha.

A boulder stood in the center of the clearing. It was pointed like a wolf's snout and flat to form a platform. Shifting to his inner wolf, Fang hopped atop the rock and crawled to the edge with heavy paws. A chorus of barks, howls, and shouts welcomed him. Fang howled at the moon that lingered with the dawn. The Pack joined until everyone participated in the eerie call.

When Fang shifted to a man, the howling ceased. Not a single whimper sounded.

• • •

"Wolves," he announced, voice projecting over the clearing. "You have made me your Alpha over these many years. Have I done anything to regret your decision?"

Barks and howls responded to indicate their undeniable loyalty.

"I'm honored to hear it." His heart heavy with the message he was about to relay. He took a deep breath. "*The Pack never turns on our own kind.* That has been ingrained in our souls for as long as the Pack has lived. Even when those have deemed it best to leave, those lone wolves have still been considered family. Only if one breaks this vow terribly have we been forced to action."

More yips of agreement filled the pause in his speech.

"Recently I have come across a dilemma that contradicts my beliefs no matter which way I turn. Many if not all of you know of my hunt for the girl, Red, the Scarlet Thief and Crimson Wraith. Some of you helped me in my search for her, despite the one who demands her. You know of whom I speak."

"You've done so much for us," an indistinct she-wolf spoke up. "It's time we returned the favor!"

A roar seconding the she-wolf's statement filled his ears. Despite their devotion, Fang was uncertain about what he had to say next. He knew he had to continue.

"Some of you already know this." He swallowed nervously. "I've only recently discovered it myself. But Red is, apparently, a wolf."

Whispers and whimpers flushed over the Pack. The question of how it happened repeated itself over and over again.

"It was my own mistake," Fang admitted. "And that mistake has since grown. When I returned to Carabosse to withdraw from her service, she proved to be the formidable manipulator some of you warned her to be. Not only did she kidnap my wife, but she threatened the lives of every wolf in this Forest. If we don't find Red, Carabosse will let my wife die and force my family under her control or otherwise slaughter the Pack."

A cacophony of vicious snarls rumbled across the clearing, accompanying roars of angry protest. Knots twisted in his abdomen. His fists clenched as he waited for the wolves to have their time of frustration. It wouldn't surprise him if some of them threatened to remove him as their leader. He wouldn't blame them. He'd led them into a slaughterhouse worse than the hunters.

Fang caught Thaddeus' eyes, the hopeless to the solemn. The older wolf turned away from him. His heart dropped, imagining the shame. But Thaddeus looked out at the crowd of angered, fearful canines.

"Listen up, dogs!" Thaddeus' voice thundered, drawing every bark silent. Fang had heard Thaddeus raise his voice few times during the span of their friendship. He'd never heard him speak this loud. "I can smell your frustration for what Fang's actions have led to. But he is our Alpha! He has done much for us over the years, protecting the Pack against the prejudices raging throughout the kingdoms..."

The words stirred the crowd. None could deny his claims.

"... Freeing us from the dictatorship of Fenrir..."

A great chorus of barks and shouts followed.

"… And rescuing those trapped and hunted by the Wolf Hunters who have taken our kind for a monstrous pest to eradicate!"

Every wolf growled, woofed, snarled, or howled in response at the name of the humans who hunted them like animals. It took nearly five minutes for the Pack to calm down enough for Thaddeus to be heard over the commotion.

"If that wolf," Thaddeus stuck his finger up at Fang, "can do all that in the prime of his youth, then you should all know he's going to get us out of this filthy mess. We owe him at the very least our loyalty, trust, and obedience in this. As for me," he looked right up into Fang's eyes, "I trust him with my life. Because what is a pack without its Alpha?!"

"*Wild!*" barked the unanimous response.

Fang grinned, stepping up beside his friend. "And what is a wolf without its pack?"

"*Alone!*" roared the answer.

Inside, Fang swelled with pleasure at such outspoken loyalty. He was eternally grateful for Thaddeus and his trust. But guilt ate at him with what he had to ask of them. Palms sweaty, he steeled himself to relay Carabosse's commands.

*****

A caw sounded from a nearby tree, making them both jump. Without hesitation, Wendy threw one of her daggers. The blow brought the bird down instantly.

Jack went to retrieve the blade for her. "Told you that you're the muscle."

Kicking dirt over the remnants of their fire, Wendy looked up at the sky. The rain had finally stopped, exposing the sun. Now that they had directions to follow, they had to get going. Any more rest would waste time.

Jack returned her dagger and then split a piece of bread between them. He appeared much better now than he had yesterday morning. The color returned to his skin, the life in his eyes. Every time she saw him, she felt relieved.

The horses fidgeted anxiously. Jack had to help Wendy up on hers again; it was too big and she had little experience riding horses. At least the horse didn't try to buck her off its back. Soon, they were both off at a steady pace east of the sun.

"Did Alice ever tell you about your birthday?" Wendy asked.

"She wished me a Happy Unbirthday and everything," Jack laughed, glancing back at her. "Boy, I used to have plans for when I turned nineteen. At least, I think I did. They kind of seem absurd now."

Wendy almost smiled. She used to have dreams of when she turned older, too. Then the years came and went, and she never got older. Dreams changed. She changed. Sometimes she wondered what would've happened if she'd let time run its course with her. But she didn't wonder enough to regret it.

"You alright back there?"

Wendy nodded, urging her horse forward to match the other's pace. "You talked in your sleep again," she voiced.

Jack didn't respond immediately. His eyes stared blankly ahead of them. When he caught her staring, he pulled a smile and adjusted their course accordingly. It didn't completely erase the empty look.

"You said her name," Wendy continued.

"Well, you know," Jack shrugged, "I'm worried about her. As strong as Rubes is, I haven't seen her as fidgety as when she is in this place. And I'm not so sure about—"

"I know, but I'm not talking about Red," she interjected. "I mean Jill."

The horses quickened their step. Again, she found Jack staring off into the distance. This time, she had to adjust their course.

"How long has this been going on?"

"Since the day I climbed back down that beanstalk."

Wendy frowned. "You haven't talked in your sleep about it before that I've heard."

He wouldn't look at her now, like he was hiding his face. But he couldn't keep the dark hurt from his voice. "You weren't there when I slept in the Facility. Kai had to wake me up all the time, when I didn't wake up screaming."

"What made you stop?"

"You, Kai, and Red," Jack responded, "and Alice. You all helped a lot. I finally stopped dreaming of it when we arrived in Wonderland."

A knot formed in her throat. Wendy wanted to say more, maybe lean over and squeeze his hand. A whiff of burning iron hit her nostrils. The horses broke into a run.

Despite not knowing what they were running from, Wendy urged her steed on. "What did Red say smelled like something burning?!"

"Was it gnomes?" Jack shouted, somehow ending up behind her. "Trolls?"

A roar and scream combined into one sound split their eardrums. Fire blasted through the trees behind them, heat pulsing against their backs.

"*Dragon!*" Jack cried. "It was a dragon!"

Chapter Twenty-Four

Guard Dogs

Esmeralda was clearly getting suspicious. No matter what she did or where she went, somehow Red found the gypsy close by watching. She tried to keep herself busy. She joined hunts and patrols, kept the children from straying too far from the rolling caravans, even helped with chores wherever she could. But when she helped Kai and Ingénu push a stuck cart from the mud, Esmeralda wasn't far with narrowed smoky eyes. When she shucked corn and split peas with Gretel and Briar, Red found Esmeralda looking from her caravan.

Red wasn't necessarily avoiding her. But she felt like the gypsy was beginning to suspect her of something that Red dreaded being revealed.

She was alone behind the line of caravans when Esmeralda at last confronted her.

"Explain yourself," Esmeralda demanded evenly. "And don't bother lying. I've seen your fear and the form it takes: a wolf, but it is not Fang as it used to be."

Red glowered, stomach tightening. "You have no right picking apart my mind."

"I have every right," she retorted, stepping closer intimidatingly. "Ever since the day you came here, you've been lying to us. You slip past any explanations as to where you've been or what happened to make you leave. You avoid the very mention of *wolf*. Your soul trembles at the sound of it."

"I've told you all you need know," Red snapped.

Esmeralda's voice lowered to a deadly whisper, "If your secrets put my people in danger..."

"I may not be of purest heart, but I'm no traitor."

"Then stop acting like one."

Droning howls split the air. Red and Esmeralda whipped around toward the front of the traveling procession that came to a hasty halt. A hollow pit formed in her abdomen.

Without need for further explanation, Esmeralda rushed toward the front on the line with Red right at her heals. All around them gypsies emerged, grabbing weapons. Children were hustled into carts. Quasimodo's caravan rocked on its wheels, but someone had barred the door and windows so he couldn't break out.

"Man your battle stations!" Jim's gruff voice bellowed somewhere ahead of them.

"We have no battle stations, Jimmy," Clopin growled, drawing his sword and loping to the front.

Red whipped her bow out and quickly strung it, arrow fitted, ready for an attack. Senses spiked. Wolves were all around, she could feel them. Kai and Alice soon joined her, both with blades drawn.

"I thought they were going to leave you alone," Alice said under her breath.

"Perhaps not everyone got the message," Red muttered.

Kai ran close. "Or this isn't about you at all."

The three slid to a stop just behind Clopin, Esmeralda, and Jim. A crowd of gypsies stood at the ready behind them, awaiting instruction. Aurore and Ingénu were ahead of them all staring at the obstacle before them.

They stood without weapons, fourteen men and women completely blocking the path. Red's nose twitched. Every single one of them reeked of wolf.

A large man stood in front of the others, hair long and stringy, eyes eerie yellow. He seemed to be the one in charge, until a smaller man stepped out from behind him. This one had a fair face, blond hair slicked back in a ponytail at the base of his neck. Eyes a darkened amber, he smiled in a way that made him appear almost trustworthy. Red detested him instantly.

"Friends," the man spoke smoothly, much too relaxed. "What's with all the fuss? My family and I come unarmed."

Clopin sneered, pushing past the royal couple to head them all. "*Oui*, except for the claws concealed under that disguise."

The man shrugged. "We cannot help what we are, just as much as you can't."

Esmeralda's hard eyes examined them all one by one, presumably deciphering what form their fears took. The man caught on quickly, wagging his finger. "Please, we know of your gifts. We shall keep ours to ourselves if you keep yours. It's only fair. All we want to do is talk."

"Talk?" Jim huffed under his breath, "Right."

Ignoring the comment he'd certainly heard, the man introduced himself, "I am Lycaon."

"Clopin," the gypsy said bluntly.

"Well, Clopin," Lycaon smiled, "perhaps you have not yet heard the news, seeing as your kind hasn't been seen in years."

"What news?" Ingénu spoke up.

"Do I smell royalty?" Lycaon's eyes twinkled. "They're always so impatient."

"Just spit it out," Jim growled.

"Woodsmen, too." He traced his thumb over his lip. "No matter. Might as well explain it, then. You're all heading for Chliobain, I assume."

"None of your business," Clopin retorted.

"So, you are going. But that just won't do."

"Why not?" Briar inquired.

"No one's allowed in or out of Chliobain," Lycaon explained.

"On whose authority?" she demanded.

"Mine of course!" He shrugged, looking around at his friends. "Well, not exactly mine. Orders are from Fang. Can't take any chances with finding the girl he's after."

Red felt her skin crawl, the grip on her bow tightening. Both Kai and Alice stepped closer. Either Fang had gone back on his word, or Lycaon hadn't heard. Whatever it was, her muscles tensed. She refused to let any wolf take her, not now, not ever.

"Your people are going to have to find somewhere else to entertain… Some of you may stay, though. I can make an exception." Lycaon's eyes flicked to Alice hungrily, who cocked her head and gave a smile that expressed exactly how much she wanted to punch him.

Clopin clenched his fists. "And if we refuse?"

He opened his arms, looking round at his small pack. "If it comes to that, we may have to bring out the claws."

Grinding his teeth, Clopin prepared to retaliate when Esmeralda grabbed his arm. The two passed a look between them in silent agreement. Turning back to the wolves, Clopin growled, "We'll be on our way, then."

Lycaon winked. "Good choice."

As soon as Clopin turned away with clenched fists, the rest of them retreated to get the carts turned around. Red cautiously walked away, aware of the few wolves hiding just off the path.

"I didn't know the gypsies housed wolves," Lycaon called after them.

Red stopped in her tracks. A chill shot down her spine.

Clopin laughed. "We don't."

"Doesn't seem like it to me," Lycaon stated, amber eyes gleaming. "It smells like you've got one right here with you."

Ticked off, Clopin spun on his heels. "Your nose needs to be checked, because there is no wolf in my family. Besides, wolves can't smell the difference between your kind and my kind anyway."

Red felt frozen, even as the others moved past her. Her foundation was unraveling under her feet.

"Most can't," Lycaon agreed. "But there are some, like me, who can."

Shaking his head, Clopin turned back to the carts with a sneer.

Her heart pounded in her ears, but she still heard the footsteps. She whipped around and grasped the arm that reached out for her. Bottle green eyes locked with amber. Lycaon's nostrils flared, a smirk on the edge of his mouth. Everything around them froze.

"It's you," he whispered, acting as if her fingernails weren't digging into his skin. His breath smelled like cinnamon. Lycaon raised an eyebrow, examining her features. "I almost didn't believe Fang actually turned his little bartering merchandise into one of us."

"I've already had the pleasure of telling him myself," Red hissed, flinging his arm to the side.

He chuckled. "Wrong move, sweetheart."

Lycaon grabbed her around the waist and spun her around so she was pressed against him. The sharp edge of a knife pushed against her throat, threatening to puncture her trachea. Gypsies went into chaos. Weapons out, angry shouts sounded, but none could pursue lest she die. Blood dripped down her throat as the blade pierced her skin.

"Don't worry, she doesn't have to die," Lycaon called to the gypsies, pulling Red back closer to the waiting wolves. "We'll just take her and be on our way. No need for fighting. Besides," he smirked, "your kind doesn't harbor my kind anyway."

That cinnamon breath brushed past her face. Her breath quickened, panic leaking into her nerves. She didn't allow herself to see their faces as the truth creeped over them. It was too late.

Calming herself, Red took the next step backwards with Lycaon. It was enough to delay the knife and feel the blade leave her skin. Instantly, she melted into the Wolf and fell out of his hold. Before he could retaliate, she whipped around and sank her teeth into his calf. Lycaon screamed.

Between her jaws, she felt his leg change. The Wolf released him and dodged the Hudson Bay wolf's strike.

Rolling for her fallen weapons, she shifted form and shot up on her knees. Her arrow aimed directly at the blond wolf's brow, impossible to miss. In two heartbeats, Lycaon changed. Amber eyes glared at her. Blood covered his calf.

The wolves behind him were all poised to intercede, teeth bared. None dared to pounce.

"You must not have heard the news," Red growled. "Fang's promised to leave me alone. Ask him yourself."

Lycaon smirked. "You may find it surprising, but I don't believe you."

"I don't *care* if you believe me," she snapped. "You and your friends are going to let us go. And if I smell or hear your kind anywhere near us, then you're going to face a lot more than just my claws." When Lycaon narrowed his eyes, Red added, "I can smell the difference between man, beast, and the mix as well."

Raising his hands, Lycaon backed away slowly. "As you wish, sweetheart."

Red kept her bow drawn until the wolves disappeared, slinking far beyond the boundaries of her senses. By then the caravans were ready to make their way back. When Red turned, she saw every single gypsy staring at her. Steeling herself, Red marched past all of them.

To Esmeralda, she muttered, "Now you know."

*****

"Why is there always a blasted bloody dragon in every blasted bloody world we go to?!"

Hooves pounded against the forest floor. The horses ran as fast as they could, weaving through trees, somehow still obeying the pull of their reins to keep them going east of the sun. Unfortunately, the fire was faster. And the dragon was more than willing to provide that.

"I mean, Giant Country may have really big bloodthirsty blokes," Jack exclaimed, ducking down close to his horse's neck, "but at least there are no ferocious flying furnaces!"

"Shut up, Jack!" Wendy snapped.

Fire blasted behind them with a sound worse than thunder. Jack cursed loudly. Ahead of him, Wendy coughed forcefully due to the smoke that filled the Forest.

He only heard the rush of water when the horses charged into the river. With only the fleeting concern of a hidden water monster, Jack slipped off his mount and into the water. The cold stung. Quickly, Wendy followed suit. Taking a deep gasp of air, Jack ducked under water just as the sound of beating wings passed overhead.

The river heated around him. His lungs burned, but he forced himself to stay under until the water cooled again. As soon as that happened, Jack emerged sputtering and splashing. From the sound of it, the dragon had moved on.

Treading water to keep his head above the surface, Jack looked around. "Wendy!"

Panic pounded with every heartbeat. The horses were gone. Wendy was nowhere to be seen.

"WENDY!" he cried.

"Jack!"

He whipped around and almost sank. Flailing, Wendy was caught in the current as it tried to drag her under. Instantly, Jack swam into the current, grabbed her, and brought her up to the surface. She gasped, shaking the water from her eyes. Neither obtained reprieve. The river pushed them forward with a strength they could barely fight. Together, they raced down the river, rolling in and out of the water.

After so long struggling to keep afloat, Jack caught hold of something reaching out into the river. He latched on, praying it wasn't a monster's leg. Pulling Wendy and himself closer, Jack glanced up just as the branch broke from its base and cascaded down with them. They went under. He didn't let go. Muscles burning, Jack pulled them both up out of the water to prop themselves up on the branch. Exhaustion took them now that they no longer had to fight the current. Jack took deep breaths, his arm still around Wendy just in case she should slip.

Gasping, Wendy raised her head. "Do you hear that?"

Jack wobbled his head, shaking the water from his ears. No matter what he did, his eardrums remained stubbornly waterlogged. Then he realized the rush and roar wasn't in his head.

Jack moaned. "Ah, don't tell me."

"Yup." Wendy frowned.

"Of course," he looked up as if he could see it himself, "a waterfall."

He rocked back and forth with all his might, trying to use the log's weight to pull them close to shore. But the river was too wide, the waters too deep, and the current too strong. There was no way to avoid it.

"We're going to have to clear it," Jack sighed turning to Wendy. "Have you ever plummeted off a waterfall before?"

She shook her head. "Only when I could fly and didn't have to worry about falling. You?"

With a sigh, Jack began instructing, "Take a deep breath, go feet first, and cover your head. As soon as you hit the water, start swimming. You don't want to end up under that waterfall, so no matter what, go downstream."

"If we do that, we'll survive?"

"I did something similar in Giant Country," Jack explained. "Let's just hope there are no rocks at the bottom."

"Lovely."

The current quickened as they drew closer to the drop. Jack held tight to Wendy for as long as he could, afraid she would drift away if he let go. Bracing himself for the fall, Jack felt his stomach tighten. He didn't feel any tension in Wendy's muscles, though. She wasn't nearly as nervous as he was. Maybe she was too used to flying to fear of falling. It could get her killed.

"Now!" Jack cried just before they fell over.

Water dropped under him, his stomach abandoning him somewhere at the top of the waterfall. He couldn't help but scream, arms and legs flailing. Halfway down, Jack remembered his own advice. He took a deep breath, covered his head and hit the water below feet first. His legs rang from the impact.

Bubbles blinded his vision. Immediately, Jack started swimming up and away from the rush of crashing water behind him. It felt like forever until he finally broke the surface, filling his burning lungs with air. Then he was under again, surrounded by water.

When he came back up, he could touch the river floor without going under. Coughing up water, Jack fell to his hands and knees on the riverbank. Then it hit him.

"Wendy," he muttered. Whipping around, he sprayed water everywhere. "Wendy!"

He flipped around and nearly fell face first in the river when he heard coughing just beside him. Relief flooded through him when he saw a waterlogged Wendy gasping for breath. He sighed and collapsed on the riverbank, catching his breath.

"We made it," Wendy breathed.

Jack opened his mouth to respond, but a snort of hot air hit his face. He couldn't close his mouth in time. Wendy laughed hysterically. Face screwed up, Jack popped open an eye to find a white and brown muzzle over his nose.

"I don't even want to know how you got down here alive," he muttered, receiving another snort in the face. He pushed away the horse's wet snout as Wendy began giggling again. He splashed her.

"Come on," she beckoned as she started to get up. "We're nearly there, I can feel it."

*****

There was an odd tension in the air ever since Red's Wolf was discovered. No one seemed to know what to do except travel. Not that they knew where they were going. But they stuck to the path where things were safer for now. As for Alice, she plucked herself a bunch of colorful flowers that were probably poisonous and went to visit Quasimodo.

On the way, she passed by the Woodsman who was telling the gypsy kids a story about his grandfather. She'd heard him tell stories about his grandfather before.

Apparently, he'd been one great adventurer, even going head to head with pirates. Alice wondered if she'd get into telling stories when her adventures were done and she had tales to share.

Remus stubbed his toe, the klutz. Gritting her teeth, Alice hopped the next few steps in pain. With a huff, she pinched her arm in retaliation. Maybe that would show him to be more careful.

Standing before the caravan with the orange horse on the door with her half-decent bouquet, Alice took a breath and knocked. It opened at her touch. She slipped inside and looked around the room.

"Hello?" she called unnecessarily.

Light filled the room from lamps and sunshine. Quasimodo wasn't hard to find. He looked up at her in surprise with mismatched eyes. As for Alice, she was more shocked to find Kai sitting in the back of the caravan.

"Hello!" Quasimodo said excitedly, tottering over to her with a great smile.

"I'm Alice," she introduced, offering the bouquet. "I'm not sure if they're particularly *safe*, but I thought these would brighten up the place."

He accepted them wondrously, his touch gentle. "Oh, thank you! I love flowers, especially the colorful ones. They hold the most joy."

The flowers were placed in a beautifully carved vase set in the window where the light could catch their petals. Kai met Alice's gaze, holding a carving knife and piece of wood. She shrugged. He did likewise.

"It's nice to meet you, Alice," Quasimodo said, turning to her once the flowers were arranged to his liking. "Please, call me Quasi."

"Pleasure to meet you as well."

"What brings you here?"

"If I'm honest," Alice sat close to Kai in a scattering of wood shavings, "a whim. Lately, I'm finding that I've been acting increasingly spontaneous."

Kai raised an eyebrow as if it was beyond an understatement. Hobbling back over to them, Quasi retrieved a knife and fresh block of lumber. Without voicing the question, Alice stared at Kai until he got the message.

"I noticed Quasi had skill in carving," Kai explained. "I thought he might show me some tricks."

Quasi blushed, lowering his gaze to his project. "I'm not all that great. I just like working with my hands. It's an easy way to pass the time." His face brightened. "But... but Kai here is good, too! Just look here..."

Bustling around the mess of blocks and shavings, he held up an intricately carved figure. Alice took it from him. It was a girl with an unfamiliar face, little flowers whittled into all the details. Petals embroidered in the dress. Blossoms braided in her hair. Alice traced her thumb over the ring on the figure's left hand.

"Is this Gerda?"

Kai nodded, but didn't look up at her.

"She's beautiful," Alice complimented, noticing the ring that peeked out from under his shirt. "I didn't know you could carve."

"My mother was a clockmaker," he explained. "She taught me a few things."

"How long has it been since you've been home?"

Icy eyes looked up at her suspiciously. "Why do you ask?"

"I told you. I'm feeling impulsive. Besides, I'm trying to figure out a mystery."

Quasi grinned, his hands working smoothly over the wood and blade. "I like mysteries."

Kai sighed, somehow discomfort etching his brow. "I think it's been about two years."

Her eyebrows shot up. She'd been trying to keep the calculations in order so she could find some clues in their pasts, as Kezia suggested. Not that she knew what it meant exactly.

"Was that before or after your time in the Snow Queen's realm?"

"Before. I haven't been to Anders since Gerda was captured."

"So, she was kidnapped around the same time Red *and* Wendy were caught by the Facility?"

Kai frowned. "What are you suggesting?"

"I'm not sure exactly," Alice admitted, placing the statuette before them. "But do you think the Snow Queen might be the Master?"

"Master?" Quasi questioned with a sudden scowl. He shook his head, roughly stabbing the block of wood in his hand. "Master is *dead!*"

Remembering the book in her father's library about Quasimodo and Notre Dame, Alice reached out and touched his scarred arm gently. "Not that master, Quasi. You needn't worry about him."

His breath slowly eased once again. Looking up at her, Quasi nodded in understanding. When she pulled back, he returned to his project. Alice stared at Kai expectantly.

Kai rubbed his scar with his knuckles. "Yes. It's possible."

Sitting back on her heals, Alice sighed and stirred her thoughts. The list of possible identities for the Master grew every day since she'd talked with Kezia: Carabosse, the Snow Queen, and two faces she'd seen when she last touched Kezia during her outburst. She still had yet to talk to Jack about possible candidates. But the warning rang through her head every time.

It will be someone they least suspect. In the back of her mind, she now found herself suspicious of everyone.

No matter where she turned, all she could see was Anne Christiansen.

Chapter Twenty-Five

West of the Moon

The first sign was the snow. It came out of nowhere, as if they'd stepped into another world. Wendy looked up at the sky. Sure enough, they were east of the sun and west of the moon all at once. Without hesitation, she urged her horse forward with Jack following.

In the center of the large patch of snow stood a cottage with frosty wild flowers growing up its walls. Thick moss blanketed the roof with dustings of snow. Lucky piggies buzzed around, squeaking at the sprites that tried to bother them. Everything about the scene seemed to defy the snow.

"Hello?" Jack called, sliding off his horse into the crusty grass to approach the door. "Hello! Are there any wizards in there?"

Wendy frowned as Jack knocked a few times with no answer. She swung her leg over and hopped off the horse. It wasn't even that cold out.

"Maybe we have the wrong house," she suggested teasingly.

"Who else would live in a cottage with magic snow and lucky piggies flying about? Carabosse? Of course not," Jack huffed, knocking on the door in steady rhythm.

She tethered the horses as best she could. All the while, there was still no answer.

Walking towards Jack, Wendy made a face. "Maybe he's not home?"

"Or pretending not to be." He pointed to the chimney. "There's smoke. No one leaves a fire going while away… if they're smart."

The smoke disappeared on cue.

"See? He heard me; now he's definitely pretending not to be home." Jack pounded on the door harder, faster. "Oi! Mister Wizard! We know you're in there!"

Making a face, he pressed his ear against the door. He shook his head. With a sigh, Jack backed away from the doorway.

Wendy raised an eyebrow. "Giving up?"

"Don't be ridiculous. I'm getting a running start." Cupping his hands over his mouth, Jack shouted at the house again, "If you don't let us in, I'm going to break the door down!"

Still no response.

"Your choice." He kicked up his feet like a bull in preparation for the charge. Wendy didn't feel good about this at all. "One!"

"Jack, I don't think…"

"Two!"

"He won't be very happy if you break his door down."

"*Three!*"

Jack gave a shout as he barreled for the door. Wendy almost covered her eyes, certain he was going to hurt himself. Just before he hit the door, it opened and he disappeared. Tumult clashed inside.

Wendy rushed up and stopped just short of the entrance to take in the scene. Jack was on the ground amongst fallen furniture with a tapestry over his head. By the door stood a man with hair slicked back away from his strong brow and a full white beard. He was huge, muscular. If nothing else, perhaps it was his sheer size that inspired his title of Bear Wizard.

If this is the Bear Wizard, Wendy thought.

"That door is made from an enchanted tree," the man's voice was so deep it was almost a growl. "You could no more knock it down than it could spring legs and dance the polka." He leaned closer to Wendy and winked. "I didn't want the lad to end up with a concussion."

Wendy smiled, finding herself instantly liking him. "Thank you for that."

"Yeah, I appreciate the concern," Jack grumbled, wrestling out from under the tapestry. "I take it you're the wizard?"

"That all depends on who's asking," he responded, his black eyes shining. They were darker than Clopin's.

Finding no harm in introducing themselves, Wendy spoke up, "I'm Wendy, and this is Jack."

Jack was still struggling to get up from the pile of furniture he'd knocked over.

"We're here to ask for your help."

"My help?" the man raised thick eyebrows. "Neither of you are old enough to remember me, and whatever legends are told don't hold a candle to the truth. Nor do I recognize either of your faces. You're not of any kingdoms in this Forest, gypsies, or wolves. I pride myself on recognizing Carabosse's goons, and you're certainly not them. And shapeshifters would never make it past the doorway. So, tell me," the man stroked his white beard as he sat in a wooden rocking-chair, "which realm do you come from?"

Wendy met Jack's eyes, unsure how much information they should reveal. He shook his head slightly. She ignored him.

"We're from England."

Jack wrinkled his nose.

The man just looked between the two of them knowingly. "But neither of you belong there."

Wendy shrugged, though Jack didn't appear comfortable in the least.

He held up his hand. "Don't tell me. Let me guess." Black eyes flicked to Wendy. "You've escaped years of age. Time itself flinches at your touch like an irritating rash. Only Neverland holds such strong powers defying time."

Now she felt a little uneasy. She'd met people who somehow knew more than they led on before: The White Queen in Wonderland, Tiger Lily in Neverland, and every single one of the gypsies. Not that she didn't trust them, at least to some extent. But she could never tell how much they *really* knew. That's what made her uneasy.

The man turned to Jack next. "There is something in your blood, a mineral that does not mix well with raw magic."

Wendy frowned at his words, remembering the strange puss in Jack's wounds. "In his blood?"

He leaned closer to Jack, who knelt frozen in his spot. "You have gold in your blood. It draws you to Giant Country, a connection you feel despite your resentment for it. I cannot begin to imagine what awful pain it must have been, and can continue to be."

She turned to Jack, confused. His eyes narrowed and his Adam's apple bobbed in a struggle to swallow. He'd never appeared so closed off before, so panicked. Wendy didn't know what to make of it.

The man leaned back in satisfaction.

"Well, since you know so much about us," Jack's voice was strained, "now it's your turn. Are you or are you not the Bear Wizard?"

"Certainly!" He smiled, the lines down his cheeks deepening. "I am called Isbjørn, the Bear Wizard, the cursed prince who can never truly escape a prison east of the sun and west of the moon no matter how many times I've left." He looked around the cottage reverently. "And whatever other exquisite titles the legends have dubbed me."

Jack righted a table beside him. "Things are about to change, Mister Wizard."

"We need you back," Wendy added.

Isbjørn narrowed his eyes, allowing the silence to stretch a moment. "I'm sorry you've come all this way, but I'm afraid I must decline."

Wendy blinked. "What?"

"You don't understand." Isbjørn clasped his hands and leaned forward. "I can't go back. If I do, Carabosse will wipe out Grimrose with all I hold dear. Maybe I'm selfish, but I will not risk it. Not after everything I've lost already."

With a huff, Jack stood and walked closer. "No, *you* don't understand. If you don't come back, Carabosse will wipe out the entire Forest. And if we're right, she could even wipe out all the realms!"

Isbjørn scowled. "What are you talking about?"

Suddenly remembering Aurore, Wendy pulled the princess' letter from her pocket. Her heart dropped slightly. It was completely soaked, the ink smudged. It was a wonder it held together at all.

"This was to explain things," she said apologetically, handing over the soaked message.

Isbjørn took it and passed a hand over it. Incredibly, the letter dried instantly and the ink seeped back into its proper place. Urgency flashed in his black eyes at the sight of the rose insignia. He broke the seal and scanned over the words in a flourish. Once finished after reading it over three times, he fell back into his chair with a hand over his face. The letter slipped out of his hands and landed on the floor soaked once again.

She didn't know what the note said, but she could only imagine. "I'm sorry," she muttered.

"Sorry?" Isbjørn huffed. "You have no reason to be sorry. You had nothing to do with this. I should never have trusted Carabosse to keep her word. Now look what my stupidity has done. Grimrose has been cast into stone, my granddaughter was kidnapped and cursed most of her life, Carabosse's hold over the Forest is stronger than ever... and now my sweet Aurore could possibly bear her own child without her family."

"Aurore's pregnant?" Wendy guffawed.

"That's what she said in her letter." Isbjørn waved his hand absentmindedly. He sighed, "This is all my fault."

"No, it's not," she insisted.

"Yeah, it is."

Wendy whipped her head around and glared at Jack. Even Isbjørn seemed strangely intrigued at the unexpected statement. But Jack didn't flinch. If anything, he stood straighter.

"Look, Mister Wizard, maybe it's not *all* your fault. Some things you probably couldn't prevent. But as for leaving and listening to the word of a bloody evil sorceress, yeah, that part is entirely your fault. Because of that, a whole lot of events took their toll. So yes, leaving, that's on you." Jack dared to come closer to Isbjørn. Even sitting down, the wizard seemed so large in comparison. That didn't stop Jack from looking down on him persuasively. "But that doesn't mean you can't try to fix things. Come back with us. Free Grimrose, defeat Carabosse, knock some bloody sense back into this Forest. Everything should work out if we have you on our side."

Isbjørn cocked his head. "What makes you so sure?"

"I've got the word of an eight-year-old girl, an old fairytale I used to know, and a shred of faith," Jack responded without hesitation. "It's not pixie dust, but I'd like to think it's enough."

Slowly, black eyes trained on Jack, Isbjørn stood to his full height. Jack had to step back a little just to give the man some space. Wendy held her breath.

"Lad, you have no idea what you're asking," Isbjørn spoke so low it was surely a growl this time.

Jack shrugged. "Ask anyone. I hardly ever know what I'm doing half the time."

His mouth twitched into almost a smile. "I like you. Both of you. You're good kids. I hope this all turns out well enough for you."

"I'd settle for *well enough*, I suppose."

"Does this mean you'll come with us?" Wendy asked hopefully.

"Yes, I'll come with you." Isbjørn nodded gruffly. "My family will not be scattered to the winds in suffering if I have anything to say about it. Now come. Get your horses. You'll follow me to Grimrose."

With a cheer of delight, Wendy spun on her heals and hastened out the door. By the time Jack followed her out, she led both horses to meet him. She supposed that they'd have to share one in order to lend Isbjørn the other, and the man was much too big to share a horse. Leaping up into the saddle, Wendy shifted forward to make room for Jack.

He was readying to join her when Isbjørn came out of the cottage and looked at them in confusion. "What are you two doing? Get on your own horse, lad."

"Do you expect to *walk* all the way to Grimrose?" Jack questioned with a frown.

"Of course not!" Isbjørn scoffed, adjusting a strange white cloak in his hands. "As you have said many times, I am a wizard! I plan on running."

Before they could comprehend his words, Isbjørn swung his white fur cloak over his shoulders and fell to his knees. He shouted in discomfort, clutching the frosty grass. His body began to grow and his skeleton changed under his skin. The white pelt melted into him. His shout turned to a guttural roar. Only his eyes never changed, black eyes that looked up at them amusedly from the face of a giant polar bear.

The horses fidgeted, nervous in the presence of such a large beast. The white bear stepped forward carefully, as if getting readjusted to his body. Hastily, Jack mounted his horse. With a huff, the white bear approached and touched his black nose to each horse's muzzle. They immediately calmed down.

Satisfied, the white bear looked up at Wendy and Jack expectantly. She smiled at him, fascinated. With that, Isbjørn turned away from his cottage and charged into the Forest. The horses followed in suit without prompting from their riders.

The snow soon fell far behind them. They never looked back.

*****

The scarlet cloak stood out like a beacon in the light of the full moon and the shadows of the Forest. Once far enough from anyone, the figure stopped. The hood was pulled up to cast darkness over her face. She drew a dagger from the folds of her cloak that shone when it caught the moon rays. Slowly, the blade slid down her white palm to leave a crimson line. She didn't even flinch. Balling her fist, she watched as five drops of blood hit the grass before her.

And she waited.

"I do hope you do not take me for a vampire."

She turned toward the voice: a woman with wild curls and dreads, hungry gold eyes, and blood in her teeth. The cloak itched annoyingly, burning. She ignored it.

The woman cocked her head. "You should know better than to wander from the path, especially during a full moon."

"I came to see you."

Her eyebrows shot up in surprise. Without a word, the girl slipped the hood off, a long blonde braid falling over her shoulder.

"Well," the woman said impressively, "I must admit, I was expecting someone else under that cloak."

She shrugged. "I wanted to get your attention."

"And you thought you could summon me with blood during the full moon?"

"It worked, didn't it?"

"To an extent. What are you called?"

"Alice. I assume you're Lupa?"

The woman held out her arms grandly with a smile. "The one and only. And I never lie."

"Neither do I, if I can help it."

Lupa again raised her eyebrows. She began to pace back and forth slowly, unable to remain still. Alice just stood patiently and evaluated the woman who she'd seen in Kezia's vision. Lupa was on her list.

"I must confess, I do not know why I am here," Lupa admitted.

"I needed to see you for myself," Alice said, eyes narrowed. "Do you really never lie?"

"I would not be where I am today if I did."

Alice tried to draw anything from the wolf's expression that could indicate deception. Unfortunately, she was completely unreadable. She had no choice but to take Lupa for her word.

"I'm looking for someone, a mysterious master of sorts," Alice confessed. "I have reason to believe you may know something about it."

Flashing her pointed teeth, Lupa chuckled. "Do you know how dangerous it is to call a wolf during the full moon alone, Alice?"

"I can imagine."

"Then I assume you should know how even more dangerous it is to do so when you only have a frightened girl and anxious boy lurking in the trees just behind you."

Alice's spine straightened, jaw tightening.

Lupa clicked her tongue. "How unwise to come with leverage."

She didn't say anything. That was enough of an answer for Lupa.

"I shall do this one thing for you, Alice," the woman crooned. "I will forgive this little nuisance and allow all three of you to leave unharmed *if* you tell me where the Wendy Bird has flown off to. But the longer you wait to answer, the chances heighten of me having a taste of some of you during this fine moon."

Uncertainly, Alice bit her lip. Lupa grinned. The Forest held its breath.

Blue eyes flashed up at the wolf. "No deal."

Lupa frowned in shock.

"You see, I have a deal of my own to propose." Alice smiled, feeling absolutely mad.

From behind her, Kai stepped from the shadows with a strange sword in both hands. It radiated power beyond the simple magic in the air. Gretel walked just behind him nervously.

Eyes widening, Lupa took a cautious step backwards. "Where did you get that?"

Alice shrugged, no longer finding the cloak uncomfortable. "We're borrowing it from a friend who'd found it in Bluebeard's treasure trove. It seemed particularly lethal."

Gold eyes shone. "You have no idea."

"So, here's the new deal," Alice continued confidently. "We will allow you to leave unharmed *if* you answer one simple question. I've heard you have a similar appreciation for questions as I do."

Trying to keep some scrap of composure, Lupa's breath shallowed as she stared at the sword that faded in and out of solidity. Silently, her gold eyes found Alice again and examined her with a new caution and intrigue. Lupa nodded in consent.

Raising her chin, Alice asked, "Are you the Master we seek?"

She smiled despite her former fear. "No. But I serve her."

With that, Lupa spun around and disappeared into the shadows. The Forest shivered, conforming to her will. A howl soon pierced the air, eerie and dangerous.

Satisfied, Alice turned back to Kai and Gretel victoriously. "Well, that turned out better than expected. It's a good thing we chose that sword."

Kai frowned. "You just let a bloodthirsty wolf escape during full moon. Do you realize we might've stopped her for good?"

"This whole plan was built on that untrustworthy word *might*," Alice pointed out.

"Innocent people could get hurt tonight, Alice."

"Less so because we interfered. I'm not sure about you, but I'll remember tonight with victory because of the lives we saved, not with defeat because of the lives we couldn't have saved anyway."

Kai grunted, still clearly upset.

"Besides," Alice added, "we were more successful than I hoped!"

"How?" Gretel spoke up, ready to leave this place and return to the gypsy camp.

"Lupa serves the Master," Kai grumbled. "Not surprising. I don't see how that gets us any further along."

Alice sighed at their ignorance. "Weren't you listening? She said that she serves *her*. Now we know the Master is female!"

Raising an eyebrow, Kai said, "That shortens the options to around half the total population of living beings."

But Alice just rolled her eyes as Gretel led them back to camp. He didn't understand. This shortened her list. However, now she didn't know what to make of the other face she'd accidentally seen in Kezia's vision. That face was a boy. She didn't know what to make of him.

*****

The white bear stopped in the center of a ring of mushrooms, breathing heavily. Jack and Wendy pulled the horses to a stop just as Isbjørn pulled off his fur cloak, human again. He grinned sheepishly.

"I'm getting too old for this," Isbjørn groaned as he lowered himself down onto the grass. "I haven't pulled a stunt like that in years. I'll need to rest a bit before we take the next leg. The fairy ring will glow if danger is near."

After slipping from his horse, Jack helped Wendy down to rest as well. It felt nice to stretch his legs. He led the horses to a creek running just past the mushrooms. Stooping down, he refilled their canteens and washed his face as the horses drank their fill. By the time he returned, Wendy and the wizard were in the midst of a conversation.

"She wasn't always like that, you know," Isbjørn was explaining, tone melancholy, "what you call *evil*. She used to be… happy, radiant, good."

"What happened, then?" Wendy asked, enthralled.

His gaze wandered as if remembering a face long forgotten. But Jack, of course, interrupted with his presence. He had a talent for interrupting things.

"What are we talking about?" Jack asked, sitting next to Wendy with some jerky to share.

Wendy accepted it gratefully. "He's talking about Carabosse."

"I'm not sure if *radiant* and *good* are words I'd associate with an evil sorceress."

"Certainly not now," Isbjørn agreed with no small measure of anger. "Carabosse has let her power consume her. At first, it was for leadership and praise. Now… I cannot imagine how it all changed. She's addicted to it, I imagine, to both power and magic. Magic and Power are not evil, mind you, nor are they good. They are only tools. But too much of anything turns to poison."

"How did you know her?" Wendy asked, interested to hear more. "Why does she hate you and your family so much?"

Isbjørn's mouth twitched. "Are you sure you want to hear an old man's tale? It could be a long one."

Wendy settled herself in the soft grass with her knees to her chest and placed her chin on her hands like an expectant child. "I love stories." Before Jack could question exactly how long this story was, she elbowed him in the ribs. "Jack likes stories, too."

His black eyes shone. "I wasn't always a wizard. Once, I was simply a prince with too much magic in his blood. A cursed prince, as it was, thanks to a witch's daughter who trapped me in a prison east of the sun and west of the moon until I married or wed her. Eventually my wife broke the curse. But broken curses never come without its side effects, and so I became the man you see before you."

"An old man?" Jack muttered.

"The Bear Wizard," Isbjørn corrected. "Age catches us all, if we're lucky."

Wendy just stared at him with more of a smile than she had before.

"Though we'd gone through our tribulations, my wife and I had a happy marriage. I had the title of Prince, but I didn't do much about it due to the peculiar situation. We lived in a small kingdom called Sol-Måne. It was many years before I happened upon the raven girl." His eyes drifted, seeing a face they couldn't. "She was leaning against a tree, not twelve years old, looking up at the ravens that flew about her. Kids from the village discovered her presence and taunted her, calling her witch and freak. She never spoke a word. She just waited for them to get close. Then, one by one, the ravens around her darted forward into the crowd of children like arrows. They scattered, screaming. I was the only one who remained.

"I took her in as my apprentice. She'd been abandoned by her family as a young girl when her powers began to emerge. The extent of her power even at that age was incredible. I helped her harness it, control it. She had such potential, such leadership. I remember once she'd gone to those very children who teased her and left with their admiration. Of course, I noticed her thirst for magic and power, how easy it was for her to slip back into impulsive ways, and I tried to help her through it."

"But you couldn't, and she turned evil because of a severe magic addiction," Jack guessed bluntly, earning another elbow in the ribs from Wendy.

Isbjørn shook his head. "No. That didn't happen until after. My wife and I had a daughter, Euna. Carabosse liked her well enough. Euna only ever smiled for her mother and Carabosse. I think it had something to do with my nose."

"Or the fact that you're part bear," Jack suggested under his breath.

"But I underestimated my situation before with the witch's daughter who'd cursed me," Isbjørn said with a growl. "She had died because of my broken curse. But I hadn't thought anything of it until I came home one day to find Euna alone crying in her crib, and a trail of blood and raven feathers leading into the Forest. The witch herself was waiting with my wife and Carabosse to avenge her daughter's death. She told me that one would die and one would live, and I had to choose. I begged and pleaded, but she was steadfast. I couldn't use my magic to save them. I couldn't do anything except choose who would die." He sighed and passed a hand over his face. "I chose Carabosse. But the witch smiled and slit my wife's throat before she vanished. Carabosse left after that, and I returned to my daughter."

Jack huffed with a scowl. "And you wonder how she turned evil..."

Isbjørn looked at him, leaned forward. "Tell me, if you were forced to choose between the woman you loved and an apprentice who trusted you, which would you choose to sacrifice?"

"I would sacrifice myself," he said without hesitation. "Every time."

"If only that were an option."

"But you'll never know, now."

"*Jack*," Wendy hissed.

Isbjørn held up his hand. "No, the lad is right. Believe me, I can never forgive myself for my actions, and I don't blame Carabosse for her hatred of me. However, that does not justify her actions, either. Perhaps I set her down the path the moment I took her off the streets or chose her to die over my wife, or perhaps it was her parents who abandoned her in the Forest, or the witch who told her a prophesy of her destruction, or the witch who kidnapped her and my wife to use as my punishment. I don't know if it's anyone's, everyone's, or no one's fault. But it has long since passed the point where the only fault for what Carabosse has become is herself."

Jack sat back, unsure what to make of it.

Wendy seemed to understand easily, though. "How do we defeat her?"

Isbjørn leaned back, stroking his beard. Black eyes dwelled on the dark sky above, the branches that cast shadows over his face. A silvery full moon was peaked from the circle of pine needles far above their heads.

Jack hoped Red was alright.

The wizard closed his eyes and sighed. "Carabosse was told that her reign would end at the hands of a disfigured human. As a means of warding this off, she cast a spell on herself that when the disfigured person killed her, then they too would die. Of course, I suspect this prophesy was false. Truly, it was Carabosse's spell that sealed her fate. Only a disfigured person will kill her, and if they do, they die."

"So, the disfigured person is the only one with the power to kill her?"

"Not that he or she is the only one who *can*, but rather the only one who will succeed. And they will die." Isbjørn shook his head sorrowfully. "This never would've happened if Carabosse hadn't cast that spell. So many lives would've been saved, terrors eradicated. But every time someone tries to stop something before it starts, they end up causing the worst of events. Always."

The mushrooms around them began to glow warily, growing brighter with every second. Jack jumped to his feet and fetched the horses. Wendy followed just behind him. Isbjørn chuckled, standing slowly and lazily shaking out his pelt.

"That'll be our cue," he announced. "Stay close."

As soon as they both mounted their horses and the white bear stood before them, they took off again. Jack looked up at the full moon and thought of Red.

Chapter Twenty-Six

Don't Close Your Eyes

"According to Gretel, we are a day away from Carabosse's fortress," Ingénu informed.

"Excellent," Clopin snapped, "now we can talk about what the devil we're going to do!"

"Was my plan not good enough?" Jim questioned with a scoff.

"Your *plan*, as you call it, went out the bloody window when we couldn't get into Chliobain! Besides, Jimmy, this is no thieves' ambush. We can't just barge in and hope all goes well."

Jim scowled, working his jaw. Red knew that look, but she didn't do anything about it. Her head hurt too much from last night.

"We cannot take on Carabosse without reinforcements," Esmeralda stated. "We must hope Wendy and Jack come through. Isbjørn and Grimrose are the only way to pull this off."

"But what about the enemy's reinforcements?" Ingénu questioned. "We have to assume Carabosse has tricks up her sleeve. After the incident outside Chliobain, we cannot rely on the element of surprise. If they work for Lupa, we should assume Carabosse has at least a small pack behind her. If they work for Fang..." He stopped briefly and turned to Red, in concern. "I apologize, Red. I know you think he changed, but if Fang still works for Carabosse, then the Pack..."

Clopin interjected, "What his highness is asking is if you are willing, no, *ready* to fight against your own kind?"

Red grit her teeth, trying her very best to keep herself under control. The effects of the full moon still weighed heavily on her, and she felt incredibly irritable. Frustration built in her chest. Four pairs of eyes looked at her expectantly, awaiting her answer.

"I am *not* the Pack," she growled. "I can and will do this whether you trust me or not. When you can all get it through her thick heads that I am not the enemy here, come talk to me."

Without another word, Red left the caravan, slammed the door behind her, and stepped into the rain. She let out a shaky breath. Tense anger threatened to consume her, and she tried to release it with every exhale. Her muscles shook. Everything ached from trying to control the Wolf last night.

When Red opened her eyes, she caught them staring. It didn't matter who, just *them*. Everyone. They either feared her for what she was or judged her for hiding it for so long. After what Kezia told her, how could she even trust herself?

She found it hard to breathe, hurrying through the caravans, then disappearing into the surrounding trees beyond the reach of those distrusting eyes. Collapsing against a trunk, she sank to the muddy ground. Knees hugged to her chest. Red leaned her head against the wet bark and let the rain fall on her face.

She wanted to cry, but the tears didn't come. She wanted to scream, but her voice didn't obey. She wanted to disappear, but even the magic didn't listen to her desires. For once, she didn't even care that she was without her cloak in the Forest. Let the monsters come.

"I don't know if I can do this anymore," she sighed.

"You're right."

Red jumped at the voice, sharp eyes finding the source instantly. Alice stood there, wet and serious. Without asking, she came over and sat down beside Red without even acknowledging the mud.

Red blinked, wondering if she'd heard it right. "What?"

"You're right."

Her brow creased suspiciously.

"What? Did you expect me to disagree?" Alice questioned.

Red hadn't expected an answer at all. But it was unusual. Maybe Kai would've agreed, but Alice?

Alice sighed as if she knew what Red was thinking. "Red, I haven't known you that long. I won't pretend that I'm close to knowing all about you. But I know how you feel."

Red hated that statement. Anytime someone tried to relate to her, they fell sorely short of it. It was a trick people used to get her to look away from her own struggles and sympathize with theirs.

"Do you?" she huffed.

But Alice didn't talk about herself. Instead, she talked about Red. "Every day in the Facility, they tried to break you and punish you for something you knew was true because the Enchanted Forest gave you marks you couldn't ignore no matter how much you might've wanted to. When there was a chance for escape, you took it despite the fact you had to expose a part of you that you were afraid for your friends to see. You continued to expose the Wolf in Wonderland when you realized you didn't have to hide it anymore, and you worked through its restraint in Neverland proving that you're still strong without it. And here, in this dreadful and miraculous place, you've somehow managed to survive and even thrive with or without the Wolf."

"I'm not sure where you're getting at."

"You are strong. But the fact is, no matter how strong you are, you can't do everything alone. Not here, not anywhere. As far as I can tell, every time you've been strong, you've had people help you along the way." Alice sighed, looking up at the rain. "You've always had people who care about you. Always. Don't pretend like you have to go through this alone."

Red looked at her, finding herself surprised more and more by Alice. But whether she meant to or not, those words sank in and branded her heart. She was glad for the rain. She was afraid her eyes were welling up.

"I think that's the longest I've heard you talk without a single question," Red voiced, the closest thing she could come to thanks without feeling petty.

Alice laughed to the sky. "I ask so many questions only because I'm willing to answer any questions if I can."

"Even if I asked what you meant when you said you knew exactly how I felt?"

"Perhaps not *exactly*. I'm not a wolf, after all. But I know what it's like when everyone seems to look at you as if you're a strange creature impossible to understand, so much so you begin to wonder if they're right."

Red frowned. "Are you really comparing my being a Wolf to your time in the Facility?"

Alice rolled her head around to look at her. Her blue eyes seemed to defy the rain that fell off her eyelashes. She raised an eyebrow curiously. "You assumed that the Facility was my first experience in an insane asylum?"

Red didn't respond. Somehow, Alice became an entirely different girl in a matter of seconds. Perhaps they were more alike than she thought.

Then Alice shifted. "But that's not why I came to find you. We figured out the Master's a woman, so I've limited down the possibilities of her identity to two people so far, and Carabosse is one of them."

"But how did you find out the Master is a woman?"

"I talked to Lupa."

Red sat up straight. "When?"

"Last night." Before Red could even begin to process this, Alice held up a hand. "We were perfectly safe. I brought Kai and Gretel, and we all came back unbitten and victorious. The only reason we didn't take you was because it was a full moon and it was Lupa. Kai didn't think that would end well."

Red felt the urge to protest, but she clamped her mouth shut. She hated it when Kai was right.

"Anyway, with this in mind, we have to go into this witch hunt as if Carabosse is indeed the Master we're looking for," Alice explained urgently. "Kai and I know slim to nothing about her or this place. We need you. So, what do you need?"

Mind racing, Red thought back to the meeting she'd just left about the attack on Carabosse. "I need to know what her reinforcements are," she decided. "We know about her, but Ingénu suspects she has tricks up her sleeve."

"That's simple enough." Alice smiled, hopping to her feet. "I don't believe you've been formally introduced to Kezia."

*****

When they arrived at Grimrose, Jack expected to find a graveyard of goblins. He found it more disturbing to find only the occasional remnants of the rock monkeys. He tried not to imagine what hungry monsters had found their dinner.

The white bear stopped just past the wall. He lazily waved his massive head from side to side, taking in the entirety of it. Despite whatever caution Jack had with Isbjørn, he felt bad for the old man. This kingdom was Isbjørn's home. Now it was reduced to a prison of stone, and he hadn't been able to stop it.

Because he left.

A chill of nostalgia suddenly shot down Jack's spine. Guilt ate at his insides as he realized who was he to judge this man? He'd caused awful things to happen to people he loved. And he left them.

Wendy urged her horse forward to stand beside the white bear. Reaching out, she easily placed a comforting hand on his shoulder. His black eyes looked back at her kindly.

Facing the road before them, Isbjørn took off in a streak of white. Jack and Wendy hastened to catch up, dashing through a cloud of sprites. Statues stared at them blankly as they zipped by. At some point, the rain receded, which was a relief.

They flew past the gates and entered the castle on horseback. By the time they slipped off their horses, Isbjørn had removed his fur and stood before the figures of the king and queen. Tears welled in his black eyes. Gingerly, the wizard touched the queen's angered face.

"I'm so sorry, my dear girl," he whispered. He took in a shaky breath, the tears only making his low voice rumble as he spoke up for them to hear, "She hardly ever smiled, you know. So strong-willed and brave, but serious beyond my comprehension. After she married Thrushbeard, she started smiling more. Each one was a gift."

Wendy's hand slipped into Jack's. He squeezed it.

Jaw set in determination, Isbjørn turned and swept to the source of the blast. He faced his son-in-law resolutely. Hesitantly, Jack and Wendy stepped back.

"Remember this," Isbjørn thundered at them, gathering his strength. "We may not always be able to do anything but stand against the atrocities that happen around us. But if you are at the precipice facing the choice to stand firm or fight…"

Isbjørn paused and the wind picked up around him. Jack waited for the rest of the old man's wisdom. But he ground his teeth as if restraining a boiling power inside until it raged.

"What?" Jack shouted over the wind, overcome with suspense. "What do you do?"

Black eyes looked up at him and winked. "That's entirely up to you."

With a jolt, Isbjørn thrust out his arms and released his spell. Magic blasted every which way. Stone melted away like rain. Thrushbeard was the first to move, charging toward Isbjørn furiously. Then he stumbled, legs stiff, and realization lit his eyes.

"Isbjørn?" King Thrushbeard blinked, taking in the sight of the wizard and his wet companions.

Before Isbjørn could explain, Queen Euna stumbled up and met her father sullenly. They looked at each other, something in their eyes Jack could not understand. Isbjørn took her hands and pressed them to his bowed head.

"You are here?" Euna asked softly.

He nodded, exposing his tears.

Gently, she removed one of her hands and lifted his chin so he wound look her in the eye. "That is enough."

It was forgiveness beyond anything Jack had ever seen.

*****

Red followed Alice to the blind girl's caravan, wondering how this plan was supposed to work. Alice knocked on the door before they stepped in. Kezia wasn't there.

Before Red could ask about it, the door opened behind them and two kids stood there: Kezia and Hansel. Both were flushed, smiling, and drenched. The lucky piggy sat curled up on Hansel's shoulder.

"You were right!" Hansel announced brightly, panting. "They're here!"

Her grin widened. "I thought so. Thanks for taking me back; I'm sorry you had to miss the rest of the game."

"Nah, that's fine." Hansel shrugged, helping Kezia into the caravan. "The rain was upsetting Lucky, anyway. See you later, Kezia!" He waved as he ran off into the rain.

Reaching out and feeling her way closer to them, Kezia's face was still flushed. She stared up at them with white eyes. "What is it you would like to know?"

Red looked at Alice uncertainly, but she silently urged her. Clearing her throat, Red turned to the girl. She was so small.

"We need to know who Carabosse's allies are," Red said at last. "If she has any tricks up her sleeve and, if it comes down to it, how can we kill her."

Kezia's smile waned. Returning to her cushion, she held out her hands. "I can show you. But we can't stay long. It hurts when they look back."

Without question for once, Alice plopped down beside the girl and beckoned for Red to join. Still unsure, Red joined. Kezia gently reached out and placed her hands on both Alice's and Red's forearms. She waited, preparing herself.

Kezia gasped and clutched them tightly. "Now."

A jolt shot up her arm and her vision blackened then changed. It was like looking through a window. Red wanted to flinch back, but the pressure in her arm held firm. She felt like a ghost, invisible and present, yet not quite *there*.

The room was black and dimly lit all around. Three people stood in the room, and she recognized two of them. Her skin crawled and gut churned, but the grip on her arm reminded her that she was watching for a reason.

A woman with raven hair and reflective eyes stood in the center of the room with arms outstretched. Eyes rolled to the back of her head. She chanted words Red couldn't understand. Powerful words. Dangerous words. Red didn't feel good at all about this ritual.

Fang stood as far away as he could, wrestling with the cuff around his wrist. But Lupa watched with hungry curiosity.

The ground shook and stone cracked. A boney, grotesque hand shot from the chasm. The thing that crawled out of the hole was beyond description, barely humanoid, pieced together with flesh, bone, earth and stone. Its eyes flamed and sparked.

Lupa stalked closer in interest as the creature squirmed on the floor and gargled out strangely. "Beautiful," she muttered, gold eyes gleaming.

Red watched in horror as more of the monsters rose from the chasm squealing.

Fang scowled. "What is this?"

The chanting woman's gaze fell on him, a small smirk on her lips. "Meet your reinforcements. Difficult to kill and in excellent supply."

A foot as thick as a tree trunk burst from the stone, sending up a spray of rubble. From the hole, a roar pierced the air.

Carabosse looked right at Red and smiled.

Chapter Twenty-Seven

Convincing a Gypsy

"The Pack *and* demons," Clopin grumbled. "This keeps getting better and better."

"I'm only telling you what I saw," Red clarified sternly. "And what I heard, from both Carabosse and Kezia."

"If Fang and Lupa are there, then the Pack cannot be far behind," Esmeralda said levelly.

"I understand that, but—"

The door burst open and in came Alice with an armload of wooden figures and Kai and Briar following just behind her. Instantly, the caravan was packed. Despite the nuisance, Alice and her companions dropped the figures onto a table in the center.

"What the devil?!" Clopin exclaimed as he wrestled away from Jim and Ingénu.

"We've got a plan," Alice announced with an accomplished grin.

"I must be losing my mind!"

"That's too bad. Maybe we can pull together a search party after the battle."

"Are you serious?" He turned to Red accusingly. "Is she serious?"

Red shrugged in response.

Clopin turned back to Alice who was trying to arrange the figures on the table, none of which looked remotely similar to typical representations for battle strategy.

* * *

He scowled, clearly losing control. *"C'est fou!* You are out of your league here, girl."

Alice froze in placing a wooden pig at the far end of the table. Slowly, she raised her eyes to meet Clopin's and straightened her spine. Even Red almost shifted on her feet from the look in Alice's eyes.

"Have any of you been in a war?" Alice asked easily, concealed bitterness in the back of her voice. "No, let me rephrase. How did you learn to fight?"

Clopin stared at her. "What does this have to do with anything?"

She placed both hands on the table. "Humor me."

Grinding his teeth, Clopin remained silent. Alice never broke her stare. When the awkward silence reached its peak, Kai cleared his throat beside her. "My father taught me."

There was another pause before Ingénu spoke up as well, "I learned growing up training to be a knight."

Briar shrugged. "I'm not a swordswoman, but I grew up in a rough area in Chliobain; had to learn to defend myself."

"I learned from my parents," Red chipped in, appreciating the discomfort this was giving Clopin. "Then I forced myself to get better."

"I wasn't taught much of anything besides what I picked up when I ended up here," Jim admitted solemnly.

Esmeralda looked at Clopin, but he wouldn't look at her. "My brother taught me."

Eye practically twitching now, Clopin narrowed his gaze. Alice wouldn't relent until finally Clopin gave in. "I've been fighting my whole life," he hissed, "from the backstreets of Paris to the steps of Notre Dame and this bloody Forest."

Satisfied, Alice shrugged. "I learned fencing growing up. Later, I had this roommate in an asylum, Rhoda. She was something of a gymnast, deemed crazy, and enjoyed teaching me while I was there. Now, I tend to improvise."

"An insane asylum," Clopin muttered. "That explains a lot."

Alice leaned against the table, looked him dead in the eye. "But the bulk of fighting I learned at war. Battles are not the same. Believe me. So don't you dare say that I'm out of my league here. I'm the only one qualified."

Jaw tight, Clopin held her gaze. Without a word, he gestured at the table invitingly. Red didn't bother to hold back her smile. Immediately, Briar and Kai arranged the pieces while Alice explained the plan. Briar interjected a few times since she was the only one of them who'd been to Carabosse's fortress before, and thus knew the layout.

Ingénu frowned, unsure. "But what you're proposing, it relies heavily on chance."

"I don't see it," Clopin grumbled, arms crossed.

"We are constantly aware of things we can't see," Briar snapped. "I'd trust something I know is right but I can't see over something I know is wrong but I can see."

"This is your best option," Kai added firmly. "If we wait around here, it won't be long before we've given the upper hand to the witch. Waiting would give her time to make more of her demon army and even strike us off guard."

"I agree," Jim spoke up, pushing past Clopin. "We should attack them before they attack us."

Ingénu sighed. "I do not like the idea of attacking before Grimrose arrives. Even without the demon army, no one knows how many are in the Pack. We are easily outnumbered."

Red shook her head, readying herself to relay the rest of what she'd learned with Kezia. "I know this is a lot to ask. This plan seems incredibly lenient on chance. But I told Alice not to come here until she confirmed with Kezia a plan with the greatest chance of success and the least amount of bloodshed."

"The *least*?" Esmeralda questioned.

Glancing at Red, Alice grimly held up her fingers. "Three. An enemy, an innocent, and an ally. The longer we wait, the higher the price. If we do nothing, still higher goes the cost."

There was a long silence as those words sunk in.

"I pray that the one enemy be Carabosse," Ingénu spoke, earning a pleased grin from his wife. "That is what I shall fight for."

Jim shrugged. "I'm too cooped up here anyway."

Esmeralda nodded solemnly, but her eyes were lowered cryptically. Red recognized that look. She was planning something.

Clopin sneered. "You're all raving mad!"

Alice snickered.

Elbowing past the others standing between him and Red, Clopin narrowed his eyes at her. "Even if this plan *does* work, you have yet to explain exactly how you suppose we get in. No one has penetrated Carabosse's fortress before. The princess here is the only exception, and that's only

* * *

because of some bloody curse of her own. We can't go skipping through the front gate!"

Red raised an eyebrow. "Leave it to me."

Remaining in the shadows, the Wolf was invisible in the night. Wrought iron gates stood over her like a giant. The fortress beyond sent chills down her spine. She was glad the full moon had passed. Facing down an army of wolves was hard enough.

She sniffed cautiously at the gate, her nose tingling. No metal. It had to be magic. Best to stay away from it, just in case it set off a warning to Carabosse for unexpected visitors.

Keeping her footsteps light, she circled the outer wall. There was no backdoor, no other means of entrance. Perhaps they could scale the wall, but there was no way of telling what lay on the other side. She couldn't smell or hear anything past it.

Resorting to Alice's backup plan, the Wolf rounded the wall again until she found a patch of foliage creeping up its side. Her heart raced and ears buzzed. Magic. Strong and unstable.

She backed into the Forest and sat in the trees. And waited. Excessive magic was always a conductor for monsters. The first to arrive were either close or powerful.

Four gnomes skittered up and sat beside the Wolf. Their diamond eyes stared at the wall, drinking in the magic like it was sugar. Still, the Wolf waited.

Her ears pricked at the soft footfalls behind her. Forcing her breath to steady even as her skin crawled, Red shifted form and remained absolutely still. The gnomes shifted uncomfortably, some even hissing at whatever monster approached.

Long fingers landed on her shoulder one by one. She didn't flinch. The grip tightened. She didn't move until she felt the bones snap and move under its skin. Even skin cells itched as they turned in on themselves.

She grasped the monster's hand fast. It seized, frozen in mid-transformation. Working her jaw and breathing heavily, Red allowed the magic to seep through the shapeshifter like a filter. The shapeshifter writhed, but she didn't relent. Spell enhancing, Red watched from behind her eyelashes as the wall flickered in and out of focus.

When her breath came short, she released the shapeshifter. It pulled back and retreated into the Forest without her ever seeing it. The gnomes skittered around in a frenzy, gnashing at the air.

Burning the spot in her memory, she shifted to the Wolf and slipped into the Forest as if she'd never been there at all.

Chapter Twenty-Eight

Ravens and Demons

Silent as the wind, every gypsy followed Red lightly and carefully through the Forest. She didn't wear her cloak, but for once she didn't feel exposed without it. Both Alice and Kai followed directly behind her, their presence calming despite everything. They encountered few ravens. But every flutter earned an archer who brought the bird down, another gypsy catching it before it hit the ground.

When they reached the illusion, Red motioned them closer. In a whisper, she warned, "There's no telling what lies on the other side. Keep alert. Prepare for anything."

As the message was passed down, Red took a deep breath, fitted an arrow, and stepped through the wall. It was like walking through mist, hardly there and gone in an instant. The others followed behind.

The courtyard was empty.

Silence lay heavily, thick as the dark. Red's muscles tensed. Cautiously, she walked closer to the fortress. Their quiet steps pounded in her ears like thunder. The hair on the back of her neck stood on end.

Alice came up beside her. "Something isn't right."

The darkness stirred. Moonlight glow rippled around them with a rustle like the cold wind against silk. Red's heart throbbed in her throat.

"Why is it so dark?" Jim muttered somewhere behind her.

"It's night; of course it's dark!" Clopin hissed.

"Even the night isn't so black," Kai said gravely, "especially with a clear sky and such a moon overhead."

The gentle crackle like sand falling on glass swept past her ears. Red's eyes flicked back and forth.

"Darkness doesn't stir," Esmeralda breathed.

The noise grew louder like a thousand whistling leaves with a soft breath against her skin. Moonlight reflected off a thousand gleaming feathers. She recognized the scent.

Diablo.

Eyes widening, Red cried out, "Shield yourselves! The ravens are upon us!"

A thousand birds' screams split the air. Legions of ravens descended upon them in a massive cloud. Red shot blindly before she was forced to resort to her blade when the ravens came with beak and talons. Stinging pain grew to burning intensity. Beating chaos completely overwhelmed her. They aimed at all angles, stabbing her ankles, scratching her arms. Red tried to shield her face with one arm and tear down ravens with the other.

Her breath cut short as she felt the birds swarm around her. She screamed, hyperventilated. They were being suffocated.

Wind blasted the feathers from her face. Blinding light pierced through the swallowing darkness. When Red dared to open her eyes, she found Briar standing in the center of the aura. Silver light radiated from her raised hands. Her eyes were swirling pools of the galaxies. Ravens swirled around her, building up the gust that blew her ginger hair around like a hurricane. But they couldn't reach her. They were spinning out of control.

● ● ●

"I have spun the fabric of the stars and skies, and I spilled my blood to enact the curse your master bestowed upon me!" Briar's voice echoed over the wind and the ravens until even the Forest beyond the wall seemed to bow from her power. "My curse has been broken. The power of starlight is mine!"

Terror screeched as a pulse of fierce light seared the ravens. It stripped the blackness from their feathers where it directly touched.

"Go back to the shadows," Briar commanded, "and do not return or melt to the darkness you've made yourselves to be!"

A tornado of black and silver ravens rushed past with a thunderclap. Cawing in fear, they flew to the Forest. The light vanished. Briar lowered her arms in exhaustion, breathing heavily. Ingénu caught her elbow before she could collapse. Everyone stared at her in utter disbelief.

Briar shrugged. "Well, I'm not sure where that came from, but I won't be able to do it again."

Recovering from the shock beating through her, Red looked around at her army. Raven bodies littered the ground. Thick blood drenched the soil. But the birds were the only corpses.

She turned to Alice who simply shrugged. "I suppose not everything can go according to plan," Alice admitted.

Without warning, the ground shook and split before them. Dirt sprayed as an enormous arm shot up from the earth. The cumbersome creature rose, revealing its massive body pieced together with earth, rock, and bone long buried. Its eyes sparked like a wildfire.

The earth cracked again, another enormous demon emerging. Smaller demons crawled out after them. Still more were coming.

Clopin shouted indistinct profanity. It was taken up as a battle cry just before they charged.

In the chaos, Red slipped away.

She met with Esmeralda around the side of the fortress as they'd discussed. In one hand, the gypsy held a stick and dagger. In the other, she held an unusual sword Red wanted to keep well away from. Without a word, Esmeralda held out the dagger. Red grimly accepted it.

"Are you sure about this?" Red asked uncertainly.

Esmeralda nodded. "Carabosse wants to be killed by someone imperfect, disfigured. So, make it quick; be certain it's permanent. Just keep away from the eyes."

Smokey eyes blazing, Esmeralda placed the stick between her teeth and bit down hard. Red steeled herself. Before she could allow herself to overthink it, she gripped the dagger and carved into her friend's face.

*****

When the battle outside began, Fang realized that whatever happened tonight, it wouldn't end here. So long as Carabosse lived, she would never release him or the Pack from her control. He knew he could never kill her. Rubbing the cuff around his wrist, Fang knew he was bound to Carabosse beyond what he could perceive. But the Pack wasn't, and neither was Zoë. If he could get them away, then at least Carabosse wouldn't be able to control the ones he loved.

But through him, she could…

His spine straightened. His heart grieved at the idea, but this could be the only way to save his wife and his people.

Spinning the plan in his mind, Fang turned to enter to room where the Pack awaited orders to attack. It was overflowing. Even the cubs were trapped here. But Lupa was not. Fang realized that was for the best.

The wolves instantly hushed as soon as they realized his presence. Thaddeus, Lev, and Quinn made their way up to him, Lycaon not far behind.

"What orders have you brought, Alpha?" Lycaon asked, his voice smooth, too anxious to spill blood this night.

Fang kept his face stone. Ignoring Lycaon, he stepped closer to Thaddeus. "Get everyone to the open-air landing behind the outer courtyard. There will be enough room, and the fresh air should ease everyone."

"What are you planning?" Thaddeus questioned, hushed.

"No wolf will die tonight if I can help it," Fang responded, his tone almost a growl. "If I am not back by first light, take the Pack and leave without me." Raising his voice so the others closest to him could hear, he declared, "Should I not return, I trust Thaddeus with command as Alpha."

Thaddeus accepted solemnly, but assured, "It will not come to that."

Fang clasped his friend's hand. "I pray not. But if so, that's what I wish."

"So it shall be."

With a final look at his friends, though Quinn and Lev seemed saddened and Lycaon's expression was solemn, Fang turned and left. He heard Thaddeus order the Pack to make for the open-air landing. His throat tightened, but he didn't turn back. Eyes darkening in determination, he left in search for Zoë.

He didn't see the gold eyes glittering in the shadows or hear the lurking figure slip into a hidden passageway completely undetected.

*****

Moving fast, Kai rolled under the giant demon's belly to split it open. His blade scratched against stone harmlessly. Taken by surprise, the demon whipped around and smashed Kai to the side. His breath abandoned him instantly. He lay gasping, aching.

At the first sign of movement, Kai rolled out of the way before the enormous foot could smash him to pieces. He scrambled to his feet and ran behind the demon. Rocks jutted out of its back in perfect footholds. Quickly, Kai leaped up onto the demon's spine and climbed, out of reach and holding on tight. He brought his blade down into the demon's skull. It went deep and stuck.

The demon thrashed about, trying to get him off. Kai held fast. But the blade had done nothing. When one of the gypsies tried to help, he drove his sword into the demon's throat and came away with a shower of dirt. The demon swept him away.

Finding himself in an impossible position, Kai held tightly to the sword in the demon's head. It wasn't until an archer put two arrows in its sparking eyes that the demon screamed in pain and fell down dead.

Picking himself up, Kai retrieved his sword. He breathed heavily.

In an instant, Kai was knocked off his feet, thrown away from a leaping humanoid creature. He looked back at his rescuer. He recognized the wild blond hair and young brown eyes.

"You shouldn't be here," Kai said to the boy, springing to his feet to stab the smaller demon through the eye. It gargled, the other eye sputtering, then went limp.

"I wanted to help," Hansel insisted, hoisting up his short sword. "I got two already! And Gretel—"

"Gretel shouldn't be here either," Kai interjected. "Where is she?"

Hansel pointed behind him. A massive demon crawled over the remains of its kin. Before Kai could raise his broadsword, a figure leaped onto the its head and drove a blade into each of its eyes. The creature fell dead in a pile of earth and rubble. The attacker whipped back her hood, exposing Gretel's pale face and fearful eyes.

"That was *amazing!*" Hansel cried enthusiastically.

Gretel brushed her short blonde hair behind her ear. Kai sighed, looking between the two stowaways. Alice's words about the victims tonight haunted him. He wasn't about to let these two be the Innocent who was to die tonight.

Sheathing his sword, Kai took Hansel around the waist and hoisted him up onto his shoulder. The kid shouted in protest, but Kai ignored him. With his free hand, he grasped Gretel's hand and dragged her behind him as he wove through the battlefield. Thankfully, she kept pace with him.

Gretel screamed, jerking back. Hansel wiggled ferociously. Whipping around, Kai found a demon dragging Gretel back by the ankle. Using his foot, Kai crushed the demon's head in. Dirt crumbled and bone cracked. Its eyes still sputtered, but it was weakened as it repaired itself. Kai helped Gretel up and they ran toward the invisible exit.

When they reached it, Kai took Hansel off his shoulder and looked at both of them grimly. "You two need to get out of here."

"But I want to fight!" Hansel argued. "Gretel killed a cannibal witch, and we fought those trolls, and—"

"This isn't a game; it's not safe."

"We're not kids," Gretel shot, expression steely as she held a firm arm around Hansel's shoulders.

A jab of déjà vu hit him at that. With a sigh, Kai said in complete seriousness, "I know. I can see that. But you need to go back, protect those who remain. If things go bad here, then we can't have this witch get her hands on the people back in the caravans."

"So, you want us to run?"

"I want you to live."

Gretel sighed, looking out at the chaos behind him. Without a word, she nodded, took Hansel's hand, and left.

When Kai stood to return to the battlefield, his gaze swept over it all. The Woodsman and Clopin stood positioned over the cracks, taking out the demons as they emerged from the earth. Relief flooded when he saw Alice alive and swinging.

He heard the roar before he realized his guard was down. Flipping around, Kai swung his broadsword into the demon's jaw. Using all his strength, he yanked out his weapon and slammed it in the side of the demon's head. Gravel sprayed. He took out its eyes and it went down.

Light blasted, blinding him temporarily. He blinked away the swimming spots in his vision, turning to find the source. For a moment, he thought he saw a polar bear standing beside him. But it was a giant of a man with a long white beard and black eyes.

"I certainly won't be doing something that big for a while," the man huffed for breath. "Now, where did everyone go?"

"*Wrong side of the wall!*"

Kai frowned. Was that Jack?

"Hurry up, then!" the old man urged. "It's only an illusion."

A thud rammed against the wall.

"Not that part!" he scolded.

Kai leaped back when someone fell through the wall illusion with a big grin on his face. "Found it!" Jack called in victory. "Did anyone call for reinforcements?"

At his words, a legion of knights flooded through the opening, charging into battle with a clamor of armor. Demons rushed to meet them. But Kai raced for the wall just as Wendy burst through.

"Kai!" Jack grinned up at him. "Little help?"

Grasping his hand, Kai pulled him to his feet. Alice soon appeared beside him, dark blood and dirt splattering her face. Wendy instantly gave them both hugs.

"I was afraid we'd be too late!" Wendy confessed.

Jack looked around. "Where's Rubes?"

With a frown, Kai turned to Alice. She chewed her lip and looked back at the fortress. No one knew. But they could guess.

*****

Red led Esmeralda through the fortress, following the scent of magic. Her hands were stained with her friend's blood. But Esmeralda didn't complain, even with her face carved and burned. Red wasn't sure it would be enough.

"Brace yourself," Esmeralda advised as they ran, her voice hoarse. "She's been known to use your worst demons against you."

"Only the worst ones?" Red muttered.

Esmeralda didn't respond.

Racing into the throne room, the doors slammed shut behind them and locked. Red's skin crawled. Esmeralda stood frozen facing the figure that awaited them in the shadows. Instantly, Red felt uneasy.

"Well, well," a deadly smooth voice crooned. "This is a pleasant surprise."

Chapter Twenty-Nine

Three

Red didn't have any time to react before Carabosse raised a hand and everything went out of focus. Her head swam. She looked to Esmeralda, but only saw a blur beside her. Carabosse herself was only shadow.

Spine tingling, Red snaked her head around until she found the one figure she could see all too clearly. He was bigger than her, muscular, with big hands that were too used to taking whatever he wanted with as much pain as possible. His bald head shone with faded black and blue tattoos. A full blue beard hung over his chest.

He was supposed to be dead.

And Red smiled. She finally understood why the monsters in the Forest always seemed to smile. Beasts only bared their teeth as a warning before they attack.

Bluebeard raised one bushy eyebrow before he too grinned under that awful beard of his. She dropped her sword, her bow, her arrows.

Red charged. He waited for her, crouched low, arms out in front of him. She ducked from a sweep of his arms, blocking every blow. She was stronger now. He couldn't hit her. At the height of his frustration, she drew a curved dagger and struck him seven times. One for each face remembered, for each girl she'd left behind.

In one swift movement, she sank the dagger in between his legs and left it there, standing straight while she watched him sink to his knees in pain. He shook at her feet, screaming. Shivering, he fell over, skin grey.

"You think he is the worst of my demons?" Red questioned, her eyes still on Bluebeard as he bled out at her feet.

When your worst demon is yourself, no one can use it against you, she thought to herself.

Bluebeard melted into the floor. Everything came back into focus.

Instantly, Red shifted and sprang for the sorceress with claws extended. Carabosse waved her hand and an invisible force tossed the Wolf to the side. Skidding to the floor, Red changed back without intending to, her hand hovering over the blade at her waist.

"I heard about your new transformation, Scarlet Thief," Carabosse smirked. "I must say, it quite becomes you."

Red sneered. A Wolf again, she bounded for the witch snarling. Again, she was thrown aside, shifting in midair, and collided with a column and collapsed. Pain throbbed down her back. Blood ran down her temple.

"Your charade nearly cost me my bounty-hunter. *Nearly*," Carabosse chuckled. "I took care of that, though."

Red crawled to her feet, feigning a limp. Retrieving her fallen bow, she had an arrow aimed instantaneously and watched it fly. Carabosse caught it in midair without flinching. The arrow turned to dust. An invisible force threw Red off her feet again. She hit her head hard. Stars danced before her eyes.

"You are so feisty, unrelenting. How admirable and completely idiotic. I am almost tempted to see how long you'd try." Carabosse's voice dripped over her like poison. "However, I cannot have you too bruised."

Spires of thorns shot out from the floor around Red, stretching up and weaving into each other to form a cage around her. She tried to break the branches, but the vines were too thick. She shot an arrow through a gap in the prison, but a thorny tendril shot up and snapped the arrow in midair. Red cursed, drawing her sword to chop her way out. It was in vain.

"Don't hurt yourself," the sorceress mocked concern.

Suddenly, Carabosse whipped around, drawing a sword hidden in her robes. The blade collided with the two swords boring down toward her. Esmeralda swept her swords away, spinning around and bringing a series of smooth blows, always on the attack, forcing the sorceress to defense. Red watched helplessly as both gypsy and witch moved in fluid motion. Swords flashed like silver moonlight.

Esmeralda used both swords to clamp down on Carabosse's, tearing them all away. She drew the one tied to her waist, the one radiating power. As if on its own, the blade drove into the belly of the beast.

Carabosse gasped, eyes bulging. Esmeralda's wounded face was grim with victory as she watched the witch's face gape at her.

Then Carabosse smiled. She cackled, her wicked face turning skyward as her laughter grew.

"Sword Kladenets? The enchanted self-swinging sword?" Carabosse grasped the blade with her hand and looked Esmeralda dead in the eyes. "It will take a lot more than a magic sword and a scarred face to kill me."

Blood oozed from her hand as she pulled the sword from her core. She tossed the sword aside, it landing with a clatter. Blood dripping from her fingertips, Carabosse leaned close and hissed in Esmeralda's ear, "You, however, are *mortal*."

Esmeralda flew backwards and hit the wall painfully. She struggled to free herself, but she was pasted to the surface. Red saw the hovering blade first, crying out a warning in vain. The sword shot forward, stopping a breath away from Esmeralda's throat. Desperately, she grasped the blade to try pulling it away. Blood dribbled down the gypsy's hands and arms.

Carabosse snickered, sweeping closer, relishing in the scene. "Why struggle?" She cocked her head. "They all seem to struggle, even when they know the inevitable. I suppose it's just desperation to cling to life, no matter how brief a time remains. They fight for those pointless seconds, those painful, fearful seconds. Fear of the unknown, it keeps us fighting. It keeps us alive."

Esmeralda scowled, wrestling against the sword. "I do not fear death."

Carabosse creased her brow curiously. "Then why do you fight it if you do not fear it?"

The gypsy's face contorted to almost pity. "Because you do."

Carabosse raised her eyebrows in surprise.

A roar sounded, quaking the walls. Red stopped her attempts of escape, peaking through the vines to find the source of the noise. A bulking figure threw himself upon Carabosse, knocking them both to the ground. Clashing bronze split the air. Carabosse whipped around to blast her attacker to bits, then froze.

Red's heart leaped to her throat.

Frozen in shock, Carabosse's hands shook as Quasimodo glared down at her ferociously.

"Quasi!" Esmeralda gasped out.

Blue and green eyes looked to her, telling a story beyond words. His expression softened.

Carabosse snapped out of her daze, shooting her hand out to cast a spell when Quasi grasped her wrist with scarred fingers. With his massive hand, he clutched the witch's throat and squeezed. Eyes bulging, Carabosse clawed at his skin with talon-like nails. She looked so helpless. Quasi hesitated, and in that moment, Carabosse unveiled a hidden knife and buried the blade in his chest.

Red froze in shock. Esmeralda screamed.

Quasimodo fell, blood flowering from his chest. Face ashen and eyes bloodshot, Carabosse smiled and turned for Esmeralda, raising a fiery hand. A blade sprouted from her abdomen and she gasped, eyes wide. Blood dribbled from the corners of her mouth. Her face contorted in pure terror.

A bell hit the back of her head with the clear, sharp bong of bronze, clattering to the ground with its edge stained crimson. Carabosse crumpled. Sword Kladenets stuck out of her spine. Black hair was soaked with blood. Quasimodo stood heaving with exhaustion behind her, then collapsed once again.

Neither got up.

The sword rattled to the floor. Esmeralda ran for her fallen friend, desperately seeking life in his ashen face. But Quasi was gone. The dragon carved knife protruded from his chest. Weeping mournfully, Esmeralda clung to Quasimodo's lifeless body.

A large raven appeared out of nowhere and settled atop Carabosse's corpse. He picked at her black hair, but no one paid him heed.

Recovering from her shock, Red slashed her blade through the thorns once again, breaking free from her prison. She took one look at the scene before her, a knot in her throat threatening to choke her. Shock overwhelmed her more than grief. It filled her with cool emptiness.

Blinking back tears, Red set her jaw, grasped her blade and bow, turned and ran. Despite the death of Carabosse, this still wasn't over.

The raven followed, leaving his dead mistress.

*****

The odds of the battle between demon and man shifted with the coming of the Grimrose battalion. But more still emerged from the cracks in the earth.

With Alice nearby to fend off any enemy, Wendy rushed to help Aurore shove a large demon off her legs. Heaving mightily, both girls could not find the strength to make it budge.

"Where's Ingénu?" Wendy questioned, driving her heels into the ground for better leverage.

Aurore shook her head. "I don't know. I lost him in the chaos of it all."

Alice chopped down a goblin that leapt toward them, the carcass landing near to stare up at her with hollowed eyes. Wendy winced, trying harder to free Aurore from the demon's mass.

"Does he know of the child?" she asked, voice strained with the effort.

"How did you...?" Aurore stopped herself before shaking her head once more. "No, not yet. It was supposed to be a surprise."

"Would he have let you fight if he knew?"

"Why do you think I haven't told him?"

"*Watch out!*" Alice cried, ducking her head.

A humungous demon flew limply through the air sailing straight for them. Wendy crouched low over Aurore. It collided with the other carcass with a smash, rolling off and away. Aurore cried out at the blow. But Wendy was pleased to find the demon had moved back from the impact, though not by much. Shoving herself against the mass again, Wendy found the challenge just as difficult as before.

When she looked up, Alice was nowhere to be seen. A horde of demons ran for them. Frantic, Wendy shuffled back, grasped Aurore's arms, and pulled with all her might. The horde was fast approaching, flaming eyes glued on them.

"Come on," Wendy groaned between her teeth, sweat running down her face. Her hands were slipping from their grasp.

"Get out of here!" Aurore urged.

Wendy shook her head, pulling all the harder. She could see Alice then out of the corner of her eye, surrounded by goblins, desperate to get back to them. But there was no time.

A guttural roar sounded behind her. Resorting to confrontation, Wendy whipped around and threw a dagger at the closest beast. It embedded itself into the demon's eye, killing instantly. She drew her sword, preparing for the attack.

With a deep roar of his own, a massive polar bear thundered into the horde of demons. King Thrushbeard appeared beside her, prepared to defend his daughter to the last. Stunned by the suddenness of the rescue, Wendy snapped out of it and returned to trying to pull Aurore out of her entrapment.

Another figure grasped hold of Aurore's arms, tugging with a greater strength than the girls'. Wendy looked up to see Ingénu, desperate to free his wife. He released Aurore, pushing himself against the troll's body. The corpse moved slightly and Wendy pulled, squeezing her eyes shut with the effort.

In that split second, there was a scream, a clamor of armor, a cry of alarm. A rush of wind swept past Wendy's face and something sprayed her arms. When she opened her eyes, she found mud covering Aurore and Ingénu. Every demon across the battlefield turned to earth, rock, and bone. Aurore was free. Ingénu embraced her firmly.

Loud explosions erupted as cracks in the ground slammed shut. Someone yelled in pain. Shuffling to her feet, Wendy joined Alice in following the cry.

"Get me out of here!" Jim barked, trying to yank himself free.

Kai found him there stuck, his leg buried in the ground where the earth had shut around it. Setting aside his sword, Kai beckoned Jack over to help. Jim grasped firmly to their shoulders as they pulled as hard as they could. Giving a shout of pain, Jim fell over exhausted. His leg was stuck fast.

Clopin trotted up, inspecting the scene thoroughly. "You seem to be in a predicament."

"You don't say," Jim grumbled.

Kai and Jack tried once again to pull him out to no avail. Clopin scratched his chin and clicked his tongue.

"Well, Jimmy." He drew his sword slowly. "We're going to have to cut it off."

"*What?!*"

"Don't squirm so much. This will hurt."

"Get that thing away from me!"

Leaving them to debate over the value of Jim's leg, Kai and Jack picked their way across the battlefield.

"Shouldn't we prevent whatever *that* is from getting out of hand?" Jack questioned.

"It shouldn't take them long to figure out he can dig himself out," Kai insisted. "We need to find the girls."

"Then we need to get inside that fortress. I'm sure that's where Red went."

Kai nodded in agreement. They jogged over to where Wendy and Alice were walking towards them. Alice's face stained in blood and Wendy's with dirt.

Alice jerked her head toward the looming fortress. "Let's go."

*****

Lupa reached the tower room before Fang using the passageways he knew not. She pulled her lips back over her pointed teeth in a smile. The girl was near gold statuary. Zoë turned stiffly to her, barely able to totter around. Gold veins gleamed in the whites of her eyes and gold crawled down her hair.

"Where is Fabien?" Zoë croaked out, her voice strained and broken so much that it came out in a whisper.

Lupa clicked her tongue, striding into the room with a dangerous gleam in her eyes. "Now, no need to fret over that." She wiggled her finger at Zoë. "Fang is fine. He is coming up now to get you." Lupa leered, "I am here to make sure he does not."

"Get me?" she managed, coughing out the words.

"Or rescue you. Either way, I cannot let that happen."

Lupa fiddled about the room, searching. She grinned upon finding the rose encased in glass. Gingerly, she lifted it from the trunk.

Zoë frowned as much as she could. "Why?"

"Oh, do not worry. You have served your purpose," Lupa assured, removing the rose from the case. Only three petals clung to the stem. "Your weakness allowed Fang to pursue his purpose. But now... Well, your presence is in the way."

Realizing what Lupa aimed to do, Zoë reached out to stop her and cried out something never spoken. Lupa crushed the rose and ground it to powder. The curse encased Zoë completely, the last to gild were her eyes. There she stood frozen in a poise of horror and desperation.

Lupa cocked her eyebrow, dusting off her hands. Footsteps hastened up the staircase. Calmly, she retreated to the concealed passageway and hid behind the door.

"Zoë!" Fang's voice echoed down the hall.

Rushing into the room, he froze suddenly as he saw the statue that remained of his love.

"Zoë," he breathed shakily.

He ran to her, hand brushing her still, cold face. She didn't respond to his call, didn't react to his touch. Her eyes looked beyond him, unaware of his presence, permanently filled with fear.

"No," Fang whispered.

Lupa waited a moment longer before protruding from the shadows.

"Fang?" She feigned surprise upon finding the scene.

Fang sniffed, turning to his aunt. She froze, truly shocked. His face was pale and eyes red. Wet tears drenched his cheeks and dripped off his chin. A brief pang of concern hit her. This broken heart exposed weakness. Grief was weakness. No anger held his composure. Only sorrow. Only weakness.

"Come," Lupa urged, taking his arm. "Nothing can be done for her."

Fang turned in a daze back to Zoë's gold form. His brow creased as if he just realized her strange pose. Lupa smirked behind his back. The seed of suspense was planted. Now was the time to let it grow. But first, they had to leave.

"Fang," she tugged on his arm slightly, "we have to go."

As if moving through murky water, Fang allowed Lupa to lead him to the passageway.

"She's gone," Fang muttered helplessly.

When her face was shrouded in the darkness, Lupa smiled in satisfaction.

*****

Red raced down the hallway, heart pounding out of her chest. She could sense them, smell them. The wolves, they were close.

"Rubes!"

She turned sharply around and found Jack running for her. Relief filled her to overflowing. Behind him, Alice, Kai, and Wendy followed after him. None of them looked seriously hurt. Alice's face was streaked with blood, Wendy was muddy, and Kai held his side as if his ribs were bruised. Jack's lip was split, but he smiled when he came up to her.

"Are you alright?" he asked, a hand on her shoulder.

Red took a shaky breath. "I will be."

"The demons turned to rubble," Alice informed once she caught up. "What happened?"

"Carabosse is dead," Red said quickly.

"Isn't that good, then?"

Red sighed, not sure how to answer that. "Quasi's dead, too."

Saying it aloud made it even more real. Her throat tightened and eyes stung with tears threatening to blur her vision.

"But Lupa's still here," she continued. "The wolves are gathering over here and—"

Something caught her ear, her voice cut short. It sounded like swirling water. And then, as if the thought stabbed her chest, Red sensed the wolves disappearing into thin air. She whipped around and shot down the hall at full speed.

"The wolves," she yelled back to the others as they attempted to follow her, "they're leaving!"

The door crashed open and Red burst into the open-air landing. The night sky seemed to swirl in front of her. She blinked, realizing it was a gaping hole in the air, a strong wind rushing from it. A grey-haired man jumped through the hole and disappeared. Only Fang and Lupa remained standing before the portal.

"Stop!" Red cried.

Fang turned and saw her, face ashen, eyes bloodshot and swollen. Red froze. She'd never seen anyone so taken by grief in her life. He frowned, hesitating. Lupa grabbed him and threw him into the swirling vortex. Behind her, Red heard the others shoot from the door. Lupa flashed her pointed teeth back at them and jumped.

A sharp caw hit the air as a blur of black feathers soared overhead. Diablo disappeared just as quickly as he'd come, vanishing into the hole.

Recovering from the shock, Red started to run for the portal despite the shout of warning behind her. The portal closed in a flash of light, forcefully blowing her back off her feet. Red collided into someone. Jack held her tight as the winds threatened to smash them against the wall and trees. Squeezing her eyes shut, Red held him back.

Everything stopped. The winds stilled, the light vanquished, and the portal disappeared.

The wolves were gone.

Red lay panting as if her breath were just beyond her reach. And she cried. Jack caressed her head, holding her close as she sobbed into his chest. She couldn't hold it back anymore. Every strength had abandoned her.

The door burst open yet again.

"We have no time to lose," an old man stated in a flourish.

Red rolled off Jack, wiping off her cheeks as if ashamed of them. Jack stood next to her, slipped his hand in hers and gave it a squeeze.

"Isbjørn?" Wendy questioned. "What—"

"We don't have a lot of time," Isbjørn interrupted. "I must urge you on." He turned to Alice who was helping up Kai. "Take out the watch."

Stunned briefly, Alice pulled the White Rabbit's pocket watch out from beneath her shirt. Isbjørn grasped it in his hands, closed his eyes, and mumbled a few words. When he released it, Red could hear the watch ticking once again.

"There," Isbjørn said kindly. "That will let it work for a few minutes, long enough for you to get out of here."

"Leave?" Red questioned with a frown. "Now?"

"Yes, now. I cannot direct where you'll end up, but you must go now. Your job is not done, not yet."

Alice raised her eyebrows. "So, Carabosse…"

"Is not the one you seek," Isbjørn finished. "Don't worry, I'll tell everyone here what they need to know. We will be prepared for the Battle of the Realms when the time comes."

"But…" Jack started.

"Go, now!" Isbjørn bellowed.

Alice stuck out the watch and the others grasped it. Red was last to clutch it before Jack pressed the button.

Chapter Thirty

Impossible Situations

"You've brought me nothing."

Lupa inclined her head before her master. "I regret to say that, no, we have not brought you Little Red. But," she crooned, "I do have news. The sorceress, Carabosse, is dead."

"And how does this concern me?"

"As you may know," Lupa went on, "she was never on our side. She merely wished to use Little Red as a bargaining chip to secure her prosperity. She may have never intended to give her up."

The Master sat silent.

"And I have brought more worthy warriors for your army."

"Warriors?" Fang snapped, glaring. "No. I will not be a part of this. I will not allow the Pack to take part in this insanity!"

"I'd watch your tongue if I were you," a woman with scarlet skirts and piles of dark hair warned. "You are not in your forest any longer."

"Then send us back," Fang growled. "I never asked to be sent here. You," he turned on Lupa, "*you* did this. How many times have I told you that I will not be a part of your schemes? I will not," he directed this on the Master, "risk the lives of my kin for *your* malicious desires."

"Your wife has died, yes?" the Master questioned as if having not heard the accusations.

Jaw clenched, Fang lowered his voice dangerously, "Do not deceive me, devil. No magic can bring back the dead, not even your dark sorcery."

"You're right," Lupa leered, "but revenge is still attainable."

Fang turned to her, silver eyes ablaze. "What revenge?"

"Why, if it was not for Little Red," Lupa shrugged, "your beloved would still be alive."

"I do not care for twisted speculation," Fang spat. "I was the one who turned Red into a wolf. I killed Midas and disposed of a chance to undo Zoë's curse a different way. And it was Carabosse who directed Midas' curse upon Zoë, and Midas who asked her to do it. Red is blameless of anything regarding Zoë."

"If you care not for the potential, then care for the inevitable," Lupa sneered. "In your grief, perhaps you could not sense who crushed the rose that was bound to your wife's fate. But I smelled the trace, the culprit." She paused, to make sure she had his attention. "It was our own dear Little Red."

His chest pressurized and stomach clenched. He shook his head. It didn't matter. It wasn't worth it.

"I don't care for revenge." Fang set his jaw. "What's done is done. Revenge will not bring Zoë back. Even if it did, revenge is only my own to take. It is only my right, only my responsibility. I will not force or ask my Pack to take on my revenge and risk their lives in doing so."

"Your Pack is that important to you?" a girl questioned, black bangs hanging over her brow. Something in her voice sounded sincere, not condescending.

● ● ●

318

A spark lit in the Master's brown and blue eyes. "Your Pack is here," the voice crooned, "in *my* world, in *my* territory, in *my* home. And from what I gather, you would die for your Pack before you put them in danger."

Fang's silence confirmed the prospect.

A cruel smile formed on the Master's face. "But would you sacrifice your Pack for a moral virtue?"

Despite his set jaw something in his eyes gave him away.

Leaning forward, the Master threatened, "If you do not join me, if you and your Pack do not do as I say, then the Pack that you care so much about, they might as well be dead already."

Clenching his fists, hopeless rage filled his heart. But no matter where he turned, Fang couldn't see a way out of this.

"What do you say, wolf?"

Fang sighed in aggravation, turning hard eyes on his new Master. "Not for your cause." He turned to his aunt. "Not for *you*." Staring at the tattoo around his ring finger on his left hand, he felt his stomach clench. "Not even for Zoë…" Raising his head, he proclaimed, "For the Pack. For my kin."

"Your chivalry is admirable," sneered the pirate in the corner.

The Master sat back in victory. "Wise choice."

Lupa bowed low. "Thank you, my liege."

Regret flickered in his heart. Rubbing the spot where his dragon cuff used to bind him, Fang realized that now he wore invisible chains, ones that the Master now held. Under his breath, Fang said for the last time, "I'm sorry, Red."

* * *

The raven that had been watching the scene below with beady eyes gave a caw in resolution. A flap of wings brought Diablo down upon Fang's shoulder, his pointed beak clicking in the wolf's ear. For the first time, Fang understood what the raven said.

Diablo had chosen his new master.

And so had Fang.

*****

Colors subsided and ticking faded as they were thrown to the ground. The light almost blinded Red after being in the dark for so long. Blue skies stretched overhead, hazy white clouds floating just over treetops. She felt so small lying there, like the world was much too vast. The woods weren't so dense around them. She could hear a creek winding its way beside them.

Slowly, Red sat up to find the others. Alice stood, dew clinging to her clothes. Jack scowled at the sky.

"Where are we?" Kai asked, rising to his feet.

Alice looked around, brushing the water from her arms. "I don't—"

A rumble shook the earth, nearly causing Kai and Alice to lose footing. Jack sat straight up, brow creased. Another ripple sent leaves falling from the trees. A flock of birds rose up like a cloud of dust, flying away screaming warning.

Fumbling slightly, Jack leapt to his feet. "We have to go. We have to go, now!"

"Why, what's wrong?" Red questioned, helping Wendy up.

"We have to go now!" Jack proclaimed, panic inking into his voice.

Another rumble in the ground, stronger this time, was followed by an even greater roar that pierced through the air and sent birds flying frantically away. They took off running.

"Giant Country," Jack cried. "We're in Giant Country!"

Acknowledgements

Thank you so much for reading this story! I realize this book is a lot darker than previous installments, but Red's character and everything that makes her called for a story with darker shadows. I enjoyed taking this journey, and though several scenes sickened me to the core, I learned a lot along the way about my characters and my own strength in taking the plunge as a writer. So, thank you for taking this journey with me.

As always, I could never do this alone.

Thank you to my incredible family for a never-ending flow of love and support. My manuscript wouldn't be nearly so stripped of typos and odd sentences if it weren't for my personal train of proofreaders. I thank them so much for their encouragement and honesty.

Thank you to my amazing friends; you have made a lasting impression on my heart. Every relationship and personality shapes the way I tell my stories. From humor to exclamations and reactions to stirring emotions, I couldn't do what I love without you.

Many thanks to the renowned authors J. M. Barrie, Hans Christian Andersen, and Lewis Carrol, as well as the unknown storytellers of "Little Red Riding Hood" and "Jack and the Beanstalk" for creating such wonderful stories that stay with us for ages. I'm blessed to add new layers to their legacies.

In this installment, I got to work with brilliant new stories and characters, and I want to acknowledge every one. Thanks to Charles Perrault's "Bluebeard" for such a horrific villain, to Perrault and the Brothers Grimm for their renditions of the fairytale "Sleeping Beauty", and to Jeanne-Marie Le Prince de Beaumont for her "Aurore and Aimée" which allowed depth to my dear Briar Rose and Ingénu, as well as Victor Hugo's "Hunchback of Notre-Dame" for beautiful characters to add to their journey. Thank you to the fairytales "King Thrushbeard", "East of the Sun and West of the Moon", "The Princess Who Never Smiled", "Hansel and Gretel", and a nod to "Molly Whuppie" and "The Little Mermaid." I enjoyed using lesser-known fairytales to bring to life. Sword Kladenets was a wonderful flavor of Russian fairytales. And I loved expanding the brilliance of Robert Louis Stevenson's "Treasure Island" through Jim Hawkins' grandson. I didn't want to contradict these classic stories, but rather plant their seeds and watch them grow.

Thank you to Vladimir Arndt and Krisana Tongnantree for the spectacular images that make up this cover, as well as Derek Murphy with his helpful tips for DIY book covers. Thank you to my friend, Hannah for helping edit my French phrases, and thanks to my proofreaders who help me see the glitches I couldn't.

And thank you to everyone who has expressed excitement for this series! I am so honored that you've picked up this book and allowed me to take you through these stories. I'm so thankful for you, dear reader.

All my thanks go to my God, who is alongside me through this journey. Above all else, I do everything for Him. May He receive all glory.

Get ready for the next adventure...

The Realms Series

Book Four

Giant Country

Emory R. Frie

...Coming Soon

Emory R. Frie is the award-winning author of debut novel, *Heart of a Lion*, and the Realms Series books, *Wonderland*, *Neverland*, and *Enchanted Forest*. Emory is attending Berry College to further pursue her writing craft. Raised in Oregon, she now lives in Georgia with her family, Scottie dog, and retired barn cat.

Made in the USA
Columbia, SC
03 September 2017